D1269870

The Knights of Derbyshire

Jane Austen's
Pride and Prejudice
Continues

by
Marsha Altman

Laughing Man Publications
New York

Dedication

This one's all for Brandy.

Introduction

Welcome, readers! Either you are returning for the fifth time or you downloaded this book by accident. Either way, I'm happy to have you. This is actually not a terrible place in the series to come in, so you're in luck. Just imagine that twenty years have passed since the events of *Pride and Prejudice* and for some reason Darcy and Elizabeth have met a number of crazy people and you'll do just fine.

In our previous books:

In *The Darcys and the Bingleys*, Elizabeth Bennet married Mr. Darcy (being of Mr. Darcy fame), and her older sister Jane Bennet married Mr. Bingley (being of Darcy's friend fame). Seriously, you did not read Pride and Prejudice? This was the book that made you regret not freshening up. At least take the movie out or something. Anyway, they proceeded to have a whole mess of kids. Fortunately, not all at the same time. The Darcys' oldest child is Geoffrey Darcy, and the Bingleys' oldest child is Georgiana Bingley.

Caroline Bingley, Charles's unwed sister, became involved with a Scottish earl, who then turned out to be a rake, and by that I mean a 19th-century scoundrel and not a gardening tool. This was all exposed in time for her to also reveal she was actually in love with the impoverished Dr. Daniel

Maddox. Dr. Maddox lost his social standing when his older brother Brian gambled away their family fortune. After some sword fighting and the bad guy getting clobbered with a candlestick, Dr. Maddox and Caroline Bingley were married, not leaving enough time in the book for them to have a mess of kids, but presumably that was coming.

In *The Plight of the Darcy Brothers*, Mary Bennet, Jane and Elizabeth's unmarried sister, returned from studying in France with child, the father being an Italian seminary student. Darcy and Elizabeth traveled through Europe to find him, on the way discovering that Darcy had an illegitimate half-brother holed up in a French monastery named Grégoire Bellamont-Darcy. Mary's would-be suitor was found and he offered her a settlement. Mary had a son, Joseph, and is currently unmarried and living with her parents. Darcy also discovered that George Wickham (the villain in Pride and Prejudice, who seduced and married Lydia Bennet, the youngest Bennet sister) was also his half-brother. Their family reunion went the worst possible way, with fratricide and a complete lack of potato salad. Lydia got over her husband's death rather quickly but was left with two children, George and Isabella Wickham. Brother Grégoire, still a monk, went to live in Austria. Dr. Maddox and Caroline Bingley had a daughter, but also adopted a son, the bastard child of the Prince Regent and a prostitute, named Frederick (the son, not the prostitute).

(There will not be a test. Just so you know.)

In *Mr. Darcy's Great Escape*, Napoleon invaded Russia, and in the tumult of war, Darcy lost track of his brother Grégoire, and Dr. Maddox lost track of his brother Brian, who was supposed to have married a Transylvanian princess but then disappeared. The two of them traveled to Austria to find them, but ended up in a Transylvanian dungeon as hostages, and their wives ended up rescuing them after locating Grégoire. Brian Maddox and his wife, Princess Nadezhda, reappeared after being missing for two years, having taken the long way home through Russia, Japan, and then a boat ride to England. So it turns out they were fine all along. No one was thrilled to hear that. They brought with them a mixed-race Japanese convict named Mugin, who I only mention because he pops up from time to time.

Lydia Bennet remarried and had a whole mess of kids with her new husband, Mr. Bradley. Kitty Bennet, the last remaining Bennet sister to be mentioned, got married to a Mr. Townsend over a whole page, because she isn't a very interesting character so I didn't spend a lot of time with her.

After the war, Grégoire Bellamont-Darcy moved to Spain, his previous monastery having been dissolved by Napoleon.

There is also a Bavarian saint named Sebald buried in Darcy's graveyard instead of his traditional home in Nuremburg, but there's a long story behind it, so just take it for what it is.

In *The Ballad of Grégoire Darcy*, Grégoire Bellamont-Darcy was forced to leave his monastery for largely political reasons, and moved to Ireland, where he met a peasant named Caitlin MacKenna. This being a historical romance series, he eventually married her but not before some dramatic things happened to pad out the book a little. They have a son named Patrick and Grégoire is a schoolteacher.

Charles Bingley and Brian Maddox went into business together, and traveled to India and the Far East, bringing back a monkey and Mugin. Unfortunately for Darcy the monkey remained, but Mugin was kicked out of England after Brian discovered he was teaching Georgiana Bingley how to fight. I'm probably bothering to mention this minor subplot for a reason.

Mary Bennet, the single mother of Joseph Bennet, married Dr. Andrew Bertrand, a doctor of French origin, and still lives in Longbourn. Mrs. Bennet died of a stroke, and after her passing, Mr. Bennet left Longbourn and took up residence in the library at Pemberley. So far, Darcy hasn't complained about any old people smells, probably because *everyone* smelled in Georgian England.

Notes on the Second Edition

Several technical and grammatical changes were made for this edition and the preview of the sixth book was added. The content of the story has not changed in any way.

I would like to thank Alex Shwarzstein, Jessica Kupillas Hartung, and Cherri Trotter for help with this edition.

If any mistakes remain, remember that only God is perfect, and He did not write this book. He's a popular enough author in His own right.

Family Trees

Bold face indicates living, *Italics* indicates deceased.

The Darcys

Henry Darcy
  (with unnamed wife)
  Gregory Darcy (never married)
  Geoffrey Darcy
    (children with *Lady Anne Fitzwilliam*)
    Fitzwilliam Darcy
      (children with **Elizabeth Bennet**)
      Geoffrey Darcy
      Anne Darcy
      Sarah Darcy
      Cassandra Darcy
      Georgiana Darcy-Kincaid
        (children with **Lord William Kincaid**)
          Viscount Robert Kincaid
      (children with *Mrs. Wickham*)
    George Wickham
      (children with **Lydia Bennet**)
      George Wickham the Younger
      Isabella Wickham
      (children with *Miss Bellamont*)
      Grégoire Bellamont-Darcy
        (children with **Caitlin MacKenna**)
          Patrick Bellamont

Assorted:

Lady Catherine de Bourgh – **Mr. Darcy's** aunt on his mother's side)
> (children with *Sir Lewis de Bourgh*)
> > **Anne de Bourgh-Fitzwilliam**
> > > (children with **Richard Fitzwilliam**, now Lord Matlock)
> > > > **Edward Fitzwilliam**, Viscount of Matlock

The Bingleys

Charles Bingley (I)
> (children with *Mrs. Bingley*)
> > **Louisa Bingley-Hurst**
> > > (married **Mr. Hurst**, no children)
> > **Caroline Bingley-Maddox**
> > > (children with **Dr. Daniel Maddox** – see *The Maddoxes*)
> > **Charles Bingley** (II)
> > > (children with **Jane Bennet**)
> > > > **Georgiana (Georgie) Bingley**
> > > > **Charles (Charlie) Bingley** (III)
> > **Elizabeth (Eliza) Bingley**
> > **Edmund Bingley**

The Bennets

Edmund Bennet
> (children with **Mrs. Bennet**)

Jane Bennet-Bingley
(children with **Mr. Bingley** – see *The Bingleys*)
Elizabeth Bennet-Darcy
(children with **Mr. Darcy** – see *The Darcys*)
Mary Bennet-Bertrand
(children with **Giovanni Mastai**)
Joseph Bennet
(children with **Dr. Andrew Bertrand**)
Margaret Bertrand
Kitty Bennet-Townsend
Lydia Bennet-Bradley (formerly Wickham)
(children with *Mr. Wickham* – see *The Darcys*)
(children with **Mr. Bradley**)
Julie Bradley
Brandon Bradley
Maria Bradley

Assorted:
Mr. Collins – nephew of **Mr. Edmund Bennet**
(children with **Charlotte Lucas-Collins**)
Amelia Collins
Maria Collins
Eleanor Collins
Jane Collins

The Maddoxes

Stewart Maddox
(children with *Mrs. Maddox*)

Brian Maddox

(married to **Princess Nadezhda of Sibui**, no children)

Dr. Daniel Maddox

(children with **Caroline Bingley**)

> **Frederick Maddox** (adopted, son of the **Prince of Wales** and *Lilly Garrison*)
>
> **Emily Maddox** (same age as Fredrick)
>
> **Daniel Maddox the Younger**

CHAPTER 1

The Problem with Mr. Wickham

1822

"MR. DARCY," said the servant. "Mr. Wickham is here to see you."

At this hour? Darcy removed his spectacles and put down his pen. "Send him in."

The servant opened the door, and George Wickham the Younger entered, his face still flushed from the cold, dark circles under his eyes. "Uncle Darcy." He bowed slowly, like a man exhausted.

"George." Darcy rose to greet him. "Please sit. You obviously require refreshment. Do you have a preference?"

"Whiskey, sir, if it's not too much trouble."

Darcy nodded, and the servant poured them two glasses and then quietly exited. Darcy took his own as George held his glass contemplatively for a moment before taking a large gulp. It struck Darcy that whiskey – single malt – had always been Wickham's preference, over brandy or gin. In looks as well, the son had the unfortunate favoring towards his father, though not quite the spitting image of him. In manners, he was entirely different. Shy, exceedingly proper, uncomfortable in unknown company – in this respect, he was a Darcy. The handicap, Darcy decided, was preferable to having his father's nature.

George was silent for a time, and Darcy thought it best not to press a man obviously in some distress. George was only a year older than his own son, and never came to Pemberley un-requested or with a complaint, as his mother did often enough. Whatever it was, the man – barely more than a boy, at eighteen – was obviously hesitant to say it.

When he did speak, he made no attempt to be anything but blunt. "I was sent down from Oxford."

Without a hint of judgment, Darcy asked, "Why?"

"I was absent for my exams, thereby failing all of my courses." He took another sip. "The head was not understanding of my excuse and I refused to resort to bribery to be allowed to take them late."

"And your excuse?"

George took another sip. "I was in Scotland; at Gretna Green." He assiduously avoided his uncle's shocked expression. "I was there to prevent the marriage of my sister to a man who was quickly revealed to be after nothing but her fortune."

Isabella Wickham was only fifteen, but already out, and her inheritance was considerable thanks to the trust fund. "Your parents knew nothing of this?"

"They encouraged it."

Darcy settled back in his chair, his mind trying to work itself around this indecipherable comment. "Mr. Wickham, I apologize, but you will have to explain that."

"Unfortunately, I cannot do so without slandering either of my parents," George said. "Which I am not wont to do. But I suppose it is necessary."

"It is."

George once again had to ready himself, as if his own words weighed him down. "Since I came into my fortune, I admit that relations with my parents have been ... strained. To be straight, my mother requested a portion of it for the family needs, and I thought the sum outrageous."

Exactly something Lydia would do, Darcy thought, but kept that to himself for the moment.

"Mr. Bradley has an income, and has a responsibility to provide for his – own children, who have always been regarded differently from myself and Isabel."

Of course, money had torn the family apart. It was not unforeseeable. Darcy had set up trust funds only for the Wickham children, who were quarter Darcys, but not for anyone else, including Lydia's three children with her new husband, to whom he was only connected by marriage. The older children had a fortune and the younger ones had a father. "I understand. Please go on."

"So – as I said, things became strained. And my sister wanted to go out and my mother didn't discourage her, and I was at Oxford and couldn't prevent it, though I did write to Mr. Bradley to ask that he say something against it, although I have no idea if he did. Anyway, a few weeks before my exams, I received a post that my sister was engaged, and they requested that I – help pay for the wedding."

It was ludicrous, but that had surely occurred to George, too. The responsibility lay with Isabella's parents, not her brother. Her own inheritance, of course, she had no access to. It would only be accessible to her future husband, and a fortune it was.

"I said that I would, despite my own feelings on the matter, if only they would delay the wedding until after the term so I could attend. They refused. She was too eager to marry, they said. Why should I deny my sister this pleasure?" He shook his head. "I didn't think I was being unreasonable."

"You were not," Darcy said carefully.

"A day before I was to sit for my first exam, I received a letter from my sister, saying that since her parents refused to put any money toward the wedding, and her intended had no funds of his own whatsoever – which made me extremely suspicious immediately – she, with the permission of our parents, was going to Gretna Green to be married. Obviously, I dropped everything and rode to Scotland, arriving a mere few hours before the ceremony. In that time, I decided to test her fiancé by saying that her inheritance was considerably smaller than she knew, to see if their love would hold up to any financial strain. Apparently it would not, because he left immediately."

Darcy had only the will to nod at this point, overcome with his own emotions.

"My sister was distraught. She could not return to Town alone, so I went with her. Upon our arrival, Mother threw a fit. I had ruined my sister's happiness. I was ruining the family by refusing to contribute anything of my grand fortune. And, I admit I was a bit ... exhausted and I might have said some things to my parents which, upon retrospection, were not entirely respectful. So they tossed me out of the house.

"I went back to Oxford and tried to explain myself and my situation, but the head would not have it. So I was told to leave. And now ..." He looked down, then up at his uncle. "I will have to set myself up in Town somewhere. I don't know."

"No," Darcy said firmly, rising from his chair and walking around the desk. "You will stay here until this is all sorted out. Which it shall be." He patted the red-eyed George on the back.

"I am sorry to inconvenience you – "

"You should not be. You are my nephew and it is no inconvenience." *My only relief is that you came here! Or god knows what would have happened to you.* "The servants will see to your things and get you settled. Now if you will excuse me, I must go inform my wife, who has already retired. Geoffrey may still be up. And if you pass the library, you may want to check to see if your grandfather has fallen asleep in there again."

"Thank you, Uncle Darcy."

Maybe it was just exhaustion, but the relief on George Wickham's face was not complete. It was, however, significant. Darcy hid his own relief and showed his nephew out of the room before heading upstairs to rouse his wife and tell her of their new guest.

~~~

George Wickham was shown to his room, where his bags were brought, few as they were, as he had ridden from Town with only as much as his horse could carry. To his surprise, he was not ready for sleep yet, still rocking from the horse. He wandered downstairs. It had begun to snow, and most of Pemberley was closed up for the night, but the library's fire was still smoldering. There was Mr. Bennet, in the armchair by the fire, half-emptied glass of wine on the table beside him and a book still in his hands.

"Grandfather Bennet," George said quietly, but he had to physically nudge him to rouse him. Mr. Bennet mumbled something and straightened his glasses so he could get a proper look at his intruder.

"George!" he said. His hair had been white for as long as George had known him, but it was even more wild, and his voice not as bold, though his tongue was not lessened by a senile brain. Mr. Edmund Bennet, of almost three quarters of a century in years, had a mind not dulled by time, even if his body was. "What a sight you are! I was not expecting you."

"My arrival was sudden," George said. "I was told to see if you'd fallen asleep in the library again."

"There are certainly worse places to fall asleep than Pemberley's library. Nonetheless, for the sake of my back and my neck, I ought perhaps to retire more properly." With George's considerable help, he got to his feet, leaning heavily on his cane. "My son is so good as to dismiss his servants when it is cold and dark. Too good perhaps, though not the worst quality in a man."

As they left the library, they did quickly locate the servants, who were ready to escort Mr. Bennet to his chambers. "Good night, George."

"Good night, Grandfather."

George did not wander the darkened hallways of Pemberley, instead heading back up the stairs. In the children's wing, he caught sight of Gawain, Geoffrey's hound, curled up obediently outside the half-opened door. "Hello, Sir Gawain," he said to the dog, who recognized him with a growl of approval. "What's this?" he tugged the fabric out of the dog's mouth with some fight.

"One of my socks, I'd imagine," said Geoffrey Darcy, emerging in the doorway. He raised a glass to his cousin. "Mr. Wickham."

"Mr. Darcy," George replied, and they both chuckled before embracing.

"It is good to see you," Geoffrey said, "for whatever reason you're here. God, I haven't spoken to anyone my age since I returned. Come in, if you'd like."

George entered the impressive chambers of Geoffrey Darcy, heir to Pemberley. And impressive they were – this was just a sitting room, with a desk for writing and piles of old schoolbooks stuffed on the shelves. "Here," Geoffrey said, offering a seat across from him at the writing table. "Would you like a drink?"

"Please." He had already had the whiskey, but unlike his cousin, he could hold his liquor. Geoffrey poured him a glass of wine from his own little personal stock. "What about Charlie? Isn't he around?"

"He's been visiting his Aunt and Uncle Maddox since we returned from Eton," he said. Charles Bingley the Third was one year younger than Geoffrey and a year behind in school. Geoffrey was finishing up his last year before Cambridge. "He came back today. Or yesterday, depending on the time." He took a large sip of his wine. "So – what brings you to Derbyshire? Other than the complete lack of things to do."

"You could go to Lambton."

"And do what? Everyone knows me at Lambton. Everyone in the county knows me, or has at least heard of me. At least you – " he broke off. "Well, I wouldn't say your name would be unknown."

"Father did have a bit of a reputation, or so I understand," George said with a smile. He had made his peace with it years ago. No, he would not be making use of any of Lambton's female offerings. His visit to the Darcys would be an exercise in celibacy. "What about your usual other half? Georgie?"

Geoffrey scowled and leaned back. "Georgie's a – she's a proper lady now. She's different."

"Really?"

"Really." But when he saw George did not relent, he added, "She at least *presents* herself as one. So no, I do not know what she's really planning. Even she won't tell me. She came out to society; she does all of the ... proper lady things that ladies have to do ... and that is all. As far as anyone knows."

So Geoffrey's foul mood was fully explained. George nodded and did not offer further commentary. "So how is your family?"

"Fine, fine." Geoffrey patted his hound on the head as he trotted up next to his owner. "Anne is rather eager to come out."

"She's young yet."

"So Mother keeps reminding her. At least Anne has the sense not to mention it within earshot of Father, unless she wants to get his mood up. Which can, at times, be amusing. As far as he's concerned, they're all to nunneries." Geoffrey paused. "What about Isabel? I heard she entered society in the fall."

"After her fifteenth birthday, yes," George said.

"Where is she now? She usually follows you everywhere. Are you intending to stay for Christmas?" He frowned. "Why *are* you here? Not that you're unwelcome."

"The story is rather long," George said, "and depressing. If you want to hear it, more wine is definitely called for."

Geoffrey, obviously starved for conversation with a peer, refilled George's glass, then his own. Slowly but surely the whole tale came out. George was surprised by the ease with which he said it, even though he had already told it once to his Uncle Darcy under more trying circumstances and with less alcohol in his overtired system. He had saved his sister. He might have lost a term at Oxford but somehow, Uncle Darcy would make everything right. That was what he always did, and in a drink-induced haze, George believed it.

Geoffrey listened to the tale with compassion, saying little but always being supportive. It was really beyond either of their scopes to understand, and at the end he had to add, "Did you really say that to your own mother?"

George found himself smiling. "Unfortunately."

"Called her a – "

"Oh God, don't say it. I never want to use that word again. I never want to *hear* that word again." He emptied his glass again. "So here I am; tossed out of University, tossed out of my own home by my own mother, and drunk off cheap wine with my cousin because I have nowhere else to go and no one else to talk to."

"This wine is anything but cheap!" Geoffrey said. "Don't smudge the honor of Pemberley! But seriously – you have money, education, a family – all right, an *extended* family – that will take care of you, and you saved your sister from the worst kind of disaster a woman can befall. Your lot's not *that* bad."

George smiled tiredly. "I suppose you're right."

CHAPTER 2

Fashion in Chatton House

CHARLES BINGLEY, forty one years of age, was finding himself to be less an early riser than he used to be. Jane was already gone when he rose that winter morning. With nothing pressing on his schedule while his business partner was abroad, he yawned luxuriously and washed his face before thinking about preparing for the day. He was still toweling his face when he heard the scream.

With less alarm than he supposed he should have had, he put on his slippers and padded out of his chambers and down the corridor, still wearing his orange kurta. The source of the noise was a collection of women's shrieks, but all he saw in the corridor was his monkey. Bingley put his hands over his ears and looked at Monkey, who screamed at him. "Monkey! *Kinasi!*" The animal obediently leapt up onto the railing and then his shoulder. "At least someone in this house listens to me," he mumbled, and with his ears still covered, he peeked into his eldest daughter's chambers.

"Papa!" It was not his oldest daughter, but his youngest, Eliza, who emerged and curtseyed to her father. "Did we wake you?"

"Of course you woke me! You probably woke half the house! What in heaven's name is going on?"

"That is precisely what I want to know!" said his beloved Jane, appearing behind his daughter. She was about as angry as Jane Bingley was capable of getting, which was admittedly not that angry, but a frightening prospect nonetheless. "Georgiana! Do you want to explain yourself?"

"Papa, you can come in," came Georgiana Bingley's voice, completely even and not exhausted, so she at least had not been howling. The occupants of the room were the three women, though one was still a girl, and a terrified maid.

Georgiana Bingley, now seventeen, was sitting before her mirror, though she rose to curtsey to her father. A robe covered her bedclothes, and she looked as she normally did. The only thing missing was her long hair, which was for the most part on the floor beside her, the scissors still in her hand. "Papa," she said respectfully, as if nothing was amiss and she was not missing most of her long locks, normally so carefully braided and put up.

Bingley paused, not quite sure what to say to his daughter at this moment, as Monkey leapt off his shoulders and into her arms. At last he said, "It seems I am a bit behind on women's fashions."

"A bit!" Jane cried, clearly disturbed by the whole incident. "Georgiana, would you like to explain to your father what you refuse to explain to me?"

"I did explain it to you," Georgie said rather unapologetically. "I cut off my hair because I was sick of putting it up. I fail to see what's hard to understand about that."

12

"Well, normally – " Then realizing there was no need to tell Georgiana what was normal behavior for someone of her age and stature, as she knew it thoroughly and clearly had no plans to abide completely by those strictures, he broke off, and started laughing.

"Charles!" Jane said.

"I'm sorry but – well, look at her." He didn't like Jane's glare, but he could hardly hold himself back. "I think we should view it positively – she did stop short of cutting it *all* off."

"*Papa!*" Eliza said. "She looks like a boy!"

Georgiana sneered at her sister.

"Don't be ridiculous, Eliza. That's hardly a respectable haircut for a man. And in that area I do actually have some experience." He knew he was in a precarious position between his wife and daughter, but knew no good way to traverse it. "Well, there's nothing we can do about it now. You can't glue it back on." He approached his eldest daughter. "I can have my man neaten up the sides a bit, I suppose. Oh, and you're confined to your room."

"Papa!"

"You can't possibly expect me to do otherwise." Nonetheless, the victory went to Georgiana, as no one could reverse what she'd done, and it would be very hard to find a wig that matched her own hair color. With a nervous glance to his wife, Bingley sighed and left the chambers to prepare for the rest of the day.

~~~

The Darcy breakfast table had undergone changes in the years, not so much in the wood itself but those present. Between Darcy at one end and Elizabeth at the other sat their two eldest children. Geoffrey Darcy was officially of age to be at the table, and Anne, who was still a child, was old enough to sit beside them and begin learning proper table manners when there were no guests. Mr. Bennet had taken residency at Pemberley since the death of Mrs. Bennet and the closing of Longbourn. Occasionally he went to Chatton House, only three miles away, but he was a homebody to the most extreme and generally liked to sleep under the same roof every night, and Darcy was happy to accommodate his father-in-law. Sarah and Cassandra Darcy were still young enough to take their own meal in the nursery.

Mr. Bennet noticed that there was another absence, however. "Am I not mistaken, Mr. Darcy, in thinking that I saw a visage of George Wickham last night when I feel asleep in the library?"

"You are not mistaken," Darcy said. "He has just come from a long journey and if he is not yet awake, I honestly cannot say I blame him."

"Is he staying with us for Christmas?" Anne said. "What about Izzy? Is she coming, too?"

"That is yet to be settled," said Elizabeth. Nothing could in fact be settled until their guest rose, but it was likely that at least he would be staying through the New Year. "Geoffrey! What did we say about feeding Gawain at the table?"

"He's not at the table," Geoffrey said, returning the hand that had fed a strip of bacon to his hound to the table. "He's beneath it."

Mr. Bennet chuckled. "He has a point."

"Papa!" But Elizabeth could neither get that angry with her father nor strict with her son when her husband was not in the mood to be. Darcy clearly had other things on his mind, no doubt all involving Wickham, and he let the incident pass without notice.

At least until Gawain, denied further scraps from his master, came to his side, sniffing at the master of Pemberley's knee.

"Don't come to me."

"But Papa," Anne said, "you feed him all the time when Geoffrey's at school!"

Now it was Geoffrey's turn to laugh triumphantly, though he had to muffle it after a stern look from his father.

Elizabeth frowned at her son but said, "You will learn, Anne, that sometimes your father does not always do the right thing and is given to moments of sentimentality after having lost his own dogs many years ago. Nonetheless, the general rule stands."

"You had dogs? What happened to them?"

"They died," he said. "Animals do not live as long as humans, for the most part."

"What about monkeys? How long do they live?"

"Too long," Darcy answered in the precise voice that made conversation – at least on that topic – cease.

15

When breakfast had passed and there was still no sign of George, Darcy ordered a tray brought up for his nephew. When it came back with only the coffee touched, he went himself to see George, only to find him coughing and sneezing over his wash bin. George attempted to apologize for his absence at breakfast, but Darcy hushed him and went back downstairs to call for a doctor, finding Elizabeth already awaiting him in his study. "He has a cold," he said. "Not all that surprising."

"I was going to write to Lydia," Elizabeth said, dismissing the servants, who closed the door behind them so the Darcys could have privacy, "but perhaps you should write to Mr. Bradley." She paced as he sat down and pulled out his ink and pen. "If George is ill, then you could inquire if his sister would like to visit him during his convalescence."

"I don't think Mrs. Bradley will much care for the idea."

"But at least now we have the excuse of illness. Not that I would ordinarily choose to make strategic use of someone's illness, but I think George would be more settled if Isabel was within more capable hands."

They had the same thoughts about Elizabeth's sister and the way she handled her own children; the nasty words did not need repeating. They had been spoken enough last night. "She may not wish to leave her mother, and drive a further wedge in the family."

"Then only suggest it, and let her come to her own decision. Or maybe Mr. Bradley will have the good sense to make it for her." Elizabeth paused in her pacing. "Darcy, if it is too great a burden to ask that we house Isabel indefinitely – "

"If it comes to that," he said, "and I will try to see that it does not, it is not a burden. Besides, it would be unfair to extend the offer to George and not to his sister, who is younger and in even more need of guidance."

Elizabeth leaned over and kissed him. "You are too good to your family."

"You are complaining?" he said with his patented smirk. "Besides, I only must write Mr. Bradley. You must write *Mrs.* Bradley."

"And Jane! That should be done first. Or, after the doctor comes. How sick is he?"

"About as much as I would expect of a man who rode to Scotland, then to Town, then to Derbyshire without much break between stops. In December. But he has no fever and I think he will manage. The doctor is just a precaution." He rose, and kissed her on the cheek. "We will manage. Somehow."

~~~

It was nearly an hour later that Geoffrey Darcy and Gawain appeared at the door to Chatton House. Normally the walk did not take him an hour, but the inch of snow on the ground and the frigid temperatures made travel a bit more difficult.

17

"Master Geoffrey!" said the doorman as he entered, and the servants rushed to attend to the flushed and sniffling young man.

"I have a letter for Mrs. Bingley," he explained to the doorman as his outer layers were removed. "Gawain, sit!" The dog obeyed so his paws could be wiped dry before he would proceed further into the house.

Mrs. Bingley quickly appeared. "Geoffrey! What are you doing out in the cold?"

He bowed. "Aunt Bingley." He handed her a letter. He did not have to explain who it was from. The Darcy seal and his mother's handwriting made it obvious enough. "Gawain needed a walk anyway. Everyone's getting a bit restless, being inside all the time."

"I know. What an awful winter to have, if December has been any indication," she said. "Is something wrong? Is everyone well?"

"Yes," he said, "except Cousin George, who came in late last night and has a cold. It's all in the letter, I imagine."

She nodded. "Please sit down and catch your breath, Geoffrey. And you are welcome to stay as long as you please if there is nothing pressing at Pemberley. Charlie is, I believe, in one of the drawing rooms."

He bowed to her again and she excused herself to read her letter. He found Charlie easily enough – he was bickering (if one could consider it bickering) with his younger brother Edmund outside the library.

18

Whatever it was, conversation ceased when Geoffrey approached. "Charlie. Edmund."

Edmund nodded to his cousin and ran off, leaving him alone with Charlie.

"What's going on?"

"Nothing," Charles Bingley the Third said with a sweet, completely unconvincing smile.

"What did she do?"

"You always assume the worst of Georgie."

"That's because I've known her all my life," he said with a smile. "So? Aside from George's arrival, this may be the most interesting thing to happen all week."

"George is here?"

"Yes, he came in last night. But don't try and change the subject."

"Well, if you want, she's in the drawing room." He gestured over his shoulder. "It should be obvious."

Even more intrigued, Geoffrey opened the double doors to the drawing room. The lone figure inside rose as her cousin and brother entered. Georgiana Bingley had been, in fact, drawing, or inking one of her pencil sketches into a more permanent medium. "Geoffrey."

He did not attempt to hide his pleasure at the amusing sight of his cousin, who looked decidedly different from when he had seen her at dinner three nights before. "Georgie."

"The barber did try to even it out," Charlie interrupted, which earned a glare from Georgiana. "I simply mean that it was worse before."

"You're not helping your case," Geoffrey said to Charlie.

"Don't say anything, because I've heard every insult that possibly could have been imagined by the mind of my sister," Georgie said, and sat back down.

"I didn't say anything! It looks nice" Geoffrey said. "But if you want to change the subject, there is some news from Pemberley. George is staying with us for ... well, I don't know, an indeterminate amount of time."

"Really?"

"He came in late last night, we had a drink and some conversation, and he woke up with a terrible cold," Geoffrey said, pacing the room, his eyes occasionally roaming to the wide windows. "Not surprising considering all the traveling he did."

"Am I going to hear it from you or do I wait to hear the censored version from Papa?" she said as the dog padded up to her. "Sorry, Gawain, but I've no food for you."

"There's little to censor, so I might as well, though I probably don't know the half of it," he said, As he paced, he related the story that a slightly inebriated George Wickham had told him the night before, from his sister going out in the fall to his being thrown from the house in Town and his flight to Oxford and then Pemberley.

Georgie did not attempt to hide her disgust with her aunt, but she did not verbalize it so readily. "Izzy's *out?* She's fifteen! She's younger than Eliza!"

"Barely, but yes. George didn't say he approved of it. They did it while he was up at Oxford."

"Where he no longer can attend."

"Father says he'll either have to find a way to make amends or try Cambridge."

"And Isabel's betrothed?" Charlie asked.

Geoffrey shrugged. "I think my parents are going to invite her for Christmas, so she can spend it with her brother. Or at least visit him while he's laid up."

"What will Aunt Bradley think of that?"

He just shrugged again.

"If he's well enough for visitors, I'll come see him immediately," Charlie said.

"Send him my regards." Georgiana couldn't visit him in his sickbed, even though they were cousins.

"I will."

"I suspect Aunt Bingley is going to take a carriage to Pemberley as soon as she finishes reading the letter from Mother. You might want to ride with her," Geoffrey suggested. "Tell her I'll be along later."

Charlie nodded and excused himself, leaving Georgiana and Geoffrey alone, aside from the servant in the corner. Georgie was absently scribbling at her current work, and he walked over to her and looked over her shoulder. "Isn't that the waterfall near Pemberley? The one with the shelter?"

"Yes," she said. "I sketched it in November." She was inking the pencil lines now.

"So where's the surprise?"

She blew on the ink to dry it, and passed him the drawing. "Look very closely."

"Where?"

"God, Geoffrey, if you can't find it, no one will."

He was tempted to scold her for the insult, but instead focused on the unfinished work. Nothing jumped out at him immediately. The original work was done with a colored pencil. "The man behind the waterfall. In the little corner there." He pointed proudly to it.

"Don't smudge it."

He smiled and took another look. "He's tiny. I know one hand has a sword, but what's in the other hand?"

"If I tell you, it stays between us."

He handed the picture back. "Of course."

"The head of his vanquished enemy. He's holding it up by the hair."

He laughed. "Some people would call you rather morbid, you know."

"I do know. Trust me, I *do* know." It was the first smile he'd seen from her today. She had always smiled less easily than he did; odd because he was a Darcy and she was a Bingley, but his father always said he'd inherited his mother's countenance and that it was for the best. "You really think it looks nice?" she said, clearly not referring to the picture.

"I'll ask for an explanation first before admitting to that."

"I got tired of putting it up. How ridiculous is it that a girl spends years growing out her hair to ridiculous lengths, only to spend ages every morning having it pinned up so neatly, and then checking all day to make sure everything's still in place. It's silly.

If showing long hair is such a detestable thing for a lady – well, then I don't have long hair."

He laughed. "I suppose you're right. So what's the real reason?"

She turned away. "You know me too well."

"Perhaps."

"It was too much effort to put it back together when it fell apart," she said. "Making myself look presentable when I returned from walking. And it ruined my balance when it would just fall down."

"Still searching for the perfect balance?" It was a metaphysical concept to Georgiana, one she had been obsessed with for reasons he never fully understood, but was willing to take at face value. "I assume you haven't found it yet, because you're injured."

She retracted her left arm, which had a bump in the sleeve from a bandage. "You know, you're the only one who noticed. And what are you doing, admiring a woman's arms, anyway? Geoffrey Darcy, you are in danger of violating propriety."

"And I would speculate that you were in danger of violating propriety when you hurt your arm," he said.

"Don't be snide."

"I'm mocking. It's different from being snide."

She didn't answer, but she didn't contradict him. That was something.

"So I assume you are being properly disciplined for the horrible transgression of ... giving yourself a haircut?"

She rolled her eyes. "*My* parents? All they did was said I couldn't leave the house until after New Years except on official outings. God, I couldn't imagine what Uncle Darcy would say."

Geoffrey tried to picture himself shaving his head and presenting himself to his father. "I don't *want* to imagine it. If it were me, I wouldn't be able to sit down for a week. Yes, you are definitely growing up in the right house."

"Speaking of right houses," Georgiana said, "do give George my regards. I don't know why Aunt Bradley would do this to him – "

"He did call her a – "

"I know!" she giggled. "Well, if he said he did, it must be true. George is a terrible liar. But besides that – "

"He has money," he said, his tone more subdued. "She wants it. And he has no obligation to give her anything significant, not while her husband's alive." He shook his head. "I've never seen a man more upset about having money than George. All right, Uncle Grégoire, but he's another matter entirely, and he's made his peace with it."

"Uncle Darcy will sort everything out," Georgie said. "That's what he does, doesn't he?"

CHAPTER 3

The Matter with Mr. Collins

"THE SOONEST we can expect a reply is probably within a week," Darcy explained to George, who was pale and sweaty, but hardly incoherent as the local doctor tended to him, ordering the servants to provide various supplies. There was little to do for a cold but sit it out. "If they respond positively, Isabella could be here by Christmas."

"Only if she wants to be," George said. "I don't want to force her to do anything else she has no wish to do. She is devastated. She was in love."

"She believed herself to be. She is not old enough to tell the difference between fleeting romance and true emotional attachment."

George leaned his head sideways to give his uncle a look.

"I am not saying she had no feelings. In fact, they could have been passionate. Nonetheless, they were not reciprocated and you were wise to act as you did. It was a great stroke of luck that you were there in time," Darcy said. When his nephew only sighed, Darcy continued, "You have more sympathy here in Derbyshire than you could possibly imagine. I rescued your Aunt Kincaid from very similar circumstances. She was not sixteen and meant to elope with a man –" Realizing that he was speaking, very awkwardly, of George's own father, he continued, "– a man who was after her fortune. Let us leave it at that. The circumstances are still painful to me. Your Uncle Grégoire would say that it was an act of God that I happened to visit her and discover the plot in time, and for once, I would agree with him about the hand of the Divine." Darcy shook his head. "I am starting to talk like him."

"Reading too many of his columns?"

"Precisely," Darcy said with a smile. "Nonetheless, at least I was seven and twenty when I had that terrible duty of consoling my sister, and a man of few pressing obligations at the time. In that way, I was very fortunate." Of course, his sister had also almost stepped into an incestuous marriage, but he didn't need to say that. He didn't know it at the time, and George didn't need to know. For strange reasons, he told George many things he was unwilling or unable to tell his own son, often because George was older, or had more weight on his shoulders at this time in his life, but this he would leave out of the family history. "You did well, George. Anyone who is not proud of you is a fool."

"My mother is less than pleased."

"I will make no further comment, but neither will I withdraw my former one." Darcy rose from his chair as there was a knock at the door. "Hopefully with all of these relatives arriving, you will still manage to get some rest, even if you have to ask me to forcibly eject them."

George smiled. "Let them in."

Darcy opened the door to his nephew Charlie, who bowed. "Uncle Darcy."

"Charles. Come to see your cousin?"

"Yes, sir."

"Your mother is here?"

"She is with Aunt Darcy."

He nodded, and left them together, returning to his study. His son, when he inquired, was still at Chatton House or on his way back. Darcy had not written Bingley personally, as he trusted Elizabeth to do so, and he had other things to see to. The doctor assured him that George was a strong boy and his health would quickly return.

Upon entering his study he withdrew a fresh piece of paper and prepared his pen, pondering how he would phrase this to Grégoire. His brother visited often, but would not be coming for Christmas. Patrick was still a toddler and traveling in the cold was not good for him, and Grégoire would only leave his wife and child for dire emergencies. The only way this would escalate to an emergency – as it seemed, the real emergency had already been averted – was if Lydia Bradley challenged his sheltering of George (and possibly Isabella) in some way, and Grégoire would be little help with that. He would still want to be informed of his nephew's doings, but his presence was not required when it was so cold and hard to travel. It did not look to be an easy winter for Derbyshire. Concerns for his tenants and land were of high priority, but Darcy shoved those aside for the day and focused on the new presence in his home and what needed to be done.

Fortunately there was no need to pen a letter to Georgiana, a task that would have been terrible indeed, as it could not be done without unintentionally forcing both of their emotions about Ramsgate to the surface. It was always painful to open wounds anew. She was not at home, but on her way to Pemberley with her husband and child for Christmas, and even if she had been delayed, she would not receive the letter before her departure. When she got here, it would be Elizabeth who would comfort her. Elizabeth was better at that. Elizabeth, as always, was invaluable. It seemed as if he had been married longer than the sum of his bachelor years, and he simply could not imagine what he would do without her. Had he been remiss in telling her that recently? Guiltily he scratched himself a note to find something special for her for Christmas.

Actions were always so much easier for him than words.

~~~

Jane Bingley's distress at the news was obvious. Elizabeth had picked a private sitting room for just that reason. "Lydia has had outbursts in the past, but to throw her son from his own house? Surely she regretted it immediately. Surely she will send someone to fetch him immediately or come herself."

"I hope for her sake that she does not come herself," Elizabeth answered. "And I do not think George particularly wishes to return to the Bradley house. The only concern he voiced to me was for his sister."

"Isabel is turning into such a charming young lady," Jane said. "She has never expressed discontent with her life in Cheapside. And she has her younger siblings to dote on." The Bradleys now had two daughters and a son, all still very young. "Mr. Bradley is a good man and has never treated her unfairly, and she has nothing to worry about concerning an inheritance."

"Apparently she has everything to worry about," Elizabeth said, "if she is to receive advice that lands her in Scotland."

"Lizzy!"

Elizabeth smiled. Jane was not naïve, just unwilling to see ill in her sister, however deserving Lydia was of it. Or at least, she would not give up her positive thoughts without a fight. "I think the events as recounted are ample proof of that. Either way, we wrote that Isabel can come to Pemberley if she wishes to see George, so it is up to her as much as it can be. And as much as she may love the Bradleys, you know how she adores her brother. Mr. Bradley is a good man, but it is only George that I can say truly has her best interests at heart."

"Poor George," Jane lamented, and Elizabeth frowned in agreement. "And now to be ill on top of everything else."

"It is only a cold. Besides, we all know colds can come about at most auspicious times."

To that, Jane could only hide her grin behind her teacup.

No more visitors arrived after the two Bingleys as they departed and Geoffrey returned from Chatton House. Mr. Bingley sent his regards but would wait for a sick visit, until he came for dinner the following evening. Darcy was reassured by his wife that nothing else could be done at this juncture; all the appropriate people had been contacted, and there was no traveling to be done for almost anyone in this weather.

Dr. Maddox would only be called if George worsened. Sir and Lady Maddox (and children) were not coming to Derbyshire for Christmas this year. They were hosting the Hursts, the Townsends, and the Bertrands for Christmas at their manor outside Cambridge, where Dr. Maddox was a full professor of very good standing in his department. The only new addition to that particular party was Mary and Andrew Bertrand's daughter Margaret, whom the Darcys had formally met at her christening in July. To their relief, Joseph Bennet had taken a liking to his little half-sister "Maggie" and was often seen holding her. The only ones missing from the picture were Brian and Princess Maddox, who were travelling on the company ship to Japan and due to return in early spring. With no children, they had time to travel widely and seemed to take great delight in doing so, and in lavishing attention and gifts upon their extended family of nephews and nieces when they returned. Nadezhda Maddox was a strong woman, a good balancing force for Brian's wild nature. He had proved a responsible business partner to Bingley, an avid scholar in all things exotic, and a loving husband. That he could not be a father seemed to not affect him, at least openly. The Maddoxes were a private couple in their strange little house outside London, and what they said to each other in Romanian or behind closed doors was anybody's guess.

The old generation was gone, with the exception of Mr. Bennet. The group that had once been young couples were now parents, some of them with children entering adulthood. They collectively braced themselves for the tumultuous years when their children would become marriageable and the entire race to marry and settle would begin anew with the next generation.

~~~

At the same time that George Wickham was riding to Derbyshire, hoping to be well-received at Pemberley, the Bellamont family received a very strange guest at their home on the Irish coast. With a bit over two weeks to Christmas, they did not expect anyone from England, much less a Rector of the Church.

Only Grégoire Bellamont recognized him immediately. "Mr. Collins." He bowed. "Do come in, sir. You must be freezing."

"Mr. Bellamont." Mr. Collins, Rector of Hunsford and heir to Longbourn, was indeed standing in the doorway, his black cloak soaked with melted snow. "Thank you for receiving me."

"It is no trouble," Grégoire said, not questioning any further until he dispensed with his self-appointed duties of washing the hands – or at least the fingertips – of his guest using a silver cup that sat by the doorway over a bin. It was an old monastic custom that he had retained and he took a perverse pleasure in the annoyed look he received as he performed it. "Welcome to our home." He handed him a towel. "You are very fortunate. We are about to serve supper. But first, is there some emergency?" Honestly, he could not conceive of a reason for the sudden appearance of Mr. Collins. "Are your wife and children in good health?"

"They are, thank you. No, there is nothing that cannot wait until after dinner."

It was not a large house and the smells from the kitchen filled the dining room, which was the next room over. "Caitlin! We have a guest!" Grégoire called out. There was a servant to take Mr. Collin's coat, but no others visible. "And Mr. Collins, I am pleased to introduce my son Patrick." With great pride he lifted Patrick off the floor in the dining room, where the boy had been playing with his wooden building blocks. "Patrick, this is Mr. Collins. It is important to welcome guests. Say hello to Mr. Collins."

Patrick, who was almost three and actually far more interested in the toy still in his hands, did manage to say, "Mitter Cowwins!"

"Very good." Grégoire kissed his son's cheek and set him back down on the floor. Almost on cue, his wife appeared in the doorway, still wearing an apron. "Caitlin, this is Mr. Collins, a cousin of Mrs. Darcy and a distinguished rector in Kent. Mr. Collins, my wife, Mrs. Bellamont."

Mr. Collins bowed to the woman before him, who eyed him skeptically before curtseying. "I hope yeh like stew."

"I do, madam."

The seating at the table was not conventional and Grégoire knew that, but he never let it bother him. He sat at the head, with his wife on his left and his son on his right, even though Patrick needed to sit on a book to reach the table, or eat standing, and usually made a mess of things. Mr. Collins was placed beside Caitlin, as it was generally the less messy side of the table.

They stood for grace. Grégoire bowed his head and said slowly, so his son could try (and fail) to mimic the words, *"Benedic, Domine, nos et haec Tua dona quae de Tua largitate sumus sumpturi per Christum Dominum Nostrum.* Bless us, Oh Lord, and these Thy gifts which we are about to receive through Thy bounty, through Christ Our Lord. Amen."

"Amen."

They sat down to dinner, which consisted of stew and some black bread. They had a much wider variety of spices than the locals had and Caitlin was getting very good at using them. Mr. Collins went on about the stew, and how flavorful it was, and though

Grégoire could not contradict him, he did cast a glance at Caitlin, who raised her eyebrow at him. He wanted to answer 'I know' but didn't feel it was appropriate. Whatever was really on Mr. Collins' mind – what had dragged him out to the middle of nowhere, Ireland, in December – would clearly not come out in casual conversation.

After dinner, Grégoire offered Mr. Collins a glass of whiskey and said, "I will be with you in a bit. However, it is time for Compline. If you wish, we have numerous books I think will be to your liking."

Mr. Collins retired to the sitting room as Caitlin went to put Patrick to bed. Grégoire tried to put his mind off his guest and retreated to the chapel. He knew the prayers by heart, but he had a book on the stand anyway.

When he returned to the main section of the house, Mr. Collins was still in the sitting room and rose to greet him. "Mr. Bellamont."

"Mr. Collins. Perhaps now you will tell me why you've come so long and so far."

Mr. Collins nodded, but did not smile. "I've been reading your column."

"Oh? I did not know it was being read in Kent."

"It so happened that I heard a most intriguing sermon by the from a fellow vicar and I asked him about it, and he immediately told me that he had pilfered it from some Papist work." He coughed. "Excuse the phrase."

Grégoire just smiled and refilled Mr. Collins' glass. "Of course. But the column is anonymous."

"Yes, but Lady Anne Fitzwilliam of ____shire is my patroness, as you may recall, since the entail on Rosings was broken. When I mentioned it to her, she said she had heard something from Mr. Darcy about how you were writing columns for Irish papers and had even been picked up by a weekly in London."

"I have."

"From there, it did not take much investigation. I have been following it ever since. I admit that I do not always understand – but anyway, that is not precisely why I am here." He paused, holding the drink in his hands as he was seated again. "May I be plain with you?"

"I am a very plain man," Grégoire said, and stoked the fire one more time before returning to his armchair.

"I have come for your blessing."

Grégoire had a hard time not breaking into laughter. "I am quite confused – have you changed your affiliation, which I last remember as being with the Church of England?"

"No, sir, I have not."

"And have you forgotten that I am no longer a man of the cloth, much less a priest, and have no powers of benediction, even if my sort of blessing were not, as you would say, Papist and heretical?"

"No, I have not." Mr. Collins played with the glass. "I usually pride myself on being a most logical and reasonable man, despite my pursuit of a career of Faith. However, I admit that there are things that I am at a loss to explain—and so is everyone else. For example, you cured Lady Catherine when she had her heart failure."

Grégoire frowned. "I did not cure her. I may have soothed her pain but she did eventually, when it was her time, die of a failed heart."

"Nonetheless, it was a miracle."

Grégoire's frown deepened. "Please do not begin down this path, Mr. Collins, as I can now see it clearly. I am not a miracle worker, no matter what everyone thinks. There is a logical explanation for every circumstance surrounding me that has been deemed a miracle," he insisted, though he was perhaps stretching the truth. He did consider his son's birth to be a miracle, as Caitlin had not expected to bear children, but that was not his doing – it was God's, and he had no way of convincing people of that. "It has caused me nothing but trouble and several times almost taken my life!" He took a gulp of his whiskey. Realizing his voice was close to anger, not at Mr. Collins but at his own history and how much pain it brought him just at the memory, he forced himself to lower his voice and its intensity. "Please, sir – tell me what it is you desire and I will tell you, plainly, that I am not capable of it and we can be done with this nonsense. I may be a Papist who believes that His Holiness the Pope holds the keys to the Kingdom of Heaven, but I do not believe in or wish to encourage superstitions."

Grégoire Bellamont rarely raised his voice; he in fact could not recall a time he was so inclined to yell that did not involve just a desire to be heard over his infant son's screaming. It seemed to have a powerful affect on the rector, who trembled but did spit out an answer, "You must understand my situation. I am a father with four daughters." When Grégoire did not respond, Mr. Collin's continued, "I am due to soon inherit the Longbourn estate, as is my right. For years I have scrupulously saved money – and I am very well paid, I admit, for the little that I do – to provide for my family and provide inheritances for my daughters, but when I come to inherit Longbourn, it will be a financial burden I will not be able to bear. It is a massive house in comparison to my home in Hunsford. If there is to be any security for my daughters, I need a son."

Grégoire raised his eyebrows. "Has Mr. Bennet died?"

"No, sir, he has not."

"Then I do not fully understand. I do know of the Longbourn entail, but to my understanding, it is not your concern until his expiration, and last I saw him, he was rather fit for his age." He took another sip. "Nonetheless, it is important to plan ahead, I suppose. Should I leave my mortal coil tomorrow, Heaven forbid, there are arrangements for a steward to manage the accounts until my son comes of age so that my wife can live comfortably here as long as she wishes." He paused. "Tell me – what does your wife have to say of this?"

"She – She shares my concerns, of course. I suppose."

Did she even know he was here? Grégoire didn't want to ask. "Does she desire a son?"

"For hereditary purposes, it is essential."

He decided to phrase the question differently. "Is she happy with the daughters she has?"

Mr. Collins now smiled. "Yes. Very much so."

"And you are as well, I presume? They are well-behaved, obedient children?"

"Yes. Yes, they are. And they take after their mother, who is very beautiful."

"And have you seen to their education?"

"Yes, of course. In particular, my third daughter is a great scholar of Greek and Latin, but they all have rudimentary knowledge of literature and religion – beyond, of course, all of the standard sewing and pianoforte and all that – "

"Of course. And they are happy in their environs?"

Mr. Collins had to consider the question. "Yes, I suppose they are. They are often in town in Kent, of course – the older ones, shopping and the like, or walking around Rosings, which is very beautiful – as you know. And my eldest daughter has a little rose garden beside my vegetables."

"So no one has expressed any discontent, any desire to move to Hertfordshire?"

He paused again. "No."

"And you said that you have saved money so fastidiously that you could provide for them decent inheritances, so that they might find good marriages?"

"Yes."

"Then it seems to me that there is many a man who would be quite envious of your position, Mr. Collins. You have a loving wife, a home you are quite fond of, a profession that suits you, and four daughters who face no great distress and seem to be, from your accounts, happy and growing into respectable ladies, as I have no doubt they will be. You have been diligent in setting aside your earnings to provide for your family, which is a very important fatherly virtue, and are rewarded with a loving family. So, why all this concern?"

Mr. Collins fumbled for an answer. It was not an easy question, which was why Grégoire asked it. He sat there quietly and gave the rector time before he answered, "T-There is the problem of Longbourn –"

"A foolish Papist ex-monk I may be, but I have some understanding of property law in England, and though you will inherit Longbourn, you have no obligation to live in it. Though I know you may not sell it, you may certainly rent it, as my brother did to Lord Richard until Geoffrey turned fifteen and the entail could legally be broken. You could even rent it out for a profit, thereby furthering your own financial interests in terms of providing for your family, who seem so well-settled in Hunsford." He continued, "When I purchased this house, my wife said it was too large. I assured her that we would need the size to host my relatives, and that I owned quite a number of books and would like the space for them." He looked to his side, and then the other. All of the walls of the room, but for the sections with windows, were lined with bookshelves. "Now we have filled this house – with books, with furniture, with pictures – but most importantly, with a child. He is perhaps not old enough to express discontent, but I cannot imagine that he would if he could. If this place were to burn in fire it would be God's will and I would move on, but for now, this house is my home in every meaning of the word and I have no desire to leave it. On the other hand, if my wife came to me and said, 'I hate this house,' I would leave it in a heartbeat. So you see, my own actions are dictated not entirely by my own desires but by the wills of those I love. I would recommend that you do the same."

This idea seemed positively new to Mr. Collins. "But the heritage of the Bennet family and the entail meant to protect it – "

Grégoire waved it off. "That entail was written by men of a previous generation who wanted to protect their own interests and keep the world the exact same way it had always been and was in their lifetime. But change is essential to the world. The only things that stay the same are God and his Divine Plan, and He has yet to inform us of its particulars, so we must keep guessing. Do not be burdened by the past and future when you have more immediate concerns – the happiness of your family, which so far, you have been so successful in providing."

Mr. Collins sat for a while. Grégoire was quite content to let him do so. In his mind, he was already composing his next column.

"How do you think of such things so easily, Brother Grégoire?" Mr. Collins said.

Grégoire looked up. "With the logic and intelligence given by God to every man, Mr. Collins."

Of course, if that was true, Mr. Collins would not be here, asking for his help. Grégoire would not say that, but instead congratulated Mr. Collins on his good decision to stay in Hunsford no matter where the die of fate was cast, and to be relieved of the burden of worrying about a son. The Englishman stayed the night, and left in the morning with many thanks that took far too long.

"What did t'at silly man want?" Caitlin asked at his side, as they waved good-bye to the rector.

"He wanted a miracle. Instead he got some cheap advice. I think I might have cheated him, my darling."

She kissed him. "Yeh sure cheat people in the nicest ways, den."

CHAPTER 4

Dark Conversation

DARCY HAD just dismissed his steward the next day when the Bingleys arrived for supper. Frowning at the clock, he chastised himself for not realizing the time earlier, called for Mr. Reed to come and brush him up quickly, and went to greet his guests.

"Uncle Darcy," Georgiana Bingley curtseyed when it came her turn.

"Miss Bingley," he said, and not another word. When he had his very discreet chance, he glared at Bingley, who just shrugged. Georgie had a very pretty bonnet covering her head, but of course that was little help. The only one who spoke of Georgie's hair was Mr. Bennet, of course, who had always said whatever he liked and would not stop at his age.

"My dear granddaughter," he said, "a man of my age can only take so many shocks in his life. Next time you decide to change sexes, please do send a note in advance."

Georgie wasn't the least bit put off, though she did color a bit. "Of course, Grandpapa."

Dinner conversation largely concerned the weather (terrible weather, even for this time of year) and Mr. Wickham's health (not quite so terrible, but certainly as concerning). They could not yet say if

Isabella Wickham would be joining the party for Christmas, but discussed the possibility.

Mr. Bennet retired early, and Darcy and Bingley escaped to the study for port. Darcy did not want to gossip about Lydia Bradley and whatever trouble she had or would cause over George's sanctuary at Pemberley, and Bingley knew it, so gladly joined in a different conversation.

"The Duke of Devonshire has made an offer on one my properties," Darcy announced. William Cavendish, 7th Duke of Devonshire, owned the other half of Derbyshire, along with many other holdings throughout the kingdom, and was probably the richest man in England. He rarely traveled up north, and the Darcys of Pemberley had always been on friendly terms with Cavendish family.

"Seeking to expand his empire?"

"On the contrary. In return, he has offered not only financial compensation, but a much larger section of land that borders mine to the east."

"What's the incentive?" Bingley asked. "I could never have imagined you discussing selling land in Derbyshire."

"The acres under discussion apparently contain, based on recent expeditions, a very rich vein of coal. So, I would say it is a fairly equal trade, from a purely financial level."

Bingley nodded. "You would pass up on a coal mine that you already own?"

Darcy, set aside his drink. "Did you hear about the mining disaster in Durham? The cave-in where twenty workers were killed?"

"I did."

"Not only was that a tragedy unto itself, but afterward, some of the other workers refused to reenter the mines without costly improvements for their safety, and were consequently fired. They looted the house of the overseer. He barely made it out alive by hiding in the forest until the constable arrived."

Bingley nodded. "I assume this is not one of His Grace's concerns."

"It was a rare occurrence. Nonetheless, it is a very high risk, albeit for a very high profit." And Darcy's good name, of course, was essential to his status as a landlord in Derbyshire.

"Then it seems as if it is a very good trade." Bingley raised his glass. "Congratulations."

"It may be the only time you ever see me contemplate selling a piece of Derbyshire that's been in my family for centuries, even for –" but he was interrupted by a knock on the door. "Come."

Geoffrey Darcy entered. "Uncle Bingley," he acknowledged, and went to whisper to his father that George was ill.

Not entirely sure why his son was trying to keep this from Bingley for the moment, but almost interested in questioning it, Darcy replied, "He has a fever?"

"Yes. And he's – talking nonsense."

Darcy nodded. "Where is the doctor?" he said in a louder voice.

"I called for him. He'd just arrived when I came to find you."

"Good," he said, rising. "Tell your mother." Geoffrey nodded and excused himself.

"George has – "

" – taken a turn for the worse, yes," Darcy said. "Unfortunately, the two best doctors I know are in Chesterton and I would be disturbing their Christmas if I called them here now, so I'd prefer not to do that unless I have to. If you would excuse me - "

Bingley nodded. "Of course."

George was Bingley's nephew as well, if only on one side, but the boy was under Darcy's care, and it was best not to crowd a sick room. Darcy bounded up the stairs past the group of children, nieces and nephews, and entered George's chambers. Only the doctor and the servants were currently there. George was propped up by pillows, a wet cloth over his forehead and his eyes hazy. "Hello, Uncle."

Darcy pulled up a seat next to him. So the boy wasn't so feverish he was speaking in tongues. "Hello, George." He tried to take his hand, but George pulled away.

"Don't touch me!" George said. "Please. Don't let him cut me." His eyes gestured to the doctor.

Darcy looked at the doctor, and then back at George. "I won't." He pulled the doctor aside, almost into the side corridor that led to the washroom. "What is it?"

"He has a high fever. There's no sign of infection, so it may just be from the cold and it should burn off. But he has been talking strangely in the past hour – "

"Geoffrey said it was nonsense."

"Fever does loosen the tongue," the doctor said, "but usually my patients don't accuse me of trying to kill them."

"In my nephew's defense, you do have some very sharp tools laid out on the bed stand."

"He has a fever, Mr. Darcy. He needs at least a preliminary bleeding."

Darcy sighed. "I didn't sanction that."

"I had no intentions of doing so until you did. He made his own assumptions. Among other things."

"Other things?"

"He told me his mother sent me to kill him. He said the nurse was drugging him so he couldn't leave – "

Darcy stopped him. "It is just the fever." He wasn't so sure, but that was none of this doctor's business. "No bleedings."

"But – "

"I have heard it argued, for and against, and I am soundly against it," he said. "And George doesn't want it. If his fever endangers his life, I will reconsider." If the fever didn't break, he would call for Dr. Maddox. The local doctor was good, but he was too traditional, and Darcy was too protective of his family to take any risks. "You are dismissed for the night. I will sit by him and make sure he does not worsen."

The doctor was intelligent enough to understand an order when it was given. He made his suggestions to Darcy and the servant and excused himself, taking his instruments with him.

"He's gone," Darcy said. "He means you no harm, George. I know part of you understands that."

George nodded.

"Someone will stay with you tonight. Your Aunt Darcy wants to see you."

"I said – I don't know what I said. To Geoffrey."

"I know."

"I didn't mean it."

"I know. He knows."

Now George was alarmed. "How does he know? *What did you tell him?*"

"I didn't – he is just very perceptive. I will tell him you are ill from your journey and he will understand." Even though George did not look convinced, Darcy rose. "I must say goodbye to my guests. Will you see your aunt?"

"Yes."

"I will return." He added, "I promise." Only then did Darcy take his leave, to find his wife and son waiting for him in the hallway. Clearly Elizabeth had managed to send the others away. "George is not well. I will stay with him tonight." He turned to Elizabeth. "Will you sit with him while I make our excuses?"

The Bingleys, of course, would understand, as they were as concerned as the rest of the family, and the evening was called short. Arranging everything, Darcy could handle. George was another story.

~~~

Elizabeth had conferred with her son in the hallway while they waited for Darcy to open the door. Apparently Geoffrey had been talking with George when the conversation took an abrupt turn to the morbid, and Geoffrey touched George's brow and found his cousin was burning up. But that was not before George accused his mother of plotting his demise, of the doctor for being part of the conspiracy, of the parade of visitors that evening to be a distraction, of some other things he didn't dare repeat or didn't understand. Only a few hours before, when the Bingleys had visited him before dinner, he had at least been coherent. Obviously he had worsened while they ate.

"You did the right thing," Elizabeth said to her son, who did look like he needed reassuring. "He will be fine. It's the fever talking." She kissed him on the forehead. "If your sisters are not asleep and want to know, tell them what I just said."

"I will."

Geoffrey rushed off, and Elizabeth braced herself and entered the room. Her nephew was not a raving maniac, as she had somehow expected. He was just lying in bed with clenched fists and a pale complexion. "Aunt Darcy."

"Hello, George." She went to feel his forehead, but he jerked away. "Would you like something to drink? You must be parched."

He just nodded.

She quickly had the servant fetch some lemonade, with plenty of ice and sugar. "It's very sweet." She set it on the side-table and George took it with shaking hands and managed to drink about half of it.

"Thank you," he said, his voice a bit less hoarse. "I'm sorry for – doing this to you. I can't seem to do or say anything right."

"You're not doing anything wrong by being ill," she assured him. "Your body is simply exhausted from your heroic efforts in Scotland. Unfortunately, there's too much Darcy blood in you to admit to any weakness."

He gave a little smirk at that. So he had not lost his senses entirely. He was, however, visibly losing what little strength he had. She took a wet towel from the servant and gently placed it on his forehead, wiping the sweat away. This time, he did not resist her. "You can rest now, George." He closed his eyes, and seemed to doze into an uneasy sleep as Darcy reentered the room. "He's just gone out."

They moved into the passageway, where they could speak and not wake him. "I sent the doctor off," Darcy said. "He was going to bleed him, and George didn't want it."

"Do you think he needs it?"

"I don't know. Dr. Maddox is against the practice of bleeding people," he said. "But this is not serious enough for him – yet. Not that I wish it to ever be that serious." He paused uneasily. "How is Geoffrey?"

"A bit spooked."

He just scowled.

"Darcy – what is it?"

"Something – from my Uncle Gregory's journals. I would show you, but Grégoire has them," he said. He did not look at Elizabeth as he said it, keeping an eye on George, now motionless but for his heavy breathing. "When he was young, he said, he had a fever and started talking nonsense. They took it much too seriously and that was the beginning of a long stream of doctors who drove him mad. They made a big deal out of almost nothing. I won't let that happen to George."

She took his hand. "It's not going to happen to George."

"Is Geoffrey still awake?"

"I imagine so."

"I'd best talk to him. Then I'll return and sit with George." He kissed her. "If he wakes, don't tell George what I just said. He'll be told when it's through."

She nodded and slipped out the door. She understood his concerns, which went beyond an ordinary cold and a fever, but that Elizabeth understood him didn't need to be said. At least, not aloud.

~~~

Pemberley was closing down for a cold winter night when Darcy located his son, saying goodnight to his eldest sister. "Papa!"

"You're up late," he said to Anne, kissing her cheek.

"Can I see George?"

"He's sleeping. As you should be."

For once, she did not put up an argument. "Good night, Papa. Good night, Geoffrey."

"Good night."

As she closed the door behind her, Darcy put a hand over his son's shoulder and escorted him to his chambers, dismissing the servants as he went. "George is asleep."

"If you want me to take a shift tonight – "

"No. In the morning perhaps, if his fever isn't broken," Darcy said. "You did the right thing by coming to me when you did." Darcy opened the secret hatch to reveal Geoffrey's stash of liquor.

"I can explain – "

"This is Pemberley, son," he said, taking out two glasses and the wine. "I know every secret nook and cranny. Sit down."

Still embarrassed, Geoffrey took a seat across from his father and accepted the glass of wine.

Darcy poured a very small amount into his own glass. "I know George said some strange things to you, and I could tell you that it was just the fever, but I would be lying. You're not a child anymore, so I feel I cannot lie to you, even when the truth is very ugly." He watched Geoffrey's expressions closely as he continued, "You remember when I brought home the casket of Uncle Gregory and explained who he was?"

"Of course."

"Do you remember when I came home from Austria?"

"A little." Geoffrey had to search his own memories. "I tried to see you, but Uncle Grégoire or Aunt Kincaid would always take me away. They said Austria made you sick."

"Yes," he said. "Austria did make me sick. It rattled me, and it took me longer to recover than it would have a different man. Mentally." He sighed. "When your Great-Uncle Gregory was young, he used to say very strange things. He recorded this in his journal. He had thoughts of which he never understood the origin – suspicious thoughts of other people. His father – your Great-Grandfather Darcy – took him to all kinds of mental doctors and they treated him, among other things, by bleeding him terribly. They never seemed to notice that it only made him worse. Eventually he became so irrational that he asked to be removed to the Isle of Man, and his wish was granted." He looked down at his untouched wine. "My father never took me to any doctors even though I was not particularly a sociable child. He had developed his own fear of them, this one completely rational. You can ask Dr. Maddox if you like, and he will explain at length why he feels the doctors of the mind do more harm than good and have no understanding of their profession, and how some things are better left alone. Anyway, we will never know, but it may have saved me from a fate like my uncle's."

He left it at that for the moment. Geoffrey was old enough to draw conclusions for himself. "...Do you think my sisters are affected?"

"I don't think so, but it's too soon to tell." It was unlikely for Anne and Cassandra, but Sarah was quiet and shy. But then, so had Georgiana Darcy been at her age. "I've suspected George was afflicted for some time, but there's nothing to be done. There's no treatment. You simply – go on."

"And Uncle Grégoire?"

He blinked, as if snapped back into reality, which he had lost for a moment. "What about Uncle Grégoire?"

"Is Uncle Grégoire – you know. Affected."

"What? Oh. No." He chuckled. "He's just a mad religious mystic. It's a different affliction entirely."

"I'm going to tell him you said that."

"I doubt he will deny it."

They shared a laugh together. After a long night, it was a good thing to share.

CHAPTER 5

Unexpected Guests

TO EVERYONE'S RELIEF, George's fever broke after one terrifying day. Darcy had written to Cambridge for Dr. Maddox's opinion, but he did not expect a reply soon enough to truly matter, and he did not request for the man to come. It was simply too close to Christmas and it was an awful thing to ask. There was nothing wrong with the local doctor, except perhaps that he was eager to bleed him, but most doctors were. Darcy fended him off long enough.

When George Wickham awoke from his stupor, the first thing he requested was a hot bath, as he had sweated through his clothes several times now. He was too weak to physically make it to the washroom himself, but when he emerged and was put back on clean sheets, he looked much recovered. He was still coughing and sneezing, and a general exhaustion kept him in bed, but he could receive visitors, and there were many to wish him well. Darcy informed him that he had also written Grégoire, but again, could not expect a reply until well after Christmas or perhaps even the new year.

Aside from his many visitors, George was well occupied by the provisions of the library during his convalescence as the week wore on. When he was strong enough to sit up and read a book, he seemed to at least feel at home in Pemberley.

He was halfway through a rereading of *Romeo and Juliet* when there was a knock on the door. "Come."

It was a servant. His family had arrived – all of them.

~~~

Of all the people Darcy was prepared to receive at Pemberley, Lydia Bradley was probably the lowest person on the list, especially looking disheveled with two screaming toddlers and an infant. She quickly passed off the baby to a male servant, who looked at the bundle in his hands with horror. Mr. Bradley was in a more stately form, as best as he could manage with Isabella Wickham beside him.

Mr. Darcy was just leaving his study, and since they had sent no word ahead of their arrival and his watchmen were not sitting outside in the cold weather and snow, his greeting of his apparent guests was haphazard at best. Still, he was Mr. Darcy of Pemberley, and knew how to receive someone (no matter how unwelcome) with dignity. After all, he had entertained Miss Caroline Bingley for years. "Mr. Bradley, Mrs. Bradley. Miss Wickham. Welcome to Pemberley. Your arrival is somewhat –"

"Where's George?" Isabella interrupted. She did not necessarily mean to be rude – the eagerness in her voice was obviously concern. "Is he all right?"

"He is on the mend. I believe he would be most eager to receive you." Certainly George would want to see his sister before his mother. Darcy only needed to twitch his head and the servants came running to attend to the Bradleys and their trunks – and judging from them, they meant to stay, at least through Christmas. Mrs. Annesley, Georgiana's former companion and present housekeeper after the death of Mrs. Reynolds, immediately appeared to organize everything and whispered to Darcy that his wife was being summoned.

Isabella Wickham was shown upstairs, but Darcy stepped in the way of the horde that tried to follow her. "Mr. Wickham is recovering from a bad cold and fever. He can only see one visitor at a time." That wasn't strictly true, but he said it anyway. As young Julia Bradley tried to run up the stairs after her older sister, Mrs. Annesley was able to grab her dress and prevent her from disobeying completely.

"Mr. Darcy!" Mrs. Bradley said. "My children will not be manhandled! Control your servants!"

Darcy glanced briefly at Mr. Bradley, who offered nothing in response to his wife's demand. "Mrs. Bradley, I assure you, the staff is well trained to handle young children. However, when I said that Mr. Wickham cannot see additional visitors, I was serious." Wondering where Elizabeth was and hoping she arrived before his temper went into full flare, he added, "Perhaps, if you find the staff unsuitable, you would like to see to your children yourself."

Fortunately Elizabeth did not tarry when called, and appeared by his side in time to embrace Julia Bradley as if she was a long-expected guest. "Hello, my darling niece! How I have longed to see you!" She turned to greet the others. "Mr. Bradley. Lydia." Through the briefest of glances to Darcy, she showed her encouragement that the situation would be handled, and saw the relief in his own gaze. "We are a bit surprised to see you, but it is encouraging to see George so well-attended by his family. Fortunately for all of us his illness has nearly passed."

"Where is my son? I must see him!" Lydia said with all of her customary drama, but with none of the anger she had apparently displayed when tossing him out of his house. While the Darcys doubted George's story, they could not help but wonder at the ensuing spectacle. "Oh! I have been so worried about him!"

Darcy cast a look at Mr. Bradley, who was holding his son Brandon. He did stammer out a response. "Thank you for hosting him."

Darcy waved off his concerns. "He is our nephew. It was the least we could do. Mrs. Bradley, I assure you, your son – "

"Has he at least been seen by a doctor?"

While he had his own reservations, he said, "The very best available at such short notice. He was exhausted from his travels, especially since, as you can see, the weather has been somewhat distressing as of late."

Pemberley in winter was still a busy house, and word had gotten out quickly. Geoffrey Darcy appeared at the top of the staircase. "Aunt Bradley.

Uncle Bradley." He very politely joined his mother and father.

"Can we offer you some refreshments?" Mrs. Annesley said, trying to draw the guests to another room.

"I would prefer to see my son."

"He is doing well," Geoffrey said. "I just came from his room. Isabel is with him right now. If you would give him a moment to collect himself - "

"I am his mother, Master Geoffrey! I bathed him when he was a child! He does not need to make himself up for me!"

"Then to compose his thoughts – "

" – which he might need to do," Darcy said, unwilling to maintain the charade of civility much longer, "considering all that has come to pass."

"Mr. Darcy – "

"Mother!" George's voice rang through the corridor, interrupting what probably would not have been a good speech for any of them. "Please." He was holding onto the railing at the top of the stairs, somewhat out of breath. Both his sister and a servant rushed to help him down the stairs, but he shook them off, slowly ambling down to join them of his own power. George Wickham was a sight – his white shirt un-tucked from his breeches, his whiskers overgrown, and his face pale from illness, but he otherwise was on his feet and not a feverish madman. "It is – good to see you. Mr. Bradley." He bowed weakly to his stepfather.

"Gewrge!" screamed Brandon Bradley after freeing himself from his father's grip as he ran to him, grabbing his legs. Geoffrey was quick to grab his cousin before he stumbled as he leaned down to say hello to the toddler.

"Hello. I wasn't expecting a reception – " He looked a bit confused at the sudden appearance of his entire family. He looked even more confused when his mother came to embrace him. "What – what are you doing here?"

"What am I doing here?" She appeared surprised. "How could I not come to my sick child?"

He nodded distractedly, and fell into her arms. Much the taller one of the pair, he had to rest his head on her shoulder.

"We came as soon as we heard," Mr. Bradley chimed in, for what it was worth.

"We'll take you home," Lydia said, "after Christmas." Apparently, she had invited her family to Pemberley. Elizabeth turned to her husband, but Darcy said nothing to approve or disapprove of the notion. He was not willing to cause a scene.

"Is that my daughter?" said another voice, as Mr. Bennet emerged from the library, his walking stick a hard tap against the marble floor. "Which one would this be? I have so many and sometimes they do sound a bit alike."

"Papa!" Lydia squealed at the appearance her father.

"I came as soon as I heard," he said, "that you came as soon as you heard. And here we are, full-circle."

"We've only just arrived," Lydia said.

"No, it must have been a full half an hour ago, for that is precisely how long it takes me to walk from the library to the next room. And I have counted," he said. "Now, aside from seeing your so-called wayward son, and no doubt intending to join us for Christmas without invitation, knowing full well Mr. Darcy is too proper a gentleman not to allow you to stay, what brings you to Derbyshire?"

Elizabeth made some attempt to hide her smile and Darcy kept his silence.

"To collect George, of course," Lydia said, "for he must collect his things before his term beings in the spring."

"Mother," George swallowed, "you know I've been sent down from Oxford."

A hint of disapproval crept on to her face as she turned back to her son. "What?"

"I told you when we came back from Scotland. I returned to Oxford to try and make amends, but they would not allow me to retake the exams."

"George! What are you to do! I told you not to interfere, and now do you see what happens – "

"Lydia," Elizabeth said quickly and very insistently, to stem the rising tide, "George did what he could and it is done. Perhaps you will have your tea now?"

"Lizzy, this is my business and you've interfered enough!" Lydia shouted, continuing before Darcy could defend his wife, "George, you will march right back to Oxford and spend whatever you must to retake those exams. You have more than enough pounds to do it and there must be one bribable Head in the entire university – "

"I will not," George said, his voice holding some power despite his earlier weakness. "It goes against my principles to bribe my way back into University."

"If he had the money, your father would have done – "

"*I am not my father!*" he shouted, abandoning his half-siblings and Geoffrey's helping hand. "My father was tossed from University for destroying a woman's virtue; I was tossed for saving my sister's! I may be cursed to look like him, but I am not my father! No matter what happens, I will not stoop to any dishonorable lows, like marrying my sister to some fortune-hunting, gambling scum – "

"George!" Isabel said, running to his side, but he was not held back. "Mama!" That protest had little effect, either. "Please don't fight over my mistake!"

Lydia and George both ignored anyone's attempts to calm them. "Isabel, you had every right to marry a man you loved. And no one had the right to force you to do otherwise."

"He was marrying her for her trust, Mother! If Uncle Darcy – "

"Yes, yes, your Uncle Darcy is such a saint for giving you all that money, because he loves you so much!" Lydia said. "You, his beloved nephew, who he harbors against your own mother. Well, perhaps you don't know this, but if your Uncle Darcy hadn't forced me to marry Wickham, you would have been a bastard!" she screamed. "So yes, I suppose you are in debt to your dear uncle, for making sure George didn't make his escape and you could be born in wedlock instead of being just another one of his countless bastard issues!"

All the color – what little there was of it – dropped from George's face like a curtain being pulled down over a window. Darcy was, on some level, impressed by George's restraint. While it was certainly beyond any and all propriety to strike one's own mother, he half expected it, since she had given him some cause. Isabel clung to George's side, burying her face in his arms, but he said nothing. There was nothing for him to say – all life, including the power of speech – seemed gone from him.

"Mrs. Bradley," came Darcy's calm voice, "you will leave this place immediately. Whether you choose to take the rest of your current family, I care not, but you have abused your hospitality to the point where I must ask you to leave Pemberley."

"Mr. Darcy – " Mr. Bradley said, trying to play peacemaker.

"My son – "

"Father!"

"Uncle Darcy – "

"Lydia." It was Mr. Bennet's voice that was finally heard above the clamor. "Mr. Darcy is master here and he can decide who to have in his home. You must take his suggestion and vacate the place immediately. I'm sure you will find Chatton House more welcoming of your misbegotten diatribes."

"Papa!"

"Mr. Darcy," Mr. Bradley said more quietly as Darcy motioned for the confused servants to begin putting their trunks back in the carriage, "please – "

"She has done enough damage for today. Perhaps next week I will be more amenable to listening to her accusations, but I will not tolerate this behavior." He turned to Isabella, realizing the immense pressure she was under. "You may stay if you wish. I think that your brother will have a more speedy recovery and this will all be resolved faster if you do."

"Darcy, you cannot keep my own children from me!" Lydia said.

"As long as they remain at Pemberley, and are both of age, I can do as I please," he said.

"Listen to him, Lydia," Mr. Bennet said, also unrelenting. "We will not have anyone else here in a rage, especially not our host."

The Bradleys were gone with the same suddenness that they had appeared. Mr. Bradley tried to talk to his stepson, but George's face was unreadable. He hugged his sister with an extra squeeze as the Bradleys left, and then went back upstairs, shut his door, and locked it behind him. When they pleaded with him to open the door so that he might receive some supper and company, he did not respond. When Darcy retrieved his master keys, he found the keyhole stuffed with a pin, barring his entrance. For three days, George would not see or speak to anyone, and ate only the food that was left for him outside the door.

What he was thinking, no one wanted to contemplate.

When he did open his door, for whatever reason he did, it was just days to Christmas. He was unwashed, unshaven, and pale beyond what he had been when he had been physically ill. He sat unmoving on his bed, and though his sister made various attempts to talk to him, he was not responsive. He remained in this stupor through Darcy's own visit, and then Geoffrey's. Word was sent from Chatton House that the Bradleys were being awkwardly received, and Lydia sent long apologies (by way of Mr. Bradley), but nothing was resolved.

Finally, Elizabeth excused the servants, shut the door, and approached her nephew alone.

"George," Elizabeth said, and seated herself on the bed next to him. He made no acknowledgment of her presence, and kept staring out the window. "What your mother said – "

"It was true," he said, now turning, his sunken eyes conveying their own response. "Mother's not good at keeping secrets, but she's a bad liar. It was true, wasn't it? My father seduced my mother with no good intentions, and if Uncle Darcy hadn't interfered – "

"Yes, that is true, I suppose, though we will never really know what your father was thinking," she said in all fairness. "That is not, however, the whole story. Lydia was young and very silly, and my mother only encouraged her to pursue officers, as it was very fashionable at the time. Even Papa refused to heed to my advice about sending Lydia to visit Brighton, away from any real chaperones. And when she ran away, she left a note saying that they were going to elope, and that they were terribly in love with each other. No doubt she thought herself in love with him, and he must have had at least some affection for her to risk the disapprobation of society by ruining an entire family's good name. She had no inheritance to offer him." When George looked away uncomfortably again, she braced herself and continued, "I confess that I was in quite the opposite quandary – I had rejected Darcy's proposal of marriage because I misjudged his character, and he could not conceive of a way to continue pursuing me that would be within the bounds of his extensive sense of propriety and good manners. He told me that when he heard about Lydia and Wickham, he blamed himself for not properly warning everyone, though in truth it was not his responsibility to tell all of Hertfordshire about your father's past. Darcy pursued them to London and found them, after all of my father and uncle's attempts had failed, and yes, he did put up a great sum to encourage your father to marry Lydia and save the family's reputation. And he paid for the living in Newcastle that would provide for Lydia and any children.

"All of this he did with the knowledge of only my Aunt and Uncle Gardiner, and the reason he gave was the same he gave to me – that he felt responsible for Wickham's deeds, even though he was not, especially since he was not even aware then that Wickham was his half-brother. My aunt told me later she knew from the start not to believe a word of it – Mr. Darcy was buying my good family's reputation so that he could possibly hope to marry me, should I see fit to judge him differently and accept a new offer. But he said not a word to me of the whole thing. I found out only because Lydia spoke of it after her wedding by mistake." She laughed sadly. "Your uncle is comfortable with actions and uncomfortable with words to the point of extremity. He was fortunate that Lydia, as you said, cannot keep a secret. My opinion of him had already changed, but this was so important to my understanding of his character. I cannot imagine how things might have gone if he had not saved Lydia's reputation, and had not been thus encouraged to pursue me further, and had not done so by amending past mistakes by also bringing Mr. Bingley back to my sister Jane. In fact, all three of our marriages came forth because of Lydia's elopement in Brighton. And with our good fortune restored, Kitty found a good husband and Miss Bingley married Dr. Maddox, and through Dr. Maddox, Mary met Dr. Bertrand – " She had not set out to make this precise speech, and was quite surprised to hear the ending out of her own lips. "*All* of this – our entire family – would not have come to be but for your mother and father's romantic entanglement, scandalous as it was at the time. From that perspective, I can only thank them for their deeds."

George and Elizabeth sat in silence, as her words were digested by both of them. When she looked up at the pale, stricken form of George Wickham, so often compared to his father in looks, she decided that those who thought so were wrong. On the surface, perhaps if he had a vicious smile on him, he was the spitting image of his father, but he never had that expression. His dark eyes were full of intelligence and thoughtfulness. He was quiet and shy even in the best of circumstances, but not ignorant of other people's feelings or the subtleties of circumstance. In character, in every way that could be possible with his background and his position in the world, he was firmly not his father. She could not imagine Lydia raising such a son. Despite his mother and his lack of a real father, he had such a firm moral character. Yet he was a troubled child, and his fortune had done nothing except give him opportunities and wealth that Lydia would covet – and he knew it. He had carried around that burden for as long as he had been aware of it.

Elizabeth knew she could assure him that they were proud of him, as Darcy often did. He was a diligent student, a gentleman, a wonderful friend to his cousins, and the best of brothers to his sister. People were lining up to say that. Even Mr. Bradley had probably said it. And yet, the one person he wanted to hear it from told him precisely the opposite.

"George." She spoke again to bring him back to attention, though it was hard to tell if he had lost it. "My sister is not without her faults, but I do not believe she is without her good qualities, either. However long it takes to remind her of them, we will persist. In the meantime, it would help us all if you stop torturing yourself. No good ever came of it. If you have any questions in that regard, ask Uncle

Grégoire sometime, and he will be happy to tell you."

But all the advice and support she could give would not let Elizabeth be his mother. Reality brought that idea to an abrupt halt. He was Lydia's son, and he always would be. She was his mother and she was the one who had to say the words. He would not settle for anything less.

CHAPTER 6

Mr. Bradley's Dilemma

MEANWHILE, the Bradleys' reception at Chatton House had been mixed. The Bingleys were always amiable, though a bit confused at the sudden appearance of the Bradley family. When the full story came out, via correspondences between the two houses of Derbyshire, reactions were even more mixed.

Mr. Bingley was a most gracious host, and whatever had occurred between Lydia and her son, he tried not to let it mar how he received his guests, who were apparently staying for Christmas. The Bradley children were easily amused by the many delights of Chatton House. Bingley had all kinds of strange Oriental items around from his travels and business, and most of them were actually quite hard to break (the ones that were not, he kept on much higher shelves or in locked cabinets). Fortunately, Monkey was practically a trained babysitter, at least until Brandon Bradley pulled on his tail a bit too hard. Then he spat in the boy's face and made a hasty retreat up into the chandelier.

"She *said* that?" Georgie asked as she comforted a trembling monkey in her arms. She, Charlie, and Eliza were conspiring with Geoffrey, who was once again playing courier, in the back room where Georgiana kept most of her art supplies.

"I was there," Geoffrey said, "otherwise I wouldn't believe it myself."

"It's *awful*," she said, scratching behind Monkey's ears as he squawked at her.

"How is George?" Charlie asked.

"He won't talk to anyone. Even Izzy."

"That's so sad," Eliza Bingley said. "But if George won't talk to his mother and he leaves in the spring, where will Izzy go?"

"Back to Town, I suppose."

"But what about getting married?"

"She can't get married without George's or my father's consent," Geoffrey said, giving Monkey a scratch on the head. "Remember, none of this came from me."

Georgiana rolled her eyes. "Of course."

~~~

With another distressing letter from Darcy about young Master George, still holed up in his room, Bingley finally called Mr. Bradley into his office. Lydia was unapproachable, but Bradley had always seemed like a sensible fellow. The old one-eyed soldier entered Bingley's study, which was hardly the tidy office of a gentleman. It was filled with treasures of the east, expensive and extraordinary.

"Mr. Bingley."

"Mr. Bradley. Do come in." He opened his liquor cabinet and poured two glasses of brandy.

The other man made no effort to appear unawares. "I assume you heard from Pemberley?"

"Yes. They are in quite a quandary over – whatever it was that passed between your wife and your stepson. My nephew." Mr. Bradley took the offered glass. "This can't go on. We're due at Pemberley for Christmas, and this situation is causing undue distress to the whole family."

"I know." And he did know, and he did look distressed. Mr. Bradley paced as Bingley sat. "Quite obviously, there has been some discord between Lydia and George in the past few months – or years, I should properly say – but this goes beyond all reason." He shook his head sadly. "I did not have any idea how the meeting with George would go, though I don't believe it could have possibly gone worse." He took a sip and kept pacing. "It is hard for me to be severe with her – you can understand how she can get. And she can be a very loving mother. She does, in fact, love all of her children."

With all things said and done, Bingley did not hold back, "She does not always show it."

"No." He grumbled the grumble of a soldier faced with a strategy unrealized. "She does compare her life to that of her sisters – all of whom seem to have succeeded beyond their wildest dreams. And because of her mistake with Mr. Wickham, she is doomed to live in poverty."

"That is obviously at least somewhat an exaggeration of the fact."

"Of course," Mr. Bradley said. "She married me knowing full well my finances, and we've never starved or suffered for lack of heat or clothing. But she was very young when this all happened. Younger than all of her sisters."

"Yes."

"I'm not trying to justify her situation – at least in terms of her relationship with her son. Her son who reminds her so much of her late husband – "

" –if she only looks at him. In every other way, he is different. Surely you can see that."

"George has matured into a gentleman who desires a higher education and a respectable living. How can I not be proud of that, even if I only had a small part of it?"

"Then you have to make her see that," Bingley said. "I'm sorry to say that, Mr. Bradley, but George is my nephew, and I saw him last week, when he was ill from all his travels and worried sick for his sister. This must be made right. If Mrs. Bradley has issues with George Wickham, she must take it up with his ghost, not the son who resembles him."

Mr. Bradley just nodded, speechless.

~~~

He had told Bingley that she could be a good mother. Mr. Bradley wasn't lying. He found his wife attending to their youngest child, Maria, named after one of her old friends from Hertfordshire, Maria Lucas. The baby was just beginning to stand up in her crib and Lydia was talking nonsense to her. It warmed his heart to see the smile on his daughter's face with her mother's attention. "Hello, Maria." He leaned over and kissed her where her soft brown hair, so like his, was starting to grow.

"She's almost ready for a nap, I think," Lydia said. "She just doesn't know it yet."

"Well, I never much understood baby-speak, so you'd best tell her."

Lydia did succeed in getting the baby to sleep. They checked on Brandon, who was still sleeping, and Julia was with one of the Bingleys' nurses. "Lydia," he said, as they took the seat by the window; it was only December and Derbyshire was deep in snow. "You know what I'm going to say."

"I must apologize to George."

"If not for George's sake – though he does deserve it for himself – then at least for the family at large."

She frowned. "I cannot take back what is true."

"George was born respectably after you married Mr. Wickham. What of it now, almost twenty years later? Why harp on such a small thing when you knew it would devastate him?"

She turned away. "You don't understand. You weren't there."

"And neither was George! He barely knew his father – he says he only has a vague memory of his father taking him to see the soldiers march, and then the funeral. Why should you make it weigh so heavily on him?"

"*Everything* weighs heavily on him. You know that. You have one good eye that can see quite well that he's sick," she said. "But oh no, they never

speak of it. No one ever talks about the Darcy illness
– "

" – Most people don't talk about uncomfortable
subjects," he said, "if they can manage it."

" – Instead they throw money at him and leave
the raising to us. And I'm told not to send him to a
doctor; that it will only make him worse. Do you
know what he said to me last summer, when he had
that fever from – "

"I was there, yes." Now it was his turn to deal
with uncomfortable subjects he didn't want to
discuss. Fever or illness loosened George's tongue,
and strange things came out: conspiracies against
him, theories about the universe; the ravings of a
madman. "He doesn't remember, and it means
nothing. He did not mean what he said. That is why
he doesn't need to apologize for it." He sighed. "We
raise him because *we're* his parents. You're his
mother and for all purposes, I am his father. If he
doesn't have us, then all of his wild thoughts that he
shares only under the influence of illness might as
well be true. Life is not perfect for anyone, Lydia.
Think of the very wealthy Darcys and their grand
estate and their hereditary madness. Or the Bingleys
with their wild children. No family is perfect."

"That doesn't excuse George."

"Excuse him from *what?*"

"You don't understand." She raised her eyes,
filled with tears. "*You can never understand.*"

Then, she made a successful retreat while he sat
there, dumbfounded.

At that precise moment, Maria decided to start crying. Wherever Lydia had gone, it was far enough away for her to not hear it, or choose to ignore it. It was Jane Bingley who entered the room. "Mr. Bradley."

"Mrs. Bingley." He hurried to his feet. "Excuse me." He picked up his daughter and took her into his arms. A nurse appeared, but he shooed her away. "She just needs to be rocked. That's all."

"I saw Lydia – "

"I know." He sighed as he tightened his grip on his daughter, rocking her back and forth. "I – she can't forgive George."

"Which George does she mean?"

Realization dawned. "Oh God."

Jane's face, usually so relaxed and calm, tightened. "I'll find her."

"You don't need to – "

"She's my sister. Yes, I need to. Mr. Bradley." She curtseyed perfunctorily and was gone, leaving him alone with his daughter.

~~~

Jane Bingley had her limits. She was understanding when her husband had some wild notion of Oriental mysticism that he wanted to tell everyone, or when her eldest daughter came back from "walking in the forest" with more cuts and bruises than she could explain. Even when her younger daughter complained that she had every right to be out if Georgie was out and didn't even want to be, or Charlie got into trouble messing around with his sister and his cousin. She was understanding when Edmund tried to copy his older brother in a stunt he was not big enough for, or when the family pet destroyed yet another dinner display by consuming half of it and stomping in the other half before it could make it to the table. But if there was one thing she would not stand for, it was the mistreatment of any of the children in her family. They were children, and had to be protected, no matter how old they got and how much clothing they grew out of and what they did with their hair. Especially a mature child who had done more than his share to protect his sister from their own mother's mechanisms – for mistreatment of such a child, there was no excuse.

"Lydia," Jane said when she finally found her sister in the sitting room, trying to concentrate on a knitting project. "We should talk."

Lydia looked up at her with pathetically pleading eyes. "Can a mother not have some peace?"

"Not when she behaves like a wicked witch and not a proper mother." Lydia's face reflected her shock at Jane's severe tone "Lydia Bradley, you cannot blame George for his father's failures anymore. He is not a target for your anger simply because he resembles his father. Mr. Wickham seduced you when you were innocent no matter how willing you were, Mr. Darcy made it possible for you to have some kind of life, and Wickham died of his own folly. If you can't make peace with that, at least spare George the brunt of it."

"What he did to me – "

" – was twenty years ago, and if he had the power to apologize when he was alive, he has none now. So curse his grave all you want and be done with it, and leave your son alone." She did not soften her tone. "George is not well, physically and mentally, and most, if not all, of his pain is your doing. Forget the Darcy curse and what you consider the guilt money he gave to your children. This has nothing to do with that. Of his own volition George saved his sister from ruin, just as his uncle did, and you would curse him for it! What must he do? Dye his hair and put on glasses? Will that redirect your irrational anger?" Jane sighed. "If you want to carry a grudge, that is your business. Do not make him carry it as well. He knows his father was a man of scorn. Nothing you say will surprise him. That does not mean you have the right to say things that you know will hurt him. For God's sake, he's your son! I would *never* willingly hurt my sons! I can't think of another person in this family who would! You will march back to Pemberley, say whatever you must to the grave of George Wickham, and then tell your son that you love him and you were foolish enough to misdirect your childish anger and your greed onto the person most wholly unworthy of it!" If that was not enough, she pointed to the door and shouted, "*Now!*"

She did not quite need to stamp her foot, and Lydia was gone. She was still poised to do so when she said, "I see you there. You are not the eavesdropper you think you are."

79

Georgiana Bingley poked her head around the corner. "Sorry, Mama. Still – "

"Not a word of this."

Her daughter for once appeared a bit intimidated. "Of course, Mama."

~~~

"Tomorrow night is Christmas Eve," Isabel Wickham said, staring out the window as her brother shaved. He still had not left his room, but was at least responsive. "Are we supposed to stay here? Should I go to Chatton House?"

"If you want to," George said, tapping the razor against the basin to get the suds off.

"I won't leave you."

"You should. If it'll upset Mother – " Before he could finish his sentence, the door creaked open.

"Mama!"

Isabel's surprise could only mean one thing. George rose and numbly bowed to his mother as she came into the room, but said nothing.

"Leave us, Isabel," Lydia said, and Isabel scurried out, leaving mother and son alone. George wiped the last of the shaving cream from his face and faced her. "Hello George." When he still offered her no greeting, she turned to the window. "You can almost see the graveyard from here."

"I suppose."

She turned to him, putting a hand on his fresh cheek. "You do look like your father."

"I know, Mother."

"There's no easy way for a woman to admit she was foolish in her youth, but I was taken in by his charms – and his smile. If only you would smile, I'm sure you would have the ladies at your feet like he did." When he squirmed, she stroked his hair. He had long sideburns, like his father. "It's not a curse to have his good looks. It's how you use them. And if your father had not misused them – well, I wouldn't have you, or Isabel, or Mr. Bradley I suppose. Do you know how he died?" She didn't give him time to respond. "He died in my arms. You know the part about him saving his half-brothers' lives by sending Dr. Maddox off. After years of neglect and –" She stopped herself. "But you don't want to hear this. You don't need the burden of your father's issues. He made you and somehow, despite the stupidity of both of your parents, you are a brilliant son. Everyone has only the highest expectations of you because you've given us every reason to believe in you. Even when I made a mistake with Izzy, you were there to stop me." She smiled through her tears. "I've never done anything in my life to deserve a son like you."

When she fell into his arms, he wrapped his around her, his first real response to her presence and the only one that fulfilled its needs.

~~~

"Papa! Just one?"

"No dear," Darcy put his hand on the shoulder of Cassandra Darcy, his youngest daughter as he closed the letter from Grégoire, wishing them all well. "It's not Christmas yet."

"Then at midnight?"

"At midnight we have church."

"After church?"

She was too big for him to easily lift, so he leaned over and kissed her. "After church we sleep. Presents are for the morning."

"Just one? The one I just got from Uncle Grégoire? *Please ...*"

He sighed. "Alright. Just the one from Uncle Grégoire." She screamed in delight and opened the box that had come from her uncle, which contained a little jewelry box made of wood. He was getting better and better at carving things. Darcy smiled at his nephew, as George was then assaulted in a similar manner by his own half-sister Julia, who had already opened her gift from him.

"George! Help me put it on!" She held up the beaded necklace he had quickly purchased for her at Lambton.

"All right." He helped her with the latch in the back.

"Thank you, George!" she said, hugging him before running off. "Mama! Mama! I found where George hid his presents for everyone!"

Geoffrey chose that time to enter, passing Julia on the way in. "I'd like to know where George's secret present hiding place is. Maybe I should follow her." He poured himself a glass of the brandy his father and cousin were sharing, and raised it in a toast. "Father. George. Happy Christmas."

"Happy Christmas," they said in unison, and agreed that with a reconciliation between all parts of the family that brought them into each other's easy company, it was a happy Christmas indeed.

CHAPTER 7

Barefoot in the Snow

IT WAS NOT the easiest Christmas ever, but it was a relief to everyone that Lydia and George were getting along. Words had been said that could not be unsaid, but the rift between them had been closed a little, enough for Pemberley to be opened to the Bradleys and the three families to enjoy the week's festivities together.

Letters arrived from all of their relations wishing them well, including one from Dr. Maddox wishing George especially well. He was relieved to hear (when he finally did hear and had time to reply) that George had returned to health, and offered to help set a date for entrance exams to Cambridge, where he was a professor, so that George could have special permission to enter midyear. Darcy was pleased by the offer, but even more by the prospect of George attending Cambridge. Of course, he expressed this only to Elizabeth: at Cambridge, George would have a protector and advisor in Dr. Maddox.

The trickier situation lay with Isabella Wickham. Though she did not openly say so and neither did her parents, there would be some awkwardness in returning to London with them, though it had been her home all her life.

"I want to live with George," she told Elizabeth in confidence, "but I know that's not appropriate. I love my parents, but..." What was left unsaid was that her loyalties lay with the person who protected her in her hour of need, not the ones who encouraged her down the road to disaster.

The Darcys conspired to take the Bradleys aside and inquire as to whether Isabel might benefit from spending some time in the country, as there would certainly be gossip about her flight to Gretna Green. In London, she would have to endure it, while if she was out of sight, people would soon forget about it and move on to the next mild scandal.

"Isabel is my darling," Lydia crooned, but Mr. Bradley put his arm around her.

"It would be better for her reputation," he said, "if her presence does not feed the scandal."

The solution came when the Maddoxes offered to take her in. They had a country house in Chesterton, but a few miles from Cambridge, where Dr. Maddox had his professorship. She would live there while George sat for his spring term, and then they would return to London for the season, where George would (and this part remained unspoken) keep an eye on his sister and make sure she was less forwardly put out to society.

It was all negotiated and settled by New Year's, at least on the surface. But Lydia had no qualms about storming into Darcy's office a few days before she was to leave and saying otherwise. "I know you're all conspiring to take my children from me."

"Your children are going to places where they will have the best possible advantages for their future happiness," Darcy replied with his customary tone of dismissal.

Lydia stormed off in search of other prey, but Elizabeth was not easily moved, either. She responded, "Every year I send my son away to Eton for his education and it breaks my heart to see him go. Nonetheless it is a necessary part of his development. George will do well at Cambridge and Isabel will do well in the country for the winter. They will both be back in Town for the Season."

Her avenues of complaint exhausted, Lydia did not attempt further disruption of the plan. She experienced some loss of composure when it was time for the family to part again, George and Isabel to the Maddox house in Chesterton, the Bradleys to Cheapside.

"I'm sure you'll do well at Cambridge. All of that reading couldn't have been for nothing," she said, which was about as good as she got at complimenting George. As she embraced him one last time, she whispered, "Take care of your sister."

He responded, "I promise."

~~~

With the Wickhams and the Bradleys gone, this time to safe harbors, a breath of relief passed over Darcy's part of Derbyshire. The wind that brought relief was also accompanied by a snowfall unparalleled in anyone's memory. And then another one. And another one. There were many dark, cold nights that winter, when Darcy closed up most of the wings of Pemberley and kept alive only the study, the library, the family's chambers, and the servants' quarters. There were days when passage between even Pemberley and Chatton House stopped completely, and the post was also held for weeks at a time, arriving in large bundles with multiple letters with different dates on them.

Derbyshire was suffering. Those who could not afford coal risked death, and with higher grain prices, lower wages, and the roads un-cleared for basic deliveries, Darcy knew it was a dangerous time. Bingley's holdings in Derbyshire did not extend past Chatton House's grounds, but Darcy was a landlord, with tenants and workers, and he saw to them all. He went out himself more than once to deliver coal and bread to his poorer tenants. Mrs. Darcy, who regularly visited the poor, did her share, but sometimes the roads were simply too dangerous, and only the most daring adventurer would wander outside. Darcy found, but would not admit, that he could no longer carry a full bag of coal, even with a walking stick, as he could in his younger days, and his joints bothered him when it got especially cold.

"You'll learn to stay by the fireplace," Mr. Bennet said. "You seem to like it so much anyway, always staring into it and playing with the fire."

What little winter game there was to be had was being quickly consumed by Derbyshire's imported wolf population, existing thanks to a misguided baronet who had thought they were dogs and let them breed. Their numbers did not grow wild because of infrequent but necessary wolf hunts, but none had taken place recently. In the winter the wolves grew more desperate, causing mothers to worry about their babies, even though no one in their right mind would leave their child on the front steps, especially if the front steps were barely clear of snow and ice. An expedition of huntsmen to shoot the wolves nearly ended in disaster, saved from freezing to death only by their stumbling into Pemberley's quarters, and they all shambled home a few days later with bad colds and no wolf hides.

More than one tenant braved the snow to ask Mr. Darcy personally for an extension on the rent due, with the price of coal and food so high, and he readily granted many extensions, recording them all. On the grounds of Derbyshire that belonged to the Duke of Devonshire, himself safely in Devonshire in the south, people were ill or dying left and right, of either starvation or exposure, and Darcy personally wrote the Duke to apprise him of the situation.

"And if he doesn't respond?" Elizabeth asked.

Darcy shrugged. His charity that winter was extensive in his own lands, far beyond the norm, and Pemberley was beginning to get stretched thin, not for the more expensive items, but for the basic ones they used every day, like firewood and grain for bread. They were never short of anything, but Darcy kept a close eye on his own stocks.

Eton's start and end were off schedule. It was not until the first thaw began that Geoffrey and Charlie returned from the winter term at Eton. Charlie still had an additional year before University, and Edmund had not started yet. Elizabeth decided to hold an open celebration at Pemberley for their tenants and servants, not a usual custom of spring, but certainly well appreciated after the harsh winter. The people flocked to Pemberley on a bright day in early March and feasted in the great hall on many bottles of wine and all sorts of things that had been stored for winter – cheese, pastries, stews and white bread. Darcy presided over it with a quiet pride and an obvious relief; only two of his tenants had died, both of them advanced in years, from the cold.

"Mr. Darcy," Old Man Jenkins, whose wife had sadly passed away the year before, not of bad conditions but of a heart attack, took the opportunity to personally shake his landlord's hand. "Without your kindness, I would not have seen this day."

Darcy nodded his thanks. He did not speak much at social gatherings, but that was either already well known by the people of Derbyshire, and now his reticence was balanced by his wife. There were inquiries after Lady Kincaid, the former Miss Darcy, and Elizabeth said she was well in Scotland with her husband and son. She did not include that another child was expected in the fall; that was not for public knowledge. Elizabeth played hostess to perfection. Her daughters were too young to stay at the event for long, as it lasted until well past their usual bedtime, so most of the attention went to young Master Geoffrey. Geoffrey, like his mother, took hosting in stride, and for that, Darcy was silently grateful as he stood in a corner. He was grateful for many things that day, but most of all, that Geoffrey was becoming the man he needed to be, and with greater ease than Darcy had.

The celebrations were called to a close before anyone got truly or embarrassingly drunk, though a few men needed the help of their wives or fellow workers to walk home, as they left with many thanks to the Darcys. The Bingleys stayed for a while longer, eager to see their long-lost relatives, and the boys retreated to their own rooms, where they could drink from Geoffrey's stash without the watchful eyes of the servants. They dropped off quickly; Edmund and Charlie were sleeping on the couch and the girls were still chatting in another room. Only Geoffrey and Georgie remained awake, quite tipsy, sitting across from each other at the card table, the bottle of whiskey between them.

"This'll be you someday," Georgiana Bingley said with a wave of her hand to sort of gesture to Pemberley at large. "Feedin' the poor an' hosting parties. And grey. Grey hair."

"My father's not all grey. Not like Grandfather Bennet."

"Grandpapa's hair is *white*. Don't you know *colors?*"

"Aren't you a *lush?*"

Georgie giggled. "Compared to my brothers, no." They glanced over at Charlie snoring on the couch, Edmund leaning on his shoulder. "Couple shots put 'em out."

"So what did you do all winter?" he said.

"What? Lady things. Painting. Drawing. Buyin' ribbons. What do you think." She pointed at him. "Don't you look at me like that, Mr. Darcy!"

"I heard you had a cold every other week."

"You heard wrong."

"I heard – "

"You've never been barefoot in the snow?"

He stared. "What? That must be painful."

"Builds strength. You place your feet in very cold water right before you go out, then cold water right when you come in, then hot water again. Aunt Nadi-sama told me."

"How does she know?"

"Uncle Brian does it. Samurai training. They have to be *tough*."

She pushed her glass away. "I think I shall be sick."

"You will?"

"Not – now." She swallowed very distinctively. "If I drink anymore though." She leaned her head against the wall.

Geoffrey stood up, steadied himself and picked her up, to which she gave no protest, and set her down more comfortably in the armchair. "You don't have to be tough, you know."

"You don't – you'll see," she said, before dropping off into sleep.

Geoffrey, who was not in much better condition than his cousin, managed to put the glasses away and cap the whiskey before he settled into his own chair. He did not fall asleep, but he was lost in thought until the servants came to collect the Bingleys for departure.

~~~

"Welcome to our home," Dr. Maddox said upon the Wickhams' arrival in January. "I hope you find it to your liking."

He knew perfectly well that that there was nothing to dislike. Lady Maddox had gone to extensive lengths to renovate the house, now called Maddox Hall, as it had no name, nor deserved one, prior to the renovations. It was tastefully done and in the latest styles, with all of the draperies and elegant tapestries well-placed and pleasing to the eye. George and Isabel's chambers were palatial compared to their house in Gracechurch Street, and when their clothing and other items arrived from London some weeks later, they hardly filled their own closets and wardrobes. The Christmas guests (the Townsends and the Bertrands) had already left, so George and Isabel passed the time with their cousins, when George wasn't studying for his exams. He studied often, even though Dr. Maddox was more than sure he would pass without trouble.

"The boy worries too much," Maddox said to his wife in private.

"His worrying, as you call it, saved his sister, so I am not one to question him about it," she answered.

Still strictly in the royal service, Dr. Maddox taught only two lectures, one on surgical basics and one on anatomy, neither of which would be in George's curriculum as a first-year student. His studies would be almost exclusively the classics and mathematics, with some logic on the side. As for George losing a semester at Oxford, Dr. Maddox replied, "No harm done. I was always more of a Cambridge man anyway."

Frederick Maddox was a year behind Charlie at Eton, and would leave for spring term about the same time the term would begin at Cambridge. Emily Maddox was not yet out like Isabel, but probably would be within a year or two. The two were nearly the same age, and became fast friends almost instantly, to George's great relief. He himself tried to get along with the Maddox boys as well as he could, but found it a challenge. Daniel Maddox Junior was not yet old enough for Eton, and had not had his growth spurt, but he was obsessed with martial activities anyway, and would fence his brother at any opportunity. He was most disappointed to learn that George was not a fencer.

"He is a wimp," Frederick whispered, but not quietly enough. In response, George stood silently, towering over him, until Frederick backed down and apologized.

Although George did not easily take to Frederick, he was surprised by the younger boy's intellect. While not inclined to his studies, when he chose to apply himself, Frederick Maddox took to learning with shocking ease and always had the highest marks in his class (despite the poorest attendance record and the worst reports about his behavior). He could talk at length about art, architecture, or any of the liberal arts and sciences, and he spoke four languages. The fact that he was more interested in booze and women (or more accurately, the prospect of them) was another matter. Even though he was well past the age that he might have expected to need them, Frederick also did not seem to need glasses, as his father did. Neither did Emily, and Danny was still much younger than Dr. Maddox had been when he began losing his sight. But the thought of it made George notice what he had never had much cause to notice before: Frederick did not resemble either of his parents. He was a twin, so he ought to resemble the family, but by some happenstance of nature he had brown hair while his parents had black and red hair and his siblings were both fair-haired. His facial features were also different, with a more distinct and almost crooked nose, and he had not the height of his father even though he was close to the age where he should be attaining it. But this, like most things, George kept to himself.

George visited Cambridge as weather permitted, to collect books for study or simply to get out of the house. He had been a monk, as far as he was concerned, since mid-December, and that was quite long enough. It was not long before he knew the best (and cleanest) house in Cambridge, and the most discreet, to take care of his needs. Unlike his father's much-maligned habits, he leaned toward monogamy. He found a woman he liked by the name of Lucille, who seemed to be both talented and free of disease, and made sporadic appointments that would increase to regular sessions once his school schedule was set and he was safely housed at Cambridge itself. He did it with no guilt; it was his only major expenditure of his fortune beyond books, and he lived so sparsely that it was hardly a dent in his income. He was a man, and he had needs. He came to that realization at sixteen and never looked back. His only great desire was to keep it from his sister and the family at large, and so far, anyone who knew had not raised issue.

At the Maddox home, he was quiet and observant, and there were other things he noticed. Lady Maddox loved to host, and they met most of the local families of note, most of them associated in some way with the university. A few girls at the table cast their eyes on George, but he reserved his energy for staring down anyone who cast eyes at his sister. When the invitations were returned, they saw the other manors and halls of the area, and George noticed that Dr. Maddox took his walking stick with him. He did not have a massive gentlemanly one – his had a smaller handle with a leather string as a handle, and a ball at the tip. Sometimes when they went to places he had never been before, he carried it around when he was inside, not using it for support but instead to find the floor and the steps. He never gave indication that his sight was fading, and could still read and write and obviously see people, but objects in the distance bothered him, or unfamiliar houses. There was a strict rule at the Maddox house not to move any of the furniture without prior permission; George figured that this was as much for Dr. Maddox to know where all the furniture was as it was in keeping with Lady Maddox's insistence on perfect décor.

Dr. Maddox showed him to the lab more than once, and for the first time, George was allowed to use the famous microscope, and to see how opium was harvested and many of the tinctures were made. He discovered that he liked it more than learning classics. He enjoyed his academic studies, but there was something to be said for learning with a practical application.

"We assumed you would go into law or the church," Dr. Maddox said to him in the laboratory one day, "but would you perhaps be interested in medicine?"

"Perhaps," George said. "I heard about your surgical lectures."

"The ones with the dissections? Well, the challenge is not to see if you can make it through the first one without being ill, young master Wickham. The challenge is to make it to the second one."

"I'll try to remember that," George said, and the lesson in tonics continued.

CHAPTER 8

Tenant Troubles

"THE ESTEEMED GEORGE WICKHAM," Darcy announced to those at the supper table, "will be attending Cambridge at the start of the spring term, having passed all of his entrance exams."

"Bravo!" Bingley said, and they raised their glasses to the young man in question. "And Miss Wickham is ...?"

"Staying with Sir and Lady Maddox until the end of his term, when they shall both return to Town."

"Capital news."

"Indeed," Darcy said, and turned to his son. "If you are looking for a roommate – "

"I'll room with George. Of course." And he looked excited to do it. Geoffrey and George had always gotten along well. In fact, Geoffrey looked relieved that he would not be entering Cambridge alone, as he'd done with Eton. He would have George, who was older and more experienced.

Darcy excused himself after dinner when his steward appeared, and they were gone a long time in the study before rejoining his wife and the Bingleys. Though the line was blurring as the children grew up, the adult Bingleys and Darcys, with Mr. Bennet, stayed together for separate conversation or entertainment after supper, while even the oldest children left, preferring to spend time with their younger siblings. "Excuse me," Darcy said, reentering the room, where Elizabeth had just finished a sonata.

"What kind of man is not present for his wife's performances?" Mr. Bennet said. "Oh, I've grown forgetful. I am that sort of man. Well, you're in good company, then."

"Did Mrs. Bennet play?" Bingley asked.

"She did," Mr. Bennet said, and shock registered on Elizabeth and Jane's faces. "She had no time for it after Kitty came along – four children, and one more on the way. But when I said performances, Mr. Bingley, I meant the type that you were accustomed to." He smiled and sipped his port. "She did play a lovely tune, though." Even though it had been several years, Mr. Bennet had never removed his black band of mourning for his wife.

"I assume Mr. Darcy only missed my performance because he was called out on important business," Elizabeth said confidently of her husband.

"Yes," he said, and left it at that, taking his seat as she agreed to play another round for her husband.

When it was time to retire, Jane went to round up her children, and in the hallway, Bingley found Darcy, who turned to him and said, "There may be some value to being in trade and not invested in land."

"I never thought I would hear you say that," Bingley said. "So now you must explain."

"It is merely rent dispute after rent dispute. I allowed so many tenants to forego their rent during the winter and now they seem to have forgotten that and are wondering why I am charging them double the month's rent now. But none of this should be unexpected. People are very good at forgetting when they owe money."

"You're not charging them interest?"

"I'd make a fortune if I did, but this was not a loan – it was an allowance for a delay in payment."

"So being too good has gotten you into some trouble?"

Darcy shrugged. "So it seems."

~~~

Geoffrey Darcy often lamented that some of his time at home between terms was always spent watching his father settle disputes, but he knew it was important. Important, but often boring, nonetheless.

In the morning Darcy saw two tenants, both of whom lived on grazing land that they rented to shepherds and then helped shear the wool in the spring. Why Darcy was seeing them both at once, Geoffrey had no idea. Scheduling, he supposed. The two men were Mr. Peters and Mr. Wallace, brothers by marriage, who had farms side-by-side and had done equally poorly in the harsh winter. They had done so badly that they asked for the postponement of their rent, and Darcy had granted it. All this the steward made note of before the two tenants entered, worn men, field laborers, with soiled boots and clothing that had been re-sewn too many times.

Nonetheless Darcy greeted them with his customary civility and bowed to his tenants. Very rarely did he let them into his study, and he had a purpose. In his ledgers he had marked off February, the month they had failed to make their rents, and next to his own signatures, Mr. Peters had signed and Mr. Wallace had made his mark. So it was there, in writing, that they owed this and last month's rent, and Mr. Peters could read.

"So there we have it," Mr. Darcy said. "It was a hard winter for everyone in Derbyshire, including those with sheep, but I understand that Mr. MacDonald purchased a new flock and will be using both of your fields for it."

"He has," Mr. Peters said, "though that's none of your business."

"As your landlord, the state of your land is my business. It is the town's business as well, as one only has to stop in a tavern to hear about Mr. MacDonald and his new flock. But the point is, you are in a much more favorable position now than you were on the first of February, and yet are still five days late on the rent."

"My lord, I admit that – "

"Don' be callin' 'im that," Wallace said. "'e's not a lord. Mr. Darcy, yes, we can make the rent. Just suppose we don't want to."

Darcy paused, and with no display of emotion that either of them could detect, said, "It is your obligation by law to pay the rent due to the owner of that property." Darcy wasn't trying to raise the tension in the room, but he himself was tense. It was one thing to not have the money. It was another to refuse it when it was due.

"What if we think the owner's been unfair to us poor commoners?"

"If you think the owner has been unfair, and was cruel and intolerant when he let you fully forego your rent when it was due, simply out of the kindness of his heart and against his own financial interests, then you may take me to court, and run up a large bill doing so before the judge tears apart your case."

Mr. Peters, an older man than his brother-in-law, rose from his seat. "John, just let him have – "

"No. I want the answer to the question," Mr. Wallace said.

"I believe I have answered it."

"Then I'll rephrase. What if we think you've been unfair and I guess the law's been unfair, protecting you and not us?" Even though Peters was tugging at his arm, he continued, "What says it tis'int our land that we been workin' on our whole lives? Because you have a piece of paper that says it's yours?"

Geoffrey watched his father sigh. "Yes, Mr. Wallace. The only reason you have been working that land – legally – is because it was rented to your father-in-law, James Peters, when he came north to look for work some thirty years ago. I remember him quite well— a good man who worked hard to provide for his family, and so has provided portions for both his son and his daughter's husband, when another man might only have collected enough to provide for the son. And with him I signed a contract of tenancy, and with you and your brother upon his death we renewed it. If you'd like me to produce the document, I would be happy to, if it is in some dispute. However, as to your larger question, these are the laws that govern our society; we would not have a society without them."

It was amazing to Geoffrey that his father could talk with increasing sternness without increasing his volume, even though there was tension enough on the tenants' side as they face the diatribe. Mr. Darcy, despite his fancy clothing and polished boots, was no dandy and could be as intimidating as he liked.

"My apologies, Mr. Darcy, sir," Mr. Peters rushed in before his brother in law could recover. "We hear things sometimes, and you know how John gets a hold of an idea. We'll pay, of course – both of us." And this time he put his hand down hard enough on John Wallace's shoulder, and they both removed their coin purses and paid the rent in full. Change was made, and they were offered tea, which they refused, and left in all expediency.

Darcy did not hesitate once they were gone. He turned to his steward. "Find out where Mr. Wallace is getting his ideas."

Mr. Hammond, Mr. Darcy's steward since the death of old Mr. Wickham, simply nodded in understanding and left.

"How do you know Mr. Wallace is listening to someone?" Geoffrey asked his father. "Everyone wants to own their own land."

"A good question. Mr. Wallace is uneducated. He can't read and he can't write, which means he relies on other people to tell him things. Clearly his family is not politically radical, as we saw from Mr. Peters. So for a radical notion to enter into his head—one that his own brother would oppose, but that he would still mention in front of me – he must have been talking to other people. While no man is incapable of independent ideas, I would suspect in this case they are someone else's."

~~~

The case of Mr. Wallace was shelved for the time being with the news that arrived the next day. There was a disaster in the very mine that Darcy had sold to the Duke of Devonshire. The mine was relatively new, and attempts to open up the new vein of iron ended with a cave-in that killed seven workers. It was not strictly Darcy's business (in fact, by selling the land he had made sure it was not), but he did pen a note to the Duke of Devonshire that there were suffering families who needed some kind of treatment and perhaps appeasement if the mine was ever to be reopened. The Duke, however, was elsewhere far in the south, so nothing would come of it for weeks. There was so much talk of the sadness among his own staff – as Pemberley was not terribly far from the mine, merely some twenty miles – that Elizabeth insisted they send some goods to the grieving families.

With that the drama of the mine, it was another day before Mr. Hammond's agents returned with the information wanted. On Saturday night, the steward passed along the information to Darcy, with Geoffrey present as well. "His name is Michael Hatcher. He's from Gloucester. He has education, and has been working presumably as a clerk or a former steward to a minor gentleman. No wife or children."

"He's a Radical?"

"I thought Owenite at first, but it turns out he's a Spencean – or at least, suspected to be one. If it could be proven, he'd be hanged."

Darcy told his son with a look that the explanation would come later. "What is he doing here?"

"That I don't know, sir. It may just be safe ground. Derbyshire has been quiet since 1817."

"His issue can't be with me, if it's mining-related," Darcy said. "Or industrial. I don't own any factories."

"I know, sir, but do remember – Thomas Spence wrote that land was to be held commonly. So as a landowner, you could be a potential target. So far I believe he has been focusing on the Duke, who has become an easier target after this disaster and his inability to offer consolation from afar, but the crowds are practically the same."

Darcy nodded. "If he is a Spencean and he's lived this long, he's dangerous. I don't want your man in danger. Or yourself."

"Understood, sir."

When the steward left, Darcy turned to his son, and offered the needed explanation. "Thomas Spence, who died a few years ago, was a Radical from Newcastle who believed in the common ownership of land and some form of what the Americans call democracy. I believe he wrote numerous tracts about it, and a society formed around him called the Society of Spencean Philanthropists, a secret society that held a rally distributing his works in 1816. The rally turned into a mob, like most of the radical rallies at the time, and they looted part of London. The Spencean leaders were put on trial for high treason and hanged. From there, they've largely disappeared, but only because there's been so much other unrest." As he explained, he paced in a way that revealed his anxiety to Geoffrey, "This man Hatcher is obviously using the original doctrine in a new form to appease the local masses, to whatever ends he intends. I tell you now, no good will come of him."

Geoffrey could find no reason to doubt his father on that.

~~~

"Nadi-sama! Brian-chan!" Georgiana Bingley rushed out of Chatton House faster than any of her siblings to greet her wayward uncle and noble aunt, embracing her aunt before the poor woman had time to take her rush hat down.

"Why do I get the affectionate kid nickname and you get the honorific title?" Brian said to his wife,

107

which only earned a glare from her. "Well, not honorific. Bad choice of words, my dear." The rest of the family caught up with Georgiana. "Mr. Bingley."

"Mr. Maddox. Your Highness." Charles Bingley gave Brian's hand a firm shake. "It is wonderful to see you home at last."

"Yes. We tried to arrive in time for Georgie's eighteenth birthday, but the winds were terrible this year." Brian removed his own hat and re-strapped it around his kimono. Unlike his trunks, his personal items were not handled or removed by the servants, including the swords in his belt. "We still got her a gift, though. Otherwise, the trip was not particularly exciting."

"No Dutch-employed commercial assassins? No fights with roving Punjab street gangs? No ninja attacks?"

"Not this trip. Sorry to disappoint." Brian bowed. "Mrs. Bingley," he said, turning to Jane.

"Mr. Maddox. Your Highness. Always so good to see you both." The Maddoxes were good friends of the family, despite the spectacle they always made of themselves, dressing and acting as they did. They only got away with it because Nadezhda was foreign and royal. "I hope you didn't come straight up here without seeing your brother."

"No, of course not. We saw him – and Mr. and Miss Wickham."

They all entered the house, and were greeted by the staff and Monkey, who squeaked happily and ran up Brian's offered arm. The servants knew not to expect Brian or Nadezhda to relieve themselves of their formidable weaponry. Brian took a seat on the settee, removing his long sword and leaning on it as they were served refreshments.

"What did Mugin have to say?" Georgiana begged, almost tugging at Nadezhda's kimono. "Did he have a message for me?"

Brian and Nadezhda exchanged glances. "Jorji-chan," Nadezhda said cautiously, "We didn't see him on this trip."

"But you always see him!"

"Japan is a big place. Much bigger than England. And they have very few horses," Brian said uncomfortably.

Georgiana frowned. She was eighteen now, too old and too intelligent for games. "You're lying."

"Georgiana!" Jane said.

"It's true," Nadezhda answered. "We did not see him. But – when we sent message, we received his sword, and a note."

"What did it say?"

"It was not for you. It was for me," Brian said. "I'm sorry, Miss Bingley."

His formality immediately told her something was wrong, but it took a moment to sink in. "It's not true!"

"I can't say where he is. I can only tell you what we just told you," Nadezhda said. "I don't believe he's dead. Something may have happened and he may be in hiding – but he wanted us to have the sword. That was what he wrote."

"He's not dead! If he wrote to you, he can't be dead!"

"We don't actually know if he wrote – "

"He's not dead!" she shrieked. Georgiana Bingley never shrieked, or had a tantrum, or ran out of the room crying – but that was precisely what she did at that moment. Bingley was so shocked by the spectacle that he never expected from his older daughter that he said nothing.

Jane rose to follow, but Nadezhda grabbed her arm. "Let her go."

~~~

Geoffrey was heading down the hill on yet another trip with his father when he saw Georgie running towards him from the direction of Chatton House, her white dress and red hair against the green hill an unmistakable image. Darcy spotted her at the same moment, and tried to find out what had happened. "Miss Bingley – " But there could be no conversation with the tear-stricken Georgiana as she grabbed hold of Geoffrey, sobbing into his chest.

"He's not dead!" she finally said. "He promised me!"

"Who's not dead?" Darcy said, alarmed. Geoffrey was too shocked to say anything.

"Mugin," she answered, sniffling. "Uncle Brian and Nadi-sama came home and they said that they sent for him and instead of him coming, they received his sword and a note saying it was theirs."

Geoffrey looked to his father, but he was waiting on the response of his son, who knew Georgie better. So Geoffrey, uncomfortable with his cousin's continued physical nearness, half embraced her, stroking her short locks. "Shh. He's not dead. If he was, that was the message they would have received. He just gave them his sword." He smiled at her. "You know Mr. Mugin. Maybe he lost the sword in a bet and had to make sure it was off the entire Continent to keep it safe. Or something silly like that."

She nodded, wanting so desperately to believe. It was only then that she realized the impropriety of the situation, and pulled herself from her cousin, wiped her tears, and curtseyed to both of them. "Uncle Darcy. Excuse me." With that she was gone, just as quickly as she had appeared.

"That was ... odd," Geoffrey said, a little hot under the collar himself.

"How does she run in those wooden sandals?"

"They're reinforced with steel."

"That does not really answer the question, but I will accept it for the time being, rather than be late." He nudged his son and they continued down the hill. "Though perhaps you should warn Miss Bingley about such displays or she may end up married to the next person she encounters while upset."

Geoffrey hoped his chuckle would defuse his blush, but it did not.

~~~

The Darcys' visit was not a hostile one by any means. Mrs. Donovan always paid her rent in kind, which was bottles and bottles of fresh milk, and it was a Darcy tradition to pick up the bottles once a month themselves instead of sending a wagon to pick up the delivery. The old widow was eager to see the young master, who was now just a few days shy of being eighteen, and Geoffrey had to endure her telling him what a nice young man he'd grown into.

Darcy stepped out onto the front porch, abandoning his son with a smirk, only to have his expression fall when he saw who was outside. Mr. Wallace, whose lands neighbored Mrs. Donovan's little plot, was standing under a tree with a man Darcy didn't recognize. Being a gentleman before anything else, he put his hands behind his back (one not far from the pistol tucked into the back of his waistcoat) and approached them, bowing. "Mr. Wallace."

"Mr. Darcy," Wallace said, not looking pleased at being discovered; in fact he looked surprised, despite it being broad daylight. "You here for the milk?"

"Of course. And would you be so kind as to introduce me to your friend here?"

Darcy suspected the name before Wallace said it. "Mr. Darcy, this is Mr. Hatcher." Darcy did not show any surprise; he had none.

"It is a pleasure to meet you," Darcy said.

"Pleasure is all mine," Mr. Hatcher said, approaching him and offering his hand. Hatcher was short and stout. He was definitely a southerner – but

112

his accent was distinctly refined, like that of Town, perhaps a lawyer or a clerk of some kind. He had overgrown hair and a downright hostile gleam in his eye, even though he was all smiles. "I hear you are the big landlord around here."

"I am Darcy of Pemberley and Derbyshire, yes, but it is really His Grace the Duke of Devonshire who holds more claims than myself."

"So I heard. Well, we won't keep you from your important business, Mr. Darcy." He saluted in a ridiculously overextended bow; nothing in Darcy's nature could allow him to return such a spectacle before they departed.

"Father?" Geoffrey's voice sounded out behind him, and he turned to his son, finally out of Mrs. Donovan's grasp. Darcy was glad his son had not been introduced to Hatcher. "Son, let's be going." Geoffrey carried the milk, and Darcy mused on his intuitions about the mysterious Mr. Hatcher.

CHAPTER 9

The Ring

IT FINALLY SEEMED to be warming up. After a long, cold winter, this brought a particular joy to everyone, even if some of the roads had been washed out by melting snow. Sawdust was tossed onto the wet roads and Lambton was alive with people as three Bingleys climbed out of their carriage. Georgiana was out and able to walk about in society with her brother, Charlie, as an escort. Eliza insisted on coming, though she wore a broad-rimmed hat and kept her hair down. Still, there was not likely to be a soul in Lambton who did not know the Bingley children and their individual statuses – for what was there to do in a country town but discuss the doings of the rich and their alternately adorable and meddlesome children?

In public at least, Georgiana was a proper gentlewoman, even if her hairstyle was a bit unusual, hidden beneath a wicker hat. She led and Charlie had to keep up with her, with Eliza walking behind them. Their mission was singular but hardly easy – find a birthday gift for Geoffrey. The delay in winter post had prevented them from ordering anything from London and his birthday was in two days. Their relatives were due to arrive from Cambridge and from London the next day.

"What do you get a boy who has everything?" Georgie said. "And don't say 'ribbons.'"

"I wasn't going to," Eliza chimed in. "We could get him a book."

"I doubt we could find one in Lambton that cannot be found in Pemberley's library."

"We could get him wine," Charlie said, and endured his elder sister's glare. "What? He drinks as much as any boy his age."

"Man. He is to be a man now. Remember that."

"Maybe *you* should remember that." This comment provoked another harsh stare from Georgiana to her brother.

"We have to get him something better than just more booze," Georgie said. "Besides, I already bought plenty." Every year, Georgie, Geoffrey, and the oldest other cousin available – usually Charlie but sometimes George – got drunk on Geoffrey's birthday, long after their parents had gone to bed. "You're nearly his age. What do *men* want for their birthdays?"

"So you admit I'm a man then?"

She rolled her eyes as they entered one of the finer establishments in town, a sort of odd-and-ends shop that sold items of refinement, like jewelry and pocket watches. "We could get him a ring," Eliza said, her gloved hand tracing the glass of the display case for signet rings and even a few wedding bands.

"We can't get him a signet ring if he's to inherit the Darcy one from his father. What will he do then?"

"Plenty of people wear two rings. Some wear more."

"He wouldn't, though. Too ostentatious," Georgie said.

"God willing, Uncle Darcy will live for many years to come. He could wear it until then," Charlie said. "It could be the 'Darcy heir' ring instead of the Darcy signet ring. And then for his son." He turned to the shopkeeper, who had little to do but listen to their conversation, though he made a pretense of reading the paper. "Mr. Harris, what would a gentleman of eighteen want for his birthday?"

Mr. Harris chuckled. "I could tell you want a gent of eighteen would really want, but that would hardly be proper in front of the ladies."

"Geoffrey's not like that!" Georgie shouted from the back of the shop, as Eliza covered her own mouth to stifle a laugh. "Don't laugh!"

"She's allowed to laugh," Charlie said. "She's just not allowed to get the joke."

"While you try to internalize and discover the stupidity of what you just said, I will try to find him a *proper* present," Georgie said. "Mr. Harris, what is this?"

"'s a signet ring, marm," he said. "Gold. I could make an engraving this afternoon if you'd like." The plate was blank.

Eliza joined her sister. "The band is funny. Is that Latin?"

Mr. Harris put on his spectacles and opened the case, lifting the ring up so the light through the window from the noonday sun hit it just right. "No. 'Tis Irish, I believe."

"What does it say?"

"Don't know." He fingered it. "It's all been here since my father let me start workin' hours in the shop 'tis all I know, Miss Bingley."

"You don't suppose it's some kind of old Irish curse?" Eliza whispered, though not particularly softly.

"Don't be ridiculous. What kind of shop would be selling cursed rings?" Charlie said.

"Not my shop, certainly," Harris defended.

"There's no such thing as magic and curses anyway," Georgie declared. "How much?"

"Who said there's no such thing as curses?" Charlie asked.

"I do. How much, Mr. Harris?"

"That's pure gold, marm. And to have it ready today would cost a sovereign. Assuming you do want a D."

"G.D.," Georgie said. "His full initials. You think you can make that fit?" The plate was not so much a proper square as a small oval, surrounded by the Irish lettering.

"I can." He took the ring and set it on his worktable. "It should take an hour. Maybe two, depending on the customers, but they're all at the rally."

Charlie opened his purse and removed a sovereign, setting it on the counter. "What rally?"

"Nothin,'" he said quickly, realizing he had mentioned something he probably shouldn't have. "Nothing for a gent like you, or ladies, certainly."

"What rally?" Georgie repeated, more insistently than her brother.

Mr. Harris gave in. "Some o' the workers are down at the tavern, listening to a man from the south talk. But you didn't hear it from me."

Georgie nodded. "We'll be back in an hour, Mr. Harris." She curtseyed and they left the shop. "Charlie, take Eliza to get an ice or something."

"I'm not a baby just because I'm not out," Eliza hissed. "You never take me along when you two get into trouble."

"Because you never think I should."

"Even I don't think you should this time," Charlie said. "Georgie, this is serious. We should wait an hour, get the ring, and then go home and tell Father."

"Tell him what? We don't *know anything*."

"Georgie!"

But she was already walking in the direction of the tavern. Charlie sighed frustratedly as she turned into an alley, and they gave in and followed their sister. "All right, Eliza, you can be look-out."

Eliza was so excited about finally getting to be in on a scheme that Charlie had to pacifying her, giving Georgiana time to sneak up to one of the windows, with no one to stop her as she opened it just a tad, so she could hear what was being said.

"Do you work hard on your land?"

"Aye!"

"Do you see any reason why someone else should claim it as their own?"

It was a bigger rally than they had ever heard to be in Lambton, not in size but in intensity. The speaker, whom they could not identify but had a sophisticated London accent, was leading the people down a logical road of thought. "He's using very leading questions," Charlie said, as he and Eliza crept closer to listen as well. "They're only going to answer 'yes' until he wants them to answer 'no' because it leads to the next question." He turned to Eliza – younger by six and twenty minutes – and explained, "Logic. I take it in school. He can present them with any body of argument and if he presents it correctly according to a logical progression, he can convince them of anything. It was how the French Revolution turned into a mob."

"That and the mass discontent of the peasant class," Georgiana said. "It's wrapping up. Let's be off."

But they were not off soon enough. They had barely gotten back onto the streets proper when the man who had been speaking emerged, and doffed his hat to Charlie. "Enjoyed the speech, sir?"

"...It was engaging," he stammered, and bowed. "Charles Bingley."

"Michael Hatcher. I suppose you've heard of me."

"I have not, Mr. Hatcher."

"Really? I'm surprised."

A voice from behind them made Hatcher look over his shoulder. "You hold your fame in high esteem for someone with dangerous notions, Mr. Hatcher." To their surprise, it was George. He bowed. "Mr. Hatcher."

"We've not been introduced," Hatcher said, now as off-guard as Charlie had been. Georgie nudged her brother, but he ignored her.

"George Wickham," George said, offering his hand. Hatcher had no choice but to shake it. George was still fairly well-dressed, but not as much as the Bingleys, and he walked differently. He was older than Charlie by three years, and more confident. "I have heard of you, Mr. Hatcher."

"And you would consider my simple notions about the rights of a man to be dangerous?"

"Thomas Spence cannot be equated with Thomas Paine. Unfortunately for you, the former's works were outlawed, though to your credit, you did deviate from them somewhat. Mr. Spence believed that land should be communal and controlled by the parish and leadership decided by vote, while you seemed to imply that these people would own their own land."

"Then I supposed I could hardly be accused of being a Spencean," Hatcher said with a nervous smile.

"Good for you, then," George said, and bowed. "If you would excuse me, I have some errands to attend to."

"Of course, Mr. Wickham." Hatcher did not show the Bingley trio his expression as he stalked off.

"George!" Georgiana said, beating the others to it. "Where were you?"

"I'd just come along to look for you when I heard about the rally. Since you weren't with Geoffrey, I assumed you must be shopping for his birthday present. As for the rally, I was in the building. The people of Lambton are not as familiar with my face." George Wickham, his father being who he was, did not spend much time in Lambton, and in addition, those who would recognize him by familiar looks were mostly women, not present in the tavern. "Come. Let's be done with whatever you have left."

They headed back to the shop. Georgiana punched her brother lightly on the side, but hard enough for him to feel it as they walked. "Why didn't you introduce me?"

"Why would I? He was clearly dangerous. I didn't want you talking with him."

"You don't get to make that decision."

"As your brother, in this case he does," George said, and endured his own punch from Georgie. Fortunately, he knew it was coming. "What I said still holds."

"Who was Thomas Paine?" Eliza said. She was not bothered by not being introduced to a random man.

"Author of the *Rights of Man*," George said. "Very different from Thomas Spence. He emigrated to America before the revolution."

By the time they returned to the shop, the work was done and the ring was carefully wrapped and placed in a box before their eyes. It would be a gift from all of the Bingley children, as George had, as he often did, acted on his own.

"I got him a book," he said.

"Of course you did," Georgie said. "What makes you think he wants a book?"

"I didn't say what kind of book," he answered. Apparently the months under the care of the Maddoxes had been kind to him, as his calm balance was restored.

The girls went into the carriage first, of course. Charlie gripped George's shoulder to stop him for a moment before they climbed in. "I've never seen you like that."

"Like what?"

"I don't know. Assertive."

"Do you have any idea how much danger you were in?" George said very seriously. "I'm the oldest, so I'm the protector. With this man about, Lambton isn't just a quiet little town. Don't come to town without an escort from now on."

Charlie chewed on this notion all the way back to Chatton House.

~~~

Despite his gregarious nature, Geoffrey Darcy wanted to keep his birthday to family and close friends, and since he spent little time in London, his friends were largely his family. He had never spent a Season in Town, being an Eton boy, and he did not want to contemplate marriage at eighteen.

While not all Geoffrey's aunts came, the Bertrands made three out of five (Lydia was invited but apparently did not wish to venture to Pemberley again) and the Maddox clan came as well, being close enough to Derbyshire to make the journey. There was a relaxed supper and many toasts, though few of his rights and privileges had changed upon his birthday. They had already happened; he was a man able to sign legal documents, be a member of clubs, play the field as an eligible bachelor, gamble, drink, and consort with prostitutes – the fact that he did few of those things was of little consequence. In fact, the most significant milestone was not to be his birthday but his University entrance in the fall, and that was the real cause for celebration. There he would learn some classics, make all the notable friends he would need for social success in life, perhaps have a bit of fun (or more than a bit), and then graduate to a life of bachelorhood and possibly matrimony before his father died and he inherited the estate. Such was the future as he imagined it. He knew what was expected of him, and he had never failed to rise to the occasion before, so everyone gladly toasted to the Darcy heir.

But the day did not begin with celebrations. It began much earlier, in the morning before the guests rose, in one of the back rooms of Pemberley.

Geoffrey Darcy relished many things about fencing, but the occasional spar with his father was not one of them. Not that there was anything particularly unpleasant about the situation, but he found it positively confounding to face an opponent who fought on his left side. His usual experiences, in his sheltered existence at Pemberley, were with his coach, and with the only one of his cousins who practiced the sport, Frederick Maddox, and both fought properly, with the right hand. But his father was left handed, or had been since an accident long ago, hazy in Geoffrey's memory, which made his right hand slightly lame; Mr. Darcy had nearly full use of it, just not to do anything precise. And fencing was indeed very precise.

Though he was in his late forties, Mr. Darcy of Pemberley had not fully abandoned his favorite sport, even at an age when it was quite appropriate to do so. Occasionally he lacked in stamina, but when the match came down to wits, he was a master. And he made it abundantly clear that if his son was to bother at all with a foil, he should become a master as well. He was remarkably patient, even with his son's occasional fit of frustration, even the time when Geoffrey actually tossed his faceguard across the room with such ferocity that it put a dent in the stone wall. The anger was not at his father, of course. It was that damned tricky left-handed foil! But his father only shook his head and said, "You will succeed. Though I would prefer if your youthful exuberance did not destroy *all* of Pemberley."

"Then you should never let me spar with Frederick again."

Darcy merely raised an eyebrow, his way of demanding a thorough explanation.

"It wasn't *my* fault."

"Or you would not have admitted to it. Does this have anything to do with the pillar I needed to replace?"

His parents were astoundingly, frustratingly clever. "Perhaps."

"And the fact that he pushed you into it?"

"You – you knew?"

"Of course," his father said, allowing the servant to take his foil and armor away. "Very little in Pemberley happens without my knowledge."

"But – you didn't say anything?"

"You admitted to me that a pillar had been destroyed and did not supply specifics. If I wanted them from you, I would have asked."

Geoffrey sat down beside his father on the bench, trying to puzzle out exactly what his father was expecting from him. There was clearly something deeper here, but he could not get at it. His father always wanted him to think things through, even when his mind was in a daze from the rush of combat, and he wanted nothing more than to dunk his head in cold water and rest for a while. Perhaps he was mistaken and nothing else was required – but it was better to be safe. "So – are you asking now?"

"As I have said, I already know the specifics. But, while we are on the topic, I would like to hear your commentary. I think it would be interesting."

Interesting. It was probably not that simple. His father was probably expecting to glean something from the reply. He knew that much. "I don't have much to say about it. Fred shoved me into the pillar and since it was wood and half-eaten by termites on the inside, it broke."

"And nothing about that strikes you as odd?"

"Well - ," *Yes!* Now he had it. "It is not gentlemanly behavior to engage in physical combat in a duel of swords."

"Correct. But it is also not gentlemanly behavior to pass judgment on another fighter. But I will take into account that until I pressed you, you clearly did not intend to, except for your original comment, which was another response to mine."

"But he's a cousin."

"So are you making a judgment on him or his fighting style? Because they are, to all effects, the same."

Geoffrey looked at him quizzically.

"A man reveals almost everything when he fights. Very few are capable of subterfuge in the heat of battle. On the most basic level, if he constantly attacks, then he wishes to either scare you or defeat you quickly. This you know."

"Right. And if he parries constantly, he is waiting for an opening."

"Yes. But it goes beyond that. If you know the fighter, you can take your knowledge of his character into account. If you don't know the fighter, you can learn a lot about him from fighting him. It requires astute observation, but it is often the key to winning a match. For example," his father said, "you are very young – "

"I'm   not   a   child!"

" – in comparison *to me*, are at an age when you

have a certain ferocity that is fueled by the particular position of being eighteen. And also, when your face is particularly flushed, I know that you are about to be too aggressive for your own good, and will fail to block. In fact, I have just told you the great secret to how I beat you, because I assure you, it is not by stamina, or skill, as my left side was, originally, my weaker side, and not the one I trained with." He gestured and the servant brought them water. "I win not because you lack any particular skill for your age, or do not have the coordination. I win because I have spent many years learning to read my opponent."

Geoffrey nodded and swallowed that particular information with his refreshment. His father seemed tired, and needed a breather anyway, even from talking. He could remember a time when his father did not have so much grey in his hair. After some silence he asked, "Did grandfather fence?"

"As a boy, I believe so. He had long given it up when I was of age."

"Then who was your partner? Uncle Bingley?"

"No, I had not met him, and he has never once fenced. I spent a great deal of my years before Cambridge sparring with your Uncle Wickham."

"I never met him, but I remember his funeral."

"You met him when you were very young and therefore simply may not remember it. I vaguely recall that Bingley hosted him at Chatton House while you were there. It was not a remarkable visit or they would have informed me so."

"What was he like?"

His father hesitated for some reason before answering. "As a fighter, very aggressive. But then again, so was I. I would say, we were equal until the day I first beat him, and then he threw down his sword and would not fence with me again. Or did not, for a long time."

"So, Fred is rather like him."

"I would hardly put them in the same category," his father said. "This is not to make a permanent judgment of Frederick. You should be very careful when making assessments of people, Son, and especially careful not to mention them to others. It can be misconstrued as gossip."

Geoffrey knew his father held gossip in very low esteem, even though everyone seemed to do it, all the time. It seemed to be the entire purpose of any social gathering, as far as he could tell.

"On the other hand," his father continued, "if you felt that your cousin was engaging in behavior that was unsafe, you should bring it to my attention, as I am responsible for your safety – and his, while he is under my roof."

"But you said already you will learn it anyway."

"Slowly and through many mediators. Entirely different than if you say it yourself. And it is partially your own responsibility to bring it forward."

"I'm confused," Geoffrey said. "Am I supposed to say it or not?"

"Well, since we've gotten this far, I suppose you should."

He swallowed and decided that he would. "I don't think Fred is very ... gentlemanly ... when he fights."

"How so? Besides shoving you into a pillar hard enough to break it."

"He is – ferocious. When he fights. He is so different from his normal self." Frederick Maddox was often mischievous and devious, but had an otherwise gentle nature.

"Both a danger and a weakness. It is important to look out for one and take proper advantage of the other – in a duel that is."

"He's so – I don't know. Different. From, say, his father."

His father said nothing.

Geoffrey took this as encouragement to continue. "Does Uncle Maddox know how to fence?"

"He does not."

"Because – I can't imagine Uncle Maddox fighting anyone. He's so proper and – not to say this isn't proper – pacifist. Fred is so different from him."

Darcy did not respond directly. After a few moments of sitting, when his breath was truly and finally caught, he slapped his son on the shoulder. "We're all different, son. The changes just happen more gradually in some than we perceive them to in others. We celebrate a year's growth, all in one day." He added, "On the other hand, the day you beat me, that will be very dramatic. And traumatic, for me."

His son smiled as he smiled, and Darcy thought inside, *But I'm looking forward to it.*

CHAPTER 10

A Gentleman of Eight and Ten

ASIDE FROM the younger children's usual boisterousness, the celebrations that day were appropriately subdued. Geoffrey was a man, which involved celebration with food and wine, and his first cigar, or at least a puff of it before he was out on the terrace, coughing, trying to breathe in some fresh air.

"I never cared for it myself," Darcy said to his son, slapping him on the back, which only brought on another round of coughing, "though it is a good idea to get used to the smoke, as it seems as though every study is filled with it."

"How is this supposed to help me digest my meal?"

"You are old enough now that I can admit to you this: Some things are utterly beyond my understanding. Most of them involve the social habits of polite society."

Geoffrey smiled at that and they returned to the study for another toast. No one else was smoking except Bingley and Brian, but their hookah produced only the scent of lemons. He was eventually excused to join his younger relatives for their own revelries, and the older generation watched him leave the study with pride.

"You all owe me a great thanks, and not for the reasons you are imagining," Mr. Bennet said, raising his glass of brandy to meet Darcy's. His son-in-law had an unusually warm smile on his face, a mixture of pride and a bit more liquor than he was accustomed to. "Without me as the last representative of my generation, the rest of *you* would be the old men."

"To that I admit I am quite grateful," said Bingley with a smile and a gesture toward his graying hair.

~~~

"It's beautiful." Geoffrey held the ring box in his hands. It was the last of the presents he opened, mainly because it was slipped in at the end.

"We didn't know what to get for you," Eliza said, "so it's from all us Bingleys."

"Thank you," he said, embracing his cousin as he put the signet ring on his finger. "What's the other writing?"

"Something in Irish, we think," Charlie said. "Even George couldn't recognize it."

"Maybe you could show it to Uncle Grégoire when he comes," George Wickham said from his corner, where he was sitting in an armchair with a book and his own glass of peach-colored brandy. Grégoire, Caitlin, and Patrick Bellamont-Darcy usually came in the late spring or summer, depending on the weather. "Do you read his columns?"

"I read a few," Geoffrey said, finally taking a seat and a bottle of wine. "Don't tell him this, but I don't understand them. They're mainly about family."

"What's wrong with family?" Emily Maddox asked.

"I mean to say, they're mainly concerning fatherhood," he said, in undertone. "Because ever since he became a father, that's what he writes about." He leaned back and took a swig from the bottle before passing it to the waiting Georgiana Bingley. "I'm not ready to be a father."

"Why is it that girls are ready to be mothers before boys are ready to be fathers?" Emily asked. "Georgie – you could be one at any time."

Geoffrey giggled; Georgiana gave her cousin a cold stare. "It doesn't happen spontaneously, you know. There's the business of courtship and marriage first."

"Hopefully," Frederick said. "Or there's the business of running to London to get a license and then marrying the next week."

"Will someone please explain to me what that means?" Emily said, and turned to her twin brother Frederick, who just smiled at her. Eliza shrugged. "Georgie – you're old enough to be thinking about these things."

"Don't remind me," she said, and took another swig. "What Fred is trying to imply is that sometimes men do stupid things and then suddenly have to marry a girl to save her reputation. Which no one in this family will be doing – right, Frederick?"

"Please. With *my* father? And *my* mother? I'd never hear the end of it," Frederick said.

"Don't think it's any different for the rest of us," Geoffrey added. "I think my father would disinherit me."

"He *can't*; you're the only son," George said, not looking up from his tome, but taking another drink straight from the crystal bottle.

"Papa would never do anything like that!" Anne Darcy said. She reached for a glass but Georgiana, who was somehow the authority for her younger cousins on this matter, shook her head and handed the bottle back to Geoffrey. Sarah and Cassandra were too young even to be in the room. There were already two girls present who were not properly old enough to drink, and that was enough.

"Of course he wouldn't," Georgiana said to console her. "Still, that doesn't mean we can't torture Frederick about it."

"Why am I the object of scorn?" Frederick asked.

"Because you brought it up," Geoffrey said, in support of Georgiana.

To that, Frederick had no answer, except to go deeper into the bottle. He was younger than the Bingley twins by a year, and he had his sister at his side to watch him, so it was not long before he dropped off and excused himself, taking his sister with him. Anne and Eliza hugged Geoffrey one last time and headed to bed. That left Charlie as the youngest, and with the lowest tolerance (aside from George, a known lush) he lasted only another hour before falling asleep on the sofa.

"Could never hold his liquor," Geoffrey said.

"He's my baby brother! Don't insult him behind his back."

"He's facing me."

"*She's* facing you is what she means," said George. "And whatever happened to Edmund?"

"They're *both* my baby brothers," Georgiana said, opening a new bottle of wine. "'cause I'm older."

"Do you remember Charlie as a baby?" Geoffrey said, pouring her another glass, and one for himself. "Because I don't."

"I remember when he was a baby," she said. "I remember because it's my first memory."

"Of Charlie?"

"No, but he was there. He was crying in the background. You were there, too, you idiot."

He grinned. "You'll have to be more specific."

She took a gulp, but did not succeed in emptying her glass before continuing, "I think we were – I don't know, three or four, maybe. You were at Chatton House and you wouldn't bathe and I said something to Mama, and I remember it because she fainted. I had never seen someone so big fall like that. I was really scared."

"What did you say?"

"I don't remember."

"You've never asked?"

"No," she looked into her glass before taking another sip. She clearly wanted to change the subject. "What's your earliest memory?"

"Mother and Father going away," he said. "Or maybe it was just Father – I don't remember if it was the time they went to Italy or when he left for Austria. I was at the docks in London to see him off. And maybe Mother."

"Why are your memories so melancholy?" George said.

"Why do you always come in with this booming voice of authority, Mr. Wickham?" Georgiana said with a giggle. "Just because you're a *year* older than us."

"More than a year."

"Wha – what's your first memory, George?" Geoffrey said, turning his head to face George.

George looked up from his book. "My father took me to see a military parade. They used to have a lot of those before the war with Napoleon ended – lots of men in red coats. He was one of them, but he wasn't marching with that regiment – or he must not have been, because I remember him holding my hand and guiding me down the streets of Newcastle. All the other times I remember were with my Mother."

"Isn't that sort of sad?" Georgiana said. "I mean, now."

"No," he answered, and took a healthy gulp from his bottle. "It was the only thing I remember him doing with me and I had a great time. Why should I be sad that I had a good time with my father?"

Neither of them could answer that properly. Finally Geoffrey said, "You're always so logical."

"And you're always impulsive, when you can get away with it. And Georgiana – no one can figure you out. We've all given up trying."

"You're not supposed to try," Geoffrey said in a voice that was beginning to be loud and slurred. "You're supposed to just think she's different an' that's that. People think too much about her."

"I'm still here!" she said, waving across the table at him.

He didn't hear her, or didn't acknowledge her, concentrating on facing George on his other side, "You're supposed to just like her for who she is, dummy. You think you're so smart. Even now – even now – why are you smirking? You smirk like my father."

"You've had too much to drink."

"No he hasn't!" Georgiana proclaimed. "I know because he's had as much as you and you're not even drunk."

"Maybe I just have a tolerance," George said quietly.

"Don't smirk at me!" Geoffrey said. His voice was not harsh – more playful. "You have my father's smirk. Only he's allowed to do that because he's my father. And me."

"Then you do it, *Mr. Darcy*."

"Don't tease him! Don't you ever tease him, George, just because he's smaller than you!" Georgiana shouted.

Finally now Geoffrey turned his head back to his female cousin. "I'm not small. You're small."

"I'm a girl. I'm allowed to be small."

"You're – not a girl. You – you're a *woman*," he said, gesturing in her general direction, "but still small."

"I could kick your arse!"

Geoffrey slammed his hand on the table. "That I do concede, young lady."

"Young lady!"

"At least I said *lady*," he said, and this time, he did smirk.

"And you're a young man, no matter what your age," George said, standing up. "And you've had a bit to drink, Mr. Darcy."

"Shut-up! I can stand!" But he couldn't. His attempts ended when he collapsed into George's arms, and Georgie dissolved into a fit of laughter in her own chair. While she was busy collecting herself, George helped Geoffrey to his room. He returned to find Georgiana standing up (somewhat unsteadily), holding his brandy. She took a swig and spit it out.

"This – this is juice! Some kind of – "

"It's peach," George said. "Peach juice. You know quite well I can't hold my liquor."

"You weasel bastard!"

"I wanted to see what you would say," he said. "I don't have many opportunities. You think you're subtle – and I admit, you are – but it's easier when you're both drunk." Knowing Georgiana had not the wits to oppose him, he called for a servant to wake Charlie so the eldest Bingleys could be carted off, home to Chatton House. He returned to his own guest chambers, still wearing the very Darcy smirk, to think for some time before finally drifting off into sleep.

~~~

Unfortunately for Geoffrey, his Eton days had trained him to be up at dawn for services, and that dawn awakening was not a pleasant one. Fortunately today he was not hurrying out of bed and had Mr. Reynolds, the grandson of Mrs. Reynolds and Geoffrey's manservant, to attend to him. Reynolds had all of the appropriate brews ready as Geoffrey lay in bed, a pillow over his head. "Thank you, Reynolds."

"Of course, sir."

"I didn't – Who carried me back last night?"

"A servant. On Mr. Wickham's orders, I believe."

He rolled over. "Oh. So it wasn't Georgie?"

"It was not, sir." If Reynolds was smirking, Geoffrey couldn't see. His vision was still a little blurry in the darkness, as the curtains had not been drawn. It would not have been the first time that Georgie, who was tiny in comparison to the heir to Pemberley, had carried him back to his quarters and passed him off to his man.

As his headache abated, or at least slowly came to a tolerable level, he sat up and ordered the curtains opened as he inspected the signet ring on his finger. Even if it was mostly inscribed in some strange Irish runes (if there were such things), it was quite beautiful in its own way.

It was a normal morning, and he was still on holiday from school. He was eighteen and a day, which was somehow less significant than the previous day. He did not feel changed in the least, except that he was older and perhaps learning how to tolerate his liquor better.

Even after lying around for some time, he was still up earlier than most of Pemberley. His sisters were not awake, nor was George, probably sleeping off his own hangover. If his mother was awake, she was off on one of her morning walks. He had a certain appreciation for early morning exercise, probably from her. "Do I have any appointments today, Reynolds?"

"No, Sir. Nothing scheduled. The master did leave a note that if you intend to go out, there is a delivery to Mr. Jenkins."

Old Mr. Jenkins, lately a widower, paid his rent on time every month but also a small addition for supplies, as on cold mornings his joints bothered him and he could not carry heavier supplies, like coal or firewood. "I'll get that over with, then."

"Very good, Sir."

He was dressed for outdoors, and took the bag of coals from the storeroom, whistling for Gawain to follow as he stepped out the servant's door and began the walk downhill to the old house, just outside the boundaries of Pemberley proper. The morning air was brisk; the dew on the tall grass still drying by the sun, so much so that Gawain was well-soaked when they finally reached the road.

"I know the feeling," Geoffrey said, as the dog looked reproachfully at him, his own boots quite wet. He set down the bag for a moment as his hound shook himself out. "Here, Boy." Gawain was now ten, getting on for a hound, but with luck he would have some active years left in him. Still, he was no puppy, and when Geoffrey knelt and stroked his head, scratching behind his ears, he noticed that the dog's hair was not as smooth and soft as it had been. "Did you at least steal some bacon from one of the cooks today?"

The noble hound's response was to jump up on his knees. Geoffrey laughed and let Gawain lick his hands. "Well, I'm as hungry as you are. We'll head straight back after this, I tell you that."

Throwing the bag back over his shoulder, he trudged the last few feet to the house, and stepped onto the porch to knock on the door. There were voices inside – multiple ones. He frowned. "Mr. Jenkins?"

The door eventually opened, and the old farmer looked at him with a surprised smile. "Master Geoffrey. I'm sorry – I was so caught up with my guests – "

"I just have your coal here – I would leave it but it's rather heavy and I wouldn't wish you to strain yourself. Do you mind if I just slip in and put it near the stove?" He had never come upon Mr. Jenkins with visitors.

"Uhm – yes. Of course, Mr. Darcy."

Geoffrey nodded and entered, proceeding straight to the kitchen. In the other room was the sound of multiple voices, but he ignored them for the moment, setting the coal down in its place. He had come just in time, too – the other bag was nearly used up. "If you need more – "

But when he turned around, the man approaching was not Mr. Jenkins. It was that man his father said was Mr. Hatcher, and behind him, more recognizable faces like Mr. Wallace and some other field laborers. "Good morning," he greeted cautiously.

"Hello, Mr. Darcy."

Jenkins stepped in. "Mr. Hatcher, this is Master Geoffrey." To which, Geoffrey tipped his hat.

"Michael Hatcher." The man didn't bow. Gawain growled softly at Geoffrey's side. "Your dog doesn't seem to like me much."

Geoffrey patted his hound with a nervous smile. "Do not mind him. He's just hungry."

Jenkins squeezed in through the hallway to come between Geoffrey and Hatcher. "Mr. Hatcher, please, he's just comin' through to give me some coal – "

"A generous offering," Mr. Hatcher said coldly, "from the giant stocks of Pemberley."

"Don't talk like that to 'im, Mr. Hatcher – that's the young master. You shouldn't – "

"I am a free man and so is he, so we can speak as we please," Hatcher said. "As for you, Mr. Darcy, I am quite aware of who you are. There is not a person in Derbyshire that does not know of the heir to the fortune of Pemberley."

"Pemberley is more than just to be measured in monetary terms," Geoffrey said, his Darcy indignation rising before he put a stopper in it. "But this is not the time to discuss it. I am due back at home and I did not wish to interrupt your meeting – "

"Hatcher," the man to his left said in a hushed voice. In the confusion of the moment, Geoffrey could not properly recall his name. "He'll tell his father."

"Don't you think I know that?"

"Tell him what? There's nothing wrong with hosting guests, Mr. Hatcher. You'll find us quite hospitable in Derbyshire," Geoffrey said, with a nervous glance to Jenkins.

"Really?" Hatcher stepped forward. "So you say I would be welcome in the great house of Pemberley?"

"If you had an issue to discuss with my father, he would be happy to see you, sir."

"But I must have an issue."

"Most people usually need *some* pretense to just up and enter someone else's house," he said. The fact that Gawain was tense at his side wasn't helping his own nerves. "I assume you have some business here that is not my own and if you'll excuse me, I will tarry no longer."

Geoffrey tried to move between the men in the narrow hallway, past Hatcher and the man he didn't know, then Wallace and the others. A man even bowed to him more respectfully, but he only made it as far as the end of the short hallway before Hatcher said, "And what if it was your business?"

He could leave. What would his father do? Think to come armed, probably – not that Geoffrey could think of drawing a gun on a man he had just met in the house of a man he knew quite well and respected. He could not think of drawing a gun on anyone. His father would try to end the conversation. "Then I would have appreciated an invitation, Mr. Hatcher."

Hatcher approached, and Gawain barked this time, and Geoffrey grabbed his collar. "Excuse me. You are right; he doesn't much care for you. He is an old dog and he is temperamental when he is hungry. We should be off."

"You really have no interest in a discussion concerning yourself, happening behind your back?"

"I have no interest in political Radicalism, Mr. Hatcher." He bowed, as if to further indicate he wished to leave as politely as possible.

But again, Hatcher engaged him, even as Geoffrey was having trouble holding Gawain at bay. "That's quite an assumption, young master. Even incisive."

"I did not mean to be. If you had – "

"If I had what?"

But this time, when Hatcher stepped forward, Gawain could not be held back. He was still a strong hound, raised for the hunt and of superior breed, and even Geoffrey could not contain him. He leapt at Hatcher, and bit into his leather shoe. "Damn mutt – " Hatcher said, and kicked Gawain, who was knocked back with a wail.

Geoffrey was not the pansy of Eton. He could throw a punch, and it took a very strong arm to catch it. "Don't touch my dog!"

Unfortunately, Hatcher had a strong arm, and he held Geoffrey's arm in a tight grip. "Don't touch me, Mr. Darcy, unless you want to face the consequences."

Mr. Jenkins hobbled up next to Hatcher. "Please, Mr. Hatcher, don't do– "

But by then Gawain had recovered, and now mercilessly leapt at the man holding his master's arm. This time, Mr. Wallace, who had been watching the exchange, drew his gun and fired.

"Gawain!" Geoffrey screamed as he pulled himself free of Hatcher at the sound of his dog's cry. From the corner of his eye, he could see Hatcher grab Jenkins' cane out from under him and raise it to strike, but that did not register until the blow came down, fast and hard on his head, and he still had not reached his dog.

Somewhere between the slam of wood into his temple and the completion of his fall backwards Geoffrey saw it all – the limping dog running off, the men shouting, Mr. Jenkins grabbing the wall for support. It all became a haze as Gawain disappeared from his vision entirely. "Go," he whispered, and hit the ground. The shock of it was too much for his head to take, and everything went black.

CHAPTER 11

The Tale of Sir Gawain

BREAKFASTING THAT MORNING at Pemberley was later than usual. Nearly everyone had been up late to their own degrees, and there was no particularly pressing business. Darcy did some paperwork before the rest of his family rose. To his surprise, the first ones at the breakfast table were his nephew and father-in-law.

"Goodness," Mr. Bennet said, "I thought we would be all alone."

"Mr. Bennet. And George – I see you weren't up too late."

George just gave a tiny smile and continued salting his eggs.

Elizabeth joined them, followed by Sarah, and eventually Anne Darcy. "Papa," she said, "have you seen Geoffrey?"

"I have not. I believe he is on an errand," Darcy said as she took her seat.

"He should show you his ring."

"What ring?"

"The Bingleys got him a signet ring," George clarified, "with his initials. It is very nice."

Darcy commented that it seemed like an appropriate gift, and breakfast continued.

"Mama," Sarah said, "are Sir and Lady Maddox coming over again tonight?"

"No, dear. We are invited to Chatton House instead and shall see them there." The Maddoxes were staying at Chatton House, and it was a rare opportunity for Anne and Sarah to see Emily Maddox, to whom they were both close in age. The only one closer was Edmund, but he was a boy, and the only one who played with boys was Georgiana. Finally, Isabel appeared for breakfast, followed by the youngest Darcy, Cassandra, who was learning table manners in the relaxed setting of a lazy morning with family. As she climbed into her seat next to her grandfather, there remained only one empty.

In fact, it stayed empty until the completion of breakfast, when Elizabeth offered to escort their daughters to Chatton House and kissed her husband good-bye. Darcy, who had actually been quite surprised that his son had it in him to do his chores so early, after what he had been informed was a very late night, was beginning to get an unsettled feeling at his son's non-appearance. Reynolds could only offer the time Geoffrey had left.

Lacking better options, Mr. Darcy asked for Mrs. Annesley, and found her in the kitchen, supervising the new serving maids.

"We've not seen the young master for some time now, Mr. Darcy," she said, gesturing over her shoulder. "He left out that way, sir."

He nodded his thanks and opened the servant exit to the bright, clear morning outside; a perfectly good

March day. So why was he so unsettled? He had been fine when he sat down to breakfast, and it was often enough that Geoffrey was not present, either sleeping in or already off with his cousins, but something unnerved him.

Maybe the boy had simply gone to Chatton House and not –

A whimper interrupted his thoughts. "Gawain," he said, squinting in the sun as he recognized the hound approaching with a visible limp. He had known that sooner or later the dog would injure himself and have to be put down – just as Darcy's dogs had been, one after the other – but he did not imagine him that old *yet*, surely?

Gawain bowed his head and made his way over to Darcy, nudging his nose hard into Darcy's knees. "What is it, boy?" He knelt down to the dog's level, and that was when he noticed the blood. Gawain had a very dark brown coat, and so it had been obscured until closer scrutiny. "What happened to you?" His second question was automatic. "Where is your master? Where's Geoffrey?"

Of course the dog could not answer him; he chided himself for thinking otherwise. But Gawain continued to nudge him, and whined as Darcy's hand found the wound. The dog seemed to have been grazed by something on his foreleg – he had been shot.

And Geoffrey was nowhere to be seen.

He did not want to send Pemberley into a panic just yet. If the servants panicked, he was more likely to, and Elizabeth was all the way at Chatton House –

her calming influence so far away from him now. He did not go inside. He picked up Gawain, carrying him in both arms as he would a very large puppy, and headed straight to the house for the huntsman. "Geoffrey is missing."

His huntsman nodded gravely, unquestioning, and handed him a rifle.

~~~

The team was assembled with all expediency. From the house he grabbed Reynolds, and with him came George Wickham, too clever to be left out of anything, even if he held a gun like it was a foreign object. Darcy wondered if he could even fire it.

Gawain's leg was splinted as a quick-fix by the huntsman, and with a party of five they started off. To no great surprise to those who knew of Geoffrey's morning errand, the still-limping Gawain headed down the hill that lead to Mr. Jenkins' land. Even though he was obviously in pain, he managed to keep ahead no matter how fast they walked, and growled when they did not keep up, eager to get on.

"Show us the way, Sir Gawain," Darcy said softly, only speaking so that some noise other than feet in the grass would be louder than the sound of his pounding heart. When they at last reached the house, all was quiet, with no smoke from the chimney, and the door closed.

The huntsman actually stopped Darcy from approaching and knocked on the door first. "Mr. Jenkins?" When there was no immediate response, he did not hesitate to open the door and enter, rifle raised.

There was no one home. There was no appearance of a fight, or anything amiss, but Gawain entered and whimpered, sniffing at the floor. "Searching for your master, are you?" George said as the men searched the house.

"It's empty, sir," the huntsman said. "'cept the coals in the stove are still warm. Someone was here this mornin.'"

Darcy charged into the kitchen, and checked the coals for himself, finding them warm but not hot, and the dirt beneath them wet, as if someone had quickly doused them. The bag of Pemberley coal was on the ground, untouched – doubtlessly the one Geoffrey had been asked to bring, as a sign of goodwill, from landlord to tenant.

"Uncle Darcy," George said, calling him back to the entrance. "Look." He pointed at the floor. "The rug."

It did not belong there. It was a nice rug, probably made by a local weaver, not the type meant to walk over with dirty boots, but it was right by the entrance, although it had probably come from the bedroom. Darcy and George knelt down and lifted it up.

On Mr. Jenkins' floor beneath it was the real mat, soiled from use, and stained with blood. The huntsman leaned over and scooped up some soil, smelled it, and confirmed that the blood was most likely not canine, but human.

Darcy briefly weighed his options for the most immediate decision – to go out with the huntsman and every other available man with the hounds to scour the woods for a trail, or to wait for Elizabeth's return from Chatton House, which would no doubt be imminent. How much practical help could his wife provide, versus how much comfort she would have to be included from the first moment? But could he really wait at home now, sitting in his castle like a useless tyrant?

He entertained himself watching the head gardener, who was too old for a chase, properly splint Gawain's leg. George carried Gawain's mat from Geoffrey's room into the study so the noble hound could rest, though the dog remained agitated.

When he had decided to await the arrival of his wife, trusting his men to begin the search competently without him, Darcy chose to go from one horrible option (watching the men leave with the hounds to search for his son) to another (informing Mr. Bennet of the situation). As usual, his father-in-law was in the library, reading, not quite ready for his mid-morning nap. "Mr. Bennet," he said with a grave bow. "I should inform you that Geoffrey is missing."

Mr. Bennet's mind was sharp, but sometimes his response was a little slow. "Was that all the commotion with the men in the hallway?"

"Yes. Elizabeth is on her way back from Chatton House. I wanted to tell her myself, but I fear the man I sent may tell her anyway."

"And you're sure this is not a prank with Miss Bingley?"

"Geoffrey is too old for pranks." He added, "Though, I wish I could say he wasn't too old, and that it is all just a joke."

Whatever Mr. Bennet had to add to that was interrupted by a cry, as Elizabeth Darcy leapt into her husband's arms as she would have when they were younger, but for much more different reasons. There was no regard for her father's presence as he embraced her tightly. "He will be all right."

"They've found him?"

"They will."

Even though she was quickly followed by her daughters and most of the Bingley clan, no one interrupted this exchange between husband and wife, as Elizabeth sobbed into his chest for several minutes before they finally separated. Darcy wiped his eyes before turning to face his guests. "They're looking for him now. I was going to go out with them – but I wanted to be here for you all," he said, turning to his three daughters. "Your brother is going to be all right."

"Then why do you have to keep *saying it*?" Cassandra Darcy wailed, and grabbed her father's waist. He didn't stop her, gripping her shoulders as he turned numbly to Bingley.

"I'm at your disposal," Bingley said before Darcy could speak. "As are the Maddoxes."

"Good," Darcy said, suddenly realizing it was promising to have both a doctor and a warrior at his side. "I'll need both."

~~~

A second party was organized, this time containing both Darcy and Bingley, along with several of Bingley's own men, to go out in the opposite direction and cover more ground. The woods around and beyond Pemberley were not like the great forests of the mainland, but they were big enough and today they seemed to go on forever. They crossed land where tenants were working in the fields or sitting on their porches, and who rushed to hear the news of why a very exclusive hunting party was out in their fields, obviously not chasing a stag. Unfortunately, none of them had seen Geoffrey Darcy that day, or Mr. Jenkins. Darcy immediately mentioned Hatcher, as he suspected that this mischief, as had all the other recent problems, somehow led back to him. If they were false suspicions, let them be so. His son was missing and that was all that mattered.

"We've seen him around," Mrs. Robinson said, "but not today. And he doesn't bother with the likes of farmer's wives. It's the men he's interested in."

"Any men in particular that have been attaching themselves to him?"

She rolled up her apron and said, "Oh, I couldn't tell ya that – I hardly leave my own house. I do wish

I could tell ya somethin' Mr. Darcy – he is such a sweet boy."

"He is," Darcy said, enjoying her use of the present tense. "Thank you." That it might be inaccurate was in the back of his mind, of course, upon seeing the blood on the floor, but the notion was too terrible to *begin* to contemplate. Yet.

When they returned, the sun was already going down. The day was just too short. He sent another group out with lanterns as he entered, but even his men had been searching for hours now and were exhausted. The first one to the door was Georgiana Bingley, but the look on his face must have told her everything.

"Papa," she whimpered, and fell into her father's arms. Darcy had never seen her so emotional – not since she was a child. "I want to help."

"You can help by comforting your aunt and cousins."

"I want to *really* help. I can't sit around."

Bingley frowned. "Georgie," he said with a swallow. Darcy wondered how he would find a way to refuse her; Georgiana had never been an easy child and she had not softened with age. "We're not letting any of the children help. If someone went after Geoffrey – "

"*I'm not a child!*" she said, and abandoned him, leaving him with his arms empty.

"Mr. Darcy," said the doorman, "A Mr. Hatcher to see you."

"Get me my rifle."

155

His servant bowed and handed over the gun. Darcy had only just relieved himself of it, and it was still loaded. He raised it at the figure in the doorway.

"This is the greeting I get?" Brian Maddox said, entering. "The other fellow is still outside. Not that I'm not accustomed to having a gun pointed at my head."

Darcy called for the huntsman on his way out, and told his manservant to keep anyone else out of the front hallway. He did raise his rifle again, as did the others (even Bingley) at the man who entered, as unaffected and confident as ever, even facing three men with rifles and one with a sword.

In fact, Mr. Hatcher didn't seem the least bit concerned at the number of weapons pointed at him. "Mr. Darcy," he said with a bow.

"Where is my son?" Darcy said, his voice only bordering on calm, as he pointed his rifle at Mr. Hatcher's forehead.

"For a member of polite society, you're sure not being very polite with your guests," Hatcher replied.

"No, I am not." Darcy cocked the rifle for emphasis. "Where is my son?"

"So you're to assume I've done something so terrible as taken him? Do you always assume the worst of people?"

"Am I wrong?"

Hatcher grinned viciously and reached into his vest pocket, pulling out a ring that shone in the lamplight. "I believe this will be familiar."

Darcy lowered his weapon long enough to snatch it from him. He had never seen it before, but it was a signet ring with the initials G.D., so he could only assume it had been the aforementioned birthday gift. How long ago that wonderful day seemed now. "There's blood on it." There was a little, smeared into the engravings.

"He's alive. If you wish him to stay that way, you might want to lower your weaponry, Mr. Darcy."

"The constable is on his way," Darcy said, "but he won't be here in time to save you from me if you don't tell me where Geoffrey is."

"And if I don't return in full health to my men, you won't be in time to save Master Geoffrey." Everything about Hatcher was cool and composed. He was holding all the cards and he knew it – and how to play them. "Now I will make my final request for an assurance of my safety by the repositioning of your many expensive weapons, and if you value his health, you might want to consider the request, and the idea of a polite discussion instead of a threat."

Everyone was waiting for Darcy – Bingley, Mr. Maddox, Reynolds, and the huntsman. The silence was so heavy that one could hear one's own breathing. At last, Darcy huffed and lowered his rifle, and the others did the same, though they were hardly set aside. "How much do you want?" he said.

"Immediately we come to the question of money," Hatcher said.

"A gentleman does not waste his *guest's* time," Darcy sneered. "You have your price. Name it."

"If you think I can be bought with bank notes, you are mistaken, Mr. Darcy. I am a representative of the people, and their demands are more complex. Yes, money is involved. Money, land, and rights. And in order to not waste my host's time, I have prepared the people's list of demands." His hand moved to the inside of his coat, and though some of the guns went back up, he did not pause, withdrawing only a scroll, tied neatly with a ribbon. "I will give you the evening to consider them." He offered the scroll to Darcy, who snatched it up but did not open it. "Obviously some of the points are negotiable. I have noted those with a mark. The others are not."

"I want to see my son."

"Then I would advise you to peruse my literature."

Darcy huffed. It was clearly taking all of his self-control – and he normally had quite a bit of it – to keep him from throttling the man before him. "I need to know he is alive."

"That you will have to take my word on," Hatcher said. "I do not believe you have another choice at this time. Yes, he is alive."

"Then why is his blood on Mr. Jenkins's floor?"

This time, Mr. Hatcher appeared to search for the appropriate answer before giving it. "He bled when we struck him. He is a more fragile boy than hard working men are used to dealing with. He has a wound on his head, but the bleeding is stopped. Nonetheless, I would not draw out these negotiations beyond what is absolutely necessary. For his health."

For his health. That Geoffrey was alive was a relief beyond measure, but how long he would likely remain so was beyond Darcy's grasp. "I will peruse your *literature*," he growled. "For my son's health, as you say. You will be here in the morning, eight o'clock sharp, and despite my instincts, you will not be harmed."

Mr. Hatcher nodded and doffed his hat, which he had never removed.

"If I do not have my son back, you are a dead man, Mr. Hatcher. In fact, even if you get everything you want, you will not escape the noose."

His opponent scoffed. "I have heard similar threats many times, but here I stand. It will take a stronger person than you to kill me, Mr. Darcy." He bowed. "Now, operating on the pretense of being a gentleman, I will take my leave. Good evening, gentlemen."

Darcy had to grab Brian's kimono to stop him from following. "Let him go."

"I could get the information out of him, Darcy."

"We can't risk it," he said. "He wouldn't have come here if he thought he was in any danger, and he was right. That said," he added in a voice that was the sort that made no one dare to challenge the veracity of the words, "by the end of this, I guarantee you he will be dead."

CHAPTER 12

Polite Society

"WHY can't I go in?"

"You just can't," George replied, as he stood guarding the study door. He knew that Georgiana Bingley would not take well to 'the adults are talking.' Plus she would probably make some comment about how that excluded him.

Georgie held up the plate in her hands. "You don't think Gawain deserves something?" On it was the best cut of meat Pemberley had to offer.

"Then let me take it in."

"Oh, so you – "

"Georgiana, I cannot deal with this now."

"*You* cannot deal with this?" she said. "Mama and Aunt Darcy are in the next room crying to death and you're the martyr? The only one hurt here is that dog. Now let me pass."

He had been told to keep people out, but he sighed, knowing she would just continue to talk at him until he relented. "Just be quiet about it."

Georgiana rolled her eyes and entered without knocking. George followed her into the study and watched her go directly to Gawain's mat, where the injured hound whined at her as she put the meat within easy reach of his snout. "Good dog. *Very* good dog," she whispered, scratching behind his ears.

The men were too absorbed in their work to take much notice of the entrance. Darcy, Bingley, and Darcy's steward, Mr. Hammond, were pouring over Hatcher's list of demands.

"He has to have a price," Darcy said, his eyes wild as they looked over the words again and again, no longer even reading them. "He has to. He can't honestly be willing to die for the people of Derbyshire."

"Between the family, we have – how much do we have now?"

"In cash? A hundred thousand by morning, if the bank will cooperate," Mr. Hammond said. "The next day at the latest."

"And that's absolutely everything we can liquidate?"

"Legally, yes."

"Uncle Darcy – "

The three of them looked up at George, who had approached nervously as Georgiana sat beside the dog behind him. "I just wanted you to know – my funds are in London, but – "

"I only wish I could say yes to that, and that it is only about money," Darcy said, "but according to the eminent Mr. Hatcher, it isn't. It's about social justice, to the point of massive charity on my behalf beyond what even I am capable of." He added, "At least not without Geoffrey's signature."

"Darcy, you can't seriously think– " Bingley started to speak, but was interrupted.

"I damn well can seriously think of it," Darcy said, "even though the legal motions would take months to break the entail even with the two of us present, and by then, Hatcher would be strung up. He must know that." He shook his head. "It has to be money."

"Or he fails to understands the laws of entail," Mr. Hammond said. "I can have the documentation ready by morning, Mr. Darcy, but it will be brief at best."

"His challenge that Pemberley isn't under entail won't hold up in any court, documents or no," Darcy said. "Or I could sign a bunch of useless forfeitures of land that won't hold." He ran his hands through his hair. "But, in answer to your question, thank you for the generous offer, but we will not be requiring cash from your accounts, George. And since this is not a public meeting ... I must ask you to remove Miss Bingley from the room."

Fortunately, Georgie knew better than to challenge her uncle, especially when he was in such distress. She curtseyed politely to him, and then ventured to speak. "I was just attending to Gawain. But – may I ask something?"

"I may not answer it, but you may ask."

"May I keep the ring? For Geoffrey?"

Darcy looked mystified by the request.

"He would want it," George said, deciding to support her to pacify her.

Their uncle didn't seem to have it in him to put up an argument to the request, and gestured with compliance. Georgie swooped in, snatched the ring, and left, dragging George out with her.

"Just promise me you won't do that again."

"I promise." She hugged him. "Thank you."

"Why did you – "

But she was already gone, and he was left to ponder her current scheme.

~~~

"Lizzy," Darcy whispered, "come to bed."

Elizabeth woke from her doze on the couch of the sitting room. Her sisters, both those by blood and by marriage, had been there to comfort her – Jane, Caroline, and Nadezhda – but she watched them grieve with her, and it was not the same. "I cannot sleep," she said, and in response to his expression, added, "warm and safe in my bed while our son is beyond reach."

"I've been informed by my doctor that I must try to get some rest before tomorrow to be at full wit," he said, "and I am afraid to even attempt such a ludicrous proposition without you."

She managed a smile. It was very late, and the others had retired to their guest rooms – no one left Pemberley that night. That they would all stay was an unspoken agreement. She accepted his hand. "You're warm."

"I had something to calm my nerves." He added, "Doctor's recommendation."

"Dr. Maddox has some very convenient recommendations."

"I am glad he is here. A great stroke of fortune."
Together, they walked upstairs, and the servants all
bowed more respectfully than usual, mindful of the
terrible situation, as the master and mistress of
Pemberley retired to her bedroom. "There is light
even in the darkness."

"You sound like Grégoire."

"It is a direct quotation, I confess. I am not that
original." Darcy dismissed his man and removed his
own clothes, crawling into bed and wrapping his
arms around her. "It cannot come to anything. He
just wants money."

"You were not so sure earlier."

"It is all I can offer him. Beyond my own life,
but that means nothing to him. He would have to kill
us all, like some kind of French Revolution done
over again, here in civilized England. He's not that
mad."

"You don't know that," she said, feeling his
heartbeat against her back, his calloused fingers
entwined with her own. "If it came down to that – "

"I would give my life for him, yes," he said.
"Would you blame me for it?"

"Blame you? I blame myself for contemplating
the idea and siding with my son over my husband."

"I am just an old, scarred man on the brink of
madness. He is – perfect." He kissed her shoulder.
"He will be a wonderful master of Pemberley,
husband, and father. Someday."

"Hopefully the husband before the father."

"Yes."

She stroked the palm of his hand, the part that was numb with all the nerves severed, and the edges that were not. "I would not blame you. I would not be happy with the arrangement, but it would be the right thing. I wouldn't curse you for it." She looked over her shoulder. "But promise me you will not let it come to that."

"I do not believe it shall."

She turned back and nudged further into his arm. "Where do you think he is right now?"

"I wish I knew," Darcy said. "They won't hurt him – beyond whatever they might have done to capture him. Hatcher will lose everything if further ... harm comes to Geoffrey. He is being taken care of. The situation requires it. He is probably asleep and in his dreams has forgotten his situation for a time."

Though neither of them could admit it, if that was true, he was the lucky one of the three of them.

~~~

The rooster had long ago crowed, but the morning mist, thick over Pemberley, had not yet cleared. The fresh air woke Darcy up, the chill almost a pleasant distraction, if such a thing was possible, as he waited on the terrace, where a table was set up. Michael Hatcher would not have entrance to Pemberley again, where the rest of the family was safe. He would sit outside for his business, as the weather was holding.

And Mr. Hatcher did appear, on time, emerging from the mist like a phantom. This time he must not have been so cocksure because he was visibly armed with a pistol in his belt. Darcy himself was not armed this morning, though Bingley was, and Darcy's master huntsman. Brian Maddox sat in his own chair, leaning his arms on his long sword, the other in his belt. With them was Mr. Hammond, with multiple cases of documents. No refreshments were offered.

"Mr. Darcy," Mr. Hatcher said, doffing his hat again. He did not look entirely the same – he was dirtier, and looked tired, although not completely exhausted. He still had that amazingly arrogant strut and self-assured tone. He wasn't introduced to the others. "I see you are prepared."

"I wish this business to be concluded," Darcy said, as unemotionally as he could manage. "I imagine you feel the same way." He gestured to the seat across from him at the little round table, and Hatcher took it. He seemed relieved to be sitting; maybe he had walked a long way. "The offer is one hundred thousand pounds, in cash. Now." He did not have to open the briefcase, or even point it out.

"I assume you are a wiser man than that, Mr. Darcy, and have at least read my materials. How you came to your conclusions, I will not bother to speculate. I am not here for my own gain. I am here for the people."

"Yes, of course, the *people*. None of whom ever appear at your side, or swear loyalty to you. In fact, everyone we can find decries you."

"The people are smarter than you believe them to be, and will not tell you what you do not want to hear, Mr. Darcy."

"Or perhaps they are more morally inclined than you believe them to be, Mr. Hatcher," he said. "Either way, since none of them are here to speak for themselves, this is between us. My offer stands. I cannot comply with your terms. If you had any understanding of the legal system – "

"The very legal system that protects your fortune - !"

" – then you would know that to sign away said fortune, I would need two signatures. One being my own, and the other being my son's, should I have one over the age of fifteen – which I do. But I see from your face that you have some understanding of the laws of entail."

"I know that laws were made to be broken, and that unjust laws are not made to be followed."

"I thought you would not listen to reason, legal or otherwise," Darcy said, and nodded for Mr. Hammond, who produced a piece of paper that was blank but for two lines at the bottom, and passed it to Hatcher. "Have my son sign the second line and return to me post-haste."

"It's blank."

"Your powers of observation amaze me, Mr. Hatcher. The terms are to be negotiated, and then I will sign. But his signature is key. Of course if he is not alive or in a condition to sign – "

"He is," Hatcher said, but he was visibly unnerved. He had not anticipated being surprised by the progress at this meeting.

"Good for you, then, because none of your noble goals of freeing the people from their tyrant noble, who is in reality not 'noble', and who provided them with food and coal all winter at his expense so they would not suffer beyond their means, will be reached without that signature. Or we could end this now, with the money, which I still believe must be your real goal."

"So you insist," Hatcher said, recovering his own indignation. He was given an attaché to protect the blank document. "Does he have a seal?"

"I have it and am authorized to use it. I only need him to sign."

He tapped on the table impatiently. "I will be waiting, Mr. Hatcher."

"You will catch cold, Mr. Darcy. I hardly intend to rush there and back and give you any indication of my hideout. I am not such a fool as that," he said. "Your son is being kept in good care – you need have no fear. And don't send your men into town – I know all of your spies and they will not catch my trail. You will wait, and I will return tonight."

"And if I don't wish to wait?"

"Well," Hatcher grinned, "that isn't your choice, now is it?" He made a fancy bow. "Mr. Darcy."

Darcy just growled under his breath as Hatcher walked away, attaché in hand.

"Do you want me to – " Bingley said, but stopped as Darcy put his head in his hands and made no motion to speak. Bingley instead put a hand on his friend's shoulder. "They're taking care of him."

"He's hurt and he can't sign," Darcy said. "I am calling his bluff – but I don't want it to be true. I want my son back."

Bingley looked at Brian, who just nodded at Darcy's assertions. Hatcher had been reluctant to take the document. "Maybe he just thinks Geoffrey won't agree to it. He won't agree to give up Pemberley – not even for his own life, God forbid."

"Maybe you're right," Brian said, more to comfort Darcy than respond to Bingley. "I'll go to town."

"He said – "

"I am not Darcy's servant or his spy. I am his eccentric relation by marriage, and if anyone has a problem with that, they will take it up with me." He put his sword back in his belt. "And I will be quite willing to take it up with them. Hatcher cannot hide forever, Darcy."

Darcy nodded softly, but did not seem to agree, as if all his energy, having been so carefully preserved for the course of the conversation, was now gone for him. Mr. Hammond and Brian both excused themselves, and left with the huntsman. It was only when they were gone that Darcy began to sob. Bingley took Hammond's seat and sat beside him, keeping a hand on his shoulder as he watched his dear friend and brother finally weep.

~~~

Before Brian went to Lambton, he went to his chambers, where his wife was waiting with her traveling clothes ready. "How do you always know what I'm going to do?" he asked in Romanian.

"Because I'm your wife," she said, handing him his *ronin gasa* hat.

They collected the reward notes – for any information surrounding Geoffrey Darcy's disappearance, or Hatcher's whereabouts, 500 pounds – put on their traveling sandals, and headed out. It was five miles to town, and the roads were extremely quiet, as if everyone was in hiding.

"Geoffrey's hurt," he said. "Hatcher knows he can't keep this going forever. Even from a minor wound, Geoffrey could die, if it gets infected."

"He said that?"

"He revealed it unintentionally. He's not as smart as he thinks." Brian looked up. "What he's up to, I have no idea. I suspect he thought the people would rise with him, and they didn't."

"Or they haven't heard of it yet."

"He must have been building this for a while – quietly. Maybe it was supposed to go differently. If Geoffrey hadn't been there to deliver the coal, they might never have crossed paths. And Gawain was with him, of course – "

" – and then if they attacked Gawain, Geoffrey would have tried something. And the only response – "

" – was to defend himself. Or themselves. Hatcher wouldn't do it alone. He's not that kind of man." He paused, his hand casually resting on his

171

blades, at the sound of a wolf howling in the distance. "There've been an awful lot of wolves about. How did they survive the winter?"

"They're the fiercest of creatures. Who knows?"

"Fiercest, huh? What about bears?"

"Bears are big and tough, but they don't plot, like wolves do," she said. Having grown up in rural Transylvania, where one of her only permitted activities was to hunt, she would know. She returned to their original topic of conversation. "But Hatcher, he would only play a high card if he had to."

"Right."

"So the kidnapping of Geoffrey – it may have been a spontaneous decision."

"And with such a violent crime, he faces exportation at least. So the stakes were high to begin with, especially if Geoffrey is injured." He glanced at his wife. "Possibly dying."

"We can only speculate."

"True."

"So, he makes outrageous demands, hoping all of his speeches will come to something and the people will act as some dreamy French peasantry and sack Pemberley," she said. "He is a romantic. And not native to Derbyshire. He appeared around the time of the mining disaster, and saw the discontent from that, but that was none of Darcy's business. The people love the Darcys of Pemberley. Even his servants readily praise him as a good landlord and master."

"So if he was to target anyone, it should have been the Duke of Devonshire, who doesn't even live *in* Derbyshire, and I doubt has visited in years. Hatcher miscalculated, and he's in a corner. So why didn't he take the money?"

"Maybe he is a real romantic."

"And thinks he is living forty years ago, in France."

They continued talking even as they walked into town, knowing full well that their mixture of Japanese and Romanian would not be understood in the least. Though Lambton was accustomed to the odd sight of the Maddoxes in full Japanese garb, they still drew some attention, especially as Brian approached the town hall, and hammered in a sign to the message board.

"Five hundred pounds?" said someone from behind. They turned to see Mr. Harris, the man who ran the jewelry and antiques shop. "I wish I had some information." He quickly corrected himself. "I wish I had the information anyway, for the young master's sake."

"So you've heard of the situation?" Brian said.

"It was the talk of the tavern last night – but no one seemed to know the specifics. I won't hesitate to tell you that. Whatever this is about, it wasn't planned to the knowledge of the people here in town."

"Thank you, Mr. Harris," Brian said with a glance to his wife. "Though sadly, it is not worth five hundred pounds. However, Geoffrey's return – or information on his whereabouts – definitely is. And Mr. Darcy intends to be good to his word."

"There isn't a person in Lambton who doesn't know Mr. Darcy is good to his word," Mr. Harris said, putting on his spectacles to read the notice properly. "I'll tell people. Gladly, for the young master."

Brian smiled. "You have no idea how good it will be for Mr. Darcy to hear that you said that."

~~~

Geoffrey Darcy woke to very few sensations, most of them unpleasant. The pounding and ringing in his head were beyond any hangover he had ever experienced, the shock of it preventing physical and mental movement. It threatened to overwhelm him, and he was unsure if more time passed, because there was only darkness, and occasionally voices, inconsistent but near. He recognized Hatcher, who was talking, and he could hear others, but only barely over the ringing sound in his head. And he was aware that he was cold, and very tired, but beyond that, there was nothing.

Why can't I open my eyes?

"Mr. Darcy? *Master* Darcy?"

It wasn't that he was too weak to respond. No, he actually couldn't respond. His body seemed to be disconnected from his mind and most of his awareness. He only had a vague sense that he was lying on something hard and being kicked. Both of these notions remained fairly abstract.

"Yeh hit him too hard. He's worth nothin' if he's dead."

"He's   not   dead."

"He will be if we leave 'im like this."

Jenkins. Geoffrey began to connect names with the voices he could hear. Jenkins, the man he'd been delivering coal to. It was coming back slowly, and it was no help to him at all.

But still, he found he couldn't speak.

"Mr. Darcy, you're making it real hard to have a civil conversation with you," Hatcher said.

Yes, so are you.

"'course if it was money we wanted, or your father wasn't an obstinate knob, this would all be over by now."

And if I could get up, that would help.

"No good. The boy's really out," said one of the other men, one he didn't recognize offhand. "Least 'e stopped bleedin.'"

I'm not a boy!

But they didn't hear him. He didn't even hear himself. All he heard was the muffled noises of the men in the room. And sometimes, he heard nothing at all.

CHAPTER 13

Doctor's Advice

"FATHER," Charlie Bingley said, standing resolutely in the doorframe to Pemberley's servant entrance, "I want to help."

"No," Bingley said without a second thought. He was out to meet the huntsman when he came back from their current round of trying to pick up Hatcher's trail. Darcy remained holed up in the study with his steward. "You'll remain inside like everyone else."

"But Father – "

"Charles!" his father said, and Charlie flinched. He could not remember hearing the sort of severity that was in his father's voice now. "You will stay inside *like everyone else*. If you want to help, comfort your cousins." He was unable to maintain that severity, softening as he patted his son on the arm. "I wouldn't want anything to happen to you."

Charlie finally nodded and stepped aside as his father turned to the huntsman and inspected the rifle. "It's been fired?"

"Stray wolves. If we weren't busy otherwise, I'd say it was time for a hunt. Not sure if we killed any, though. We didn't pursue."

Bingley left to pass the news on – not that there was much to tell. Charlie himself left the servant's quarters and returned to the sitting room upstairs, where the Darcy, Bingley, and Maddox children were supposed to be. Instead he found only Georgiana. "They went down for dinner," she said of the others. "What did Papa say?"

"He said no again."

Georgie huffed and sat down on the settee.

"It's not as though he would have let *you* help," Charlie said. "You know he wouldn't."

Georgie fingered her necklace. Instead of her usual Indian charm box, the gift from her father that lit up when she pushed down on the top, she had Geoffrey's ring on a silver chain around her neck. "Do you want to actually help?"

"Of course."

"Then shut the door."

He reluctantly did, and they were truly alone. "This is not the time for childish pranks."

"I am not a child," she said. She wasn't; she was eighteen, just like Geoffrey, even two weeks older. "If you want to be of actual help, you can help me."

"By doing what? Listen to their conversations? You already spy on everyone. You probably know more about what's going on than I do."

She laughed at that. "True, but that isn't what I meant." She reached into her purse and pulled out a piece of paper, which she handed to Charlie. "I need everything on the list."

"You're not allowed to go outside!"

"I didn't say I was going outside. I just said I need everything on the list. And that's why I can use your help." She rose. "Now we're late to dinner."

"Is this a childish prank to break tension or something more terrible?" Charlie said.

"Do you want to know the answer?"

"Probably not," he said, and followed her to dinner.

~~~

The Darcys supped alone. Darcy would not leave his study, as if the pile of legal papers and contracts in front of him would provide an answer if he only stared at them long enough. Elizabeth, for once, abandoned her duties as hostess to be at her husband's side, not wanting him to be alone, even though at every other moment his steward had been there. Still, neither of them had much of an appetite. As the sun began to decline, more time passed since Hatcher's disappearance without any sign or word from him. The constable was to arrive in the morning, but they had little faith that he could help them. The Kincaids and the Bellamonts would not have even received their letters yet, much less be on their way to Pemberley, a disheartening thought, for even Grégoire's distant prayers would have been some consolation to them.

They ate in silence until a sudden knock at the door, startling them and worsening their agitated nerves. "Come," Darcy said, his hand unconsciously falling on Elizabeth's.

Mrs. Annesley entered. "A Mr. and Mrs. Richardson to see you, sir."

"The tenants?"

"Yes, ma'am."

Darcy and Elizabeth exchanged glances. "Send them in." They rose as the tenants entered the room. "Good evening, Mr. Richardson. Mrs. Richardson." Darcy tried to maintain his restraint. He must be polite and inquire after their four young children, as if he had all the time in the world. Maybe Elizabeth would do that.

Fortunately, Mr. Richardson took the initiative before Darcy could open his mouth. "We're so sorry ta hear 'bout your son, Mr. Darcy. Mrs. Darcy." He bowed again and held his hat in his hands. "'Tis a real muddle."

"We don't know anythin' ta tell ya, Mr. Darcy, but we felt real bad with what happened to a fine young lad like Master Geoffrey, so we made you ... well, we didn' have much, but we made you a cake."

Elizabeth accepted the basket gratefully. "Thank you, Mrs. Richardson, for your kind thoughts, and lovely cake. It is very reassuring that people are not inclined to listen to Mr. Hatcher's propaganda."

"Hatcher? That man comin' about our town, spoutin' nonsense?" Mr. Richardson said. "Nobody I know took that man real seriously, Mr. Darcy, and now that he went and snatched a lad – if I saw 'im, I'd turn 'im in myself."

"That is very comforting to hear," Elizabeth replied again, seeing Darcy too emotional to speak. The Richardsons did not keep them any longer from their dinner and excused themselves, leaving the Darcys with their cake.

"You're not a bad landlord," Elizabeth said, kissing Darcy before the steward entered. "You're a good man."

"I wish only to convince someone else of that," he said, and on cue, the steward announced the arrival of one Mr. Hatcher, come alone, waiting for him at the entrance.

"I wish to go with you," Elizabeth said, "if he sees how distraught – "

"I don't want him to see that," Darcy said with more force than he was accustomed to with Elizabeth. "Please, Lizzy," he whispered, "it is hard enough for me to talk to this man as it is."

She nodded and reluctantly stayed in the room as he left to greet his *guest*.

~~~

As Darcy approached the open doors, Brian Maddox had just returned, Bingley was of course ready at his side, and Dr. Maddox was waiting in the wings. He did not welcome Hatcher in, instead walking up to him on the front steps so he did not enter Pemberley proper. There were no greetings. "Well?"

Hatcher produced the paper, still blank but for a scrawl where Geoffrey's signature should have been. "It's not my fault he's a heavy sleeper – "

Darcy grabbed Hatcher by his collar, lifting him ever so slightly off his feet and shaking him in fury. *"What did you do to my son?"* Hatcher was a stout man, and at least a decade younger than Darcy, but

181

he was not as tall or as passionate at this particular moment, and his face was red from strangulation by the time Bingley and Brian managed to pull Darcy away. "I will not be manhandled in my own house!" It took him a moment to recover himself, shaking out his coat as Hatcher stumbled and rubbed his throat, but no one rushed to help *him*. "Now – what have you done to my son? And be plain about it for once. Dr. Maddox will hear your account."

Brian nodded to his brother, who came up behind Darcy as Hatcher began to speak. "That dog – when he attacked me, one of my men shot him, so the boy tried to strike me, and I hit him in the head. Here." He pointed to his temple. "He's alive, but he won't wake."

"Is he bleeding?" Dr. Maddox asked. His professional voice was comforting in its own strange way, all calm and seriousness.

"He bled a little, but it stopped. And there's some bruising."

Darcy did not hesitate to reach into his coat and pull out a small pistol, pointing it directly at Hatcher's forehead. "Take me to Geoffrey."

"I'll make a concession – "

"*You will take me to my son!*"

"You shoot, and he'll be dead before you find him. You know that." Hatcher swallowed when Darcy did not lower his pistol. "I'll let the doctor see him."

"I'll go," Dr. Maddox said, stepping forward, "as long as we leave before Caroline hears about it. And I need to bring plenty of lamps."

Darcy hesitated, lowering his pistol and whispering to the doctor, "You do not have to risk yourself for me again."

"I want to do it, for Geoffrey. But I'm night-blind. I'll need a lot of light."

"We have plenty of light," Hatcher said. "I'll bring him back as soon as he finishes his assessment."

Darcy, with mere moments to assess the situation, closed his eyes and nodded. "All right. Doctor – "

But Dr. Maddox already had his bag in hand and called for his coat. Before he could leave, Brian drew his blade and held it to Hatcher's throat, drawing just the smallest bit of blood. "If you don't bring him back, I will hunt you to the ends of the earth."

"And he's been to the ends of the earth," Bingley said.

Dr. Maddox and his brother embraced before he left with Hatcher, disappearing into the night. Darcy nearly collapsed, but Bingley caught him. "My only request," he said, "is that someone other than I tell Lady Maddox what just happened."

~~~

Hatcher had another man with him, at the edge of the grounds, where the real road began, and two horses. With so little light, Dr. Maddox couldn't see him clearly, and doubted he would recognize him anyway. "You don't have to do this," he said as the other man tied his hands behind his back. "I won't fight you."

"You can't blame me for taking precautions," Hatcher said, and they blindfolded him, even though without his glasses and in the dark of night, he was completely blind anyway. Between the horse ride and the number of times they spun him around, by the time they reached their destination, he had no proper idea where they were, except that it was extremely secluded. His hands were untied, which allowed for circulation to return to them as he was led into what appeared to be a tent.

They removed his blindfold and returned his glasses. It was still too dark for him to see much as the man with Hatcher opened up the doctor's case and started removing the sharp objects, taking them out of the doctor's reach.

"Those are just my surgical tools."

"If you need 'em, let me know."

"I need more light."

They brought in more torches for him, until there was quite enough light for him to finally see. He was in a small tent, obviously designed mainly to keep him from seeing where he was in the woods. On the ground, wrapped in blankets, was the first familiar form he could see besides Hatcher.

"Geoffrey." When the form before him did not respond, he had to try not to despair. Geoffrey Darcy, still wearing his waistcoat, lay on his side, his hands tied tightly behind his back. Not that he was going anywhere; he was completely unresponsive when Dr. Maddox probed him.

He had no sharp tools to cut Geoffrey's bonds and so held the lantern up to the boy's face. There was a bruise and swelling above his left eye, not far from the hair line, and dried blood that had dripped down across his forehead. "Geoffrey, can you hear me? It's Dr. Maddox." He pushed up the boy's lids, but his eyes were rolled back into his head. "Unfortunately I've not come here to rescue you." He looked a bit closer at the wound along his hairline. That at least would need cleaning. He turned to his bag, and retrieved a much stronger pair of glasses that he now used for close inspection, and his smelling salts. Geoffrey's breathing was shallow, and Maddox had to hold the bottle right up against his nose before the boy got a whiff. There was some visible nasal reaction, but still he did not wake. "He's not woken at all?"

"No," said Hatcher. "I've had someone with him the whole time."

"Has he spoken in his sleep?"

"No."

Dr. Maddox removed a metal bowl from his bag and handed it to Hatcher. "Fill it with clean water, if you have a source. That or alcohol."

His captor left silently, closing the tent flap behind him. Dr. Maddox sighed and began checking Geoffrey for other wounds, but he appeared to have none. "Geoffrey, if you can hear me, we're doing everything we can to free you." He added, thinking it might ease his mind, if some part of it could hear, "And Gawain is all right. The bullet just grazed him." He began pulling out his bandage cloth. "Miss

Bingley has your ring, as I understand. She's keeping it safe for you, and she'll be very upset if you don't come back to claim it soon."

Hatcher returned with water, which Maddox tasted. It was cold and fresh, obviously from a stream. It was not boiled, but it would have to do. Dr. Maddox cleaned his hands as best he could. "Scissors," he said, and Hatcher put his tiny scissors into the waiting palm. Dr. Maddox wet the cloth and wiped the blood from Geoffrey's forehead. He snipped away at some of the hair that was caught in the dried blood, and moved slowly up against the hairline, to see how far the swelling went. "There's a sharp object that looks like a small pike made of steel. I need it."

"Why?"

"I need to see what the swelling is."

Hatcher sighed and handed him the object in question, which he delicately used to pierce the swelling. There was only a little bleeding, and some pus around the wound, but still no reaction from Geoffrey,. Dr. Maddox pushed down on the wound gently, and some of the swelling went down. Sighing, he took a fresh cloth and held it against the bleeding spot. "I think you were lucky and managed not to smash his skull and pierce his brain. Nonetheless he does have a very serious concussion." When the bleeding had stopped, he put down a bandage and tied it around Geoffrey's head. It was unnerving to hold the young man in his arms and feel him limp like a corpse. "Is he hurt anywhere else?"

"No."

"Did you check?"

"*Yes.*"

Dr. Maddox wasn't interested in Hatcher's attitude, though it was notably more subdued than it had been at Pemberley. "More light," he ordered, and Hatcher came forward and held a lantern right over him as he went though his bag and found a small glass bottle of sugar and a spoon. He put a little sugar and water onto the spoon. "Open his mouth."

"What?"

"Just do as I say."

Like most men, Hatcher was inexperienced in the field of medical science and listened readily to a doctor's demands, opening Geoffrey's mouth. Dr. Maddox put the sugar solution under the boy's tongue. "Does he swallow?"

"We didn't want to try."

Dr. Maddox nodded reluctant approval. It was more likely that the boy would choke. He rubbed Geoffrey's neck. "Do you have a cot or something to keep him off the ground?"

"I could get something."

He stroked Geoffrey's hair, the bit of it that was far away from the wound. He kept his locks a bit longer than absolutely fashionable, and his hair was colored like his father's but curlier. "I suppose you won't listen to me when I say you'd best send him home."

"How long does he have?"

"He could very well live or very well die. It's not a question of time. However, in these bad conditions, he could contract any number of illnesses. Even a cold could kill him now, in such a state."

Hatcher sat down on a box in the corner. "You understand that I can't give him up."

"From your viewpoint, perhaps. But from any kind of moral, human, or medical position, no, I cannot understand it. He's concussed and, perhaps, slowly dying. He's more likely to contract something in the open woods than safe in his bed. Make the deal with Mr. Darcy and be done with it."

"He won't make the deal we want."

Dr. Maddox kept his tongue in check. He was still, strictly speaking, captive. "Make *a* deal with him if you expect to get anything at all. Or, in my honest opinion, your best bet is to deliver Geoffrey and run. The Darcy holdings are complex and you cannot go into long negotiations with Geoffrey in this condition. You know that, I know that, and Darcy already suspects it." In the distance, he heard a wolf howl, but ignored it. "Keep him dry and warm, and raise him off the ground. If he gets a fever, deliver him to Pemberley, because he's no bargaining chip to you then." He poured water into the bottle of sugar. "Put a spoonful of this under his tongue twice a day. Not *on* his tongue. Under it. Do you understand?"

"Yes."

The doctor was reluctant to release Geoffrey, but he knew he had to get back to Darcy, and there was little else he could do here. "This is all I can do." He stood, switching the magnification glasses for his normal bifocals. "Even if I stayed here with him, he still could die at any time, and then there won't be an army in the world that can save you. So whatever nonsense is between you and Darcy, you'd best end it."

He wished it was brighter in the tent, or his vision was better, so he could see if Hatcher was frightened. He suspected that he was.

~~~

Pemberley was still lit up when Dr. Maddox was returned, and the horses galloped away with Hatcher and his man. Hatcher was in no mood to talk but said he would return in the morning. Dr. Maddox could not see his timepiece, only the lights of Pemberley in front of him, and a bright red, unmistakable figure that came rushing out and grabbed him, and if she had any strength, would have lifted him right up and throttled him instead of hugging him fiercely.

"How dare you!" Caroline Maddox cried into his shoulder, not loud enough for the others that were approaching to hear. "How dare you put yourself in danger! What would I have done without you?"

"I wasn't in danger."

"You – I couldn't – " But she muffled her own tears by snuggling into his arms, and he returned the embrace.

The first man to arrive, carrying the lantern, was Darcy. He couldn't see precisely, but he guessed that it was, from his stature and how he was dressed.

189

"I've seen to him," Dr. Maddox said in answer to the unasked question. "I think we'd best discuss the rest inside, but he is alive, Darcy. Concussed, but alive."

"Thank God for that," Darcy said, and led them inside.

CHAPTER 14

The Wolves of Derbyshire

"WHAT DO YOU think he's thinking right now?" Cassandra Darcy, the youngest of the three Darcy girls, stared out the glass window at the moonlit sky.

"You heard Dr. Maddox say he's sleeping," Sarah Darcy said. Anne, older and more openly affectionate, took their little sister in her lap.

"He's probably having a pleasant dream, then," Anne said to Cassandra. "He's dreaming about playing with Gawain or fishing with Charlie."

"He's not afraid?"

"Geoffrey's *never* afraid," Anne assured her.

Their nurse entered followed immediately by their mother, who announced that it was time for bed.

"No!" Cassandra said, climbing off Anne's lap and running to her mother. "I want to stay up and wait for Geoffrey!"

"Dearest, I promise you, if he comes home tonight, I will wake you first. But until then, you'd best get your rest."

"I bet Georgie gets to stay up!"

"Miss Bingley is fast asleep, just like the rest of your cousins soon will be. In fact, she specifically requested a different room so she could have quiet from all the noise the men are making, and be better rested for tomorrow. And I won't have you adding to the noise. Now off to bed, all of you!" She kissed them each as Nurse saw them off, even though they gave great protest. She turned at a knock on the door. "Come."

It was George Wickham. "Aunt Darcy."

"George."

"I just wanted to see – if the girls are all right."

"As can be expected," she said, turning away from him quickly enough to wipe away her own tears that had begun to form. "Thank you, George. You can turn in now."

"I didn't know I also had a bedtime."

"You're my nephew and you're in my home, so I have every right to enforce it," she said.

"There's nothing else I can do?"

She smiled. "You can tell me why I saw Charlie carrying a ladder up the stairs when he thought no one was looking."

He shrugged. "Your guess is as good as mine."

"Watch over him, will you?"

"I'll do my best."

She kissed him on the cheek before returning to the first floor, where she waited for her husband to finish the meeting in the study.

~~~

"He's in bad shape, Darcy," Dr. Maddox said. "I know you too well to lie to you. He needs medical attention immediately – more than I could give at their hideout."

"Can you tell us anything about it?"

The doctor sighed and took the offered glass of wine. "It is very deep in the forest. I couldn't hear any signs of civilization at all, just their horses. They had him in a tent – a temporary one. There was no floor."

"Was it well-stocked?"

"Yes. And near a fresh water stream."

"There are dozens of them around here," Bingley said.

"How many men were there?"

"At least three. Maybe four. I didn't know the other man I saw clearly, and the others weren't in the tent, so the encampment must be larger – they may have an outside fire going."

"Was he old, the other man?" Darcy said. "White hair?"

"No."

"Not Jenkins, then."

"But he's still missing," Bingley said. "One can only assume he's either there of his own free will or he's as much a prisoner as Geoffrey."

"Sadly, I would think the latter," Darcy said. "He's an old man, but he's no fool. He wouldn't fall into Hatcher's plan so easily, even if he had been listening to him speak. And he's always liked Geoffrey – otherwise I wouldn't have given asked Geoffrey to go there." He frowned and shook his head. "Could you wake him at all?"

"No. Nor do I think I could do so here. However, I don't think the skull is cracked. My main concern is that the woods can get very cold and wet in the

193

night and it's not for anyone in his condition. That, and he hasn't had sustenance in two days now because he can't swallow." He sighed. "I told Mr. Hatcher to give it up, but he refused. But he is in a corner and he does know that." He added, "I did hear wolves."

"It seems like there are wolves everywhere."

Darcy nodded. "Anything else?"

"Sadly, no." Dr. Maddox finished off his wine. "Brian?"

All eyes turned to Brian Maddox, who had spent most of the day making the rounds in Lambton and the villages of Derbyshire. "There are definitely at least three of them. There's Hatcher himself, and Mr. Wallace, who hasn't been seen recently by his wife or brother. His brother said he left early that morning and hasn't shown up since. And no sign of Mr. Jenkins, but he has no long-standing prior associations with Mr. Hatcher, who rolled into town about the same time as the mine disaster. Did you write His Grace?"

"Yes, but I can hardly expect a reply from the Duke in time to help with this, if he would do anything at all."

Brian nodded. "Either way, Hatcher's been renting a room over the tavern in Lambton but he hasn't been there since Geoffrey was taken. He must have had this place in the woods staked out ahead. A man like him would always have *somewhere* to run."

"The others?"

"There are two field workers who were close with him, or at least were seen a lot with him, one of whom is the son of a tenant of yours named Mr. Graham. The eldest, I believe. I spoke with his father and mother and they said he was always a bit of a stray. The other is a seasonal hand, named Mark Blackwood, who worked in the mine, but survived the disaster, and lived in town. But he's been known to travel in and out when he's out of work, so it might not be reliable that he's with Hatcher," Brian said. "We posted signs all over town– everyone knows about the reward, and many expressed their concerns over 'the young master.'" He did his best impression of a local Derbyshire accent. "These demands of Hatcher's – they're nonsense, correct?"

"He wants me to forfeit all of my land in Derbyshire, including Pemberley, which is to be turned into a communal home for the poor. The rest will be turned over to the current tenants." Darcy held up the paper. "It lists their individual holdings in great detail, so he has clearly spent some time on this, with a complete list of names and the parcels they are to receive at my bequest. Though the tenants themselves might not be aware of it, of course. I am to return to my townhouse in London and be content. He has refused the offer of money. Of course I could write up a bunch of useless deeds – in fact, I am having my steward do so as we speak – but Hatcher must know they will not hold up in any court with the entail intact. Only about thirty percent of my own holdings in Derbyshire are not part of my entail, and even those could be challenged as not binding documents, as they were signed under duress." He sat back in his grand chair. "What is he thinking?

What could he possibly want that is within the realm of possibility for me to give him?"

"His very plan leaves him without anything of worth," Bingley said. "Maybe he is a true revolutionary. Good of the people and all that."

"Or he intends to take Pemberley for himself once you are gone. As if that could ever be," Brian said. "I'll kill him myself before I see that happen."

"You will have to wait in line for that honor, I think," Dr. Maddox said. "Behind Darcy, Bingley and a number of angry women."

"He said he will be back in the morning," Bingley said to Darcy. "Perhaps he will be more amenable to a monetary offer when he better assesses the situation with Geoffrey."

"Promise him the moon if you like," Brian said. "Mr. Darcy, I swear to you I will do everything in my power to make sure that after he's delivered Geoffrey, he doesn't make it out of the shire alive."

Darcy just looked up at Brian, standing now so tall and serious compared to the tired, world-weary father missing a son, and nodded his thanks.

~~~

Mr. Hatcher did not arrive early, but he did come alone. The stakes remained where they were, and he felt safe enough with one pistol and the threat of Geoffrey's death upon his non-return to approach Pemberley with no apprehension. Darcy, who had been sitting on his heels all morning, raced out to find the man dirtied and bloodied. Darcy had to resist the urge to inquire after his health. He didn't care whether Hatcher lived or died, though seeing the man in such a state was a curious thing.

"I was attacked by a wolf," Hatcher said, referring to the claw marks on his face and his general state. "A wild animal. How are you today, Mr. Darcy?" He looked around him. "Where are your men?"

"Do I need them? Are you intending to shoot me and be done with it? Because if you do, you won't make it back to the road."

Hatcher laughed. He looked tired. In fact, he was breathing heavily. Obviously he had been doing some running, perhaps from the wolf he had mentioned. Or perhaps it was another one of his games. "Bring your people out and let me see them."

"And why should I?"

"Just do it, Darcy. I'm in no mood for games."

"Neither am I. Nor am I in the mood to take orders. We're here to discuss my son and I will not parade all of Pemberley before you before we do it."

Hatcher laughed and wiped off some blood that was dripping into his eyes. "Where's that crazy one? The one who dresses like a woman?"

"I do not!" Brian Maddox said, storming out. "They're pleated pants."

"Mr. Maddox, please," Darcy said.

Hatcher took a good look at Brian and even took a step towards him, but Brian had a hand on his swords, and that was enough to make Hatcher back away again. "All right. The Irish one?"

"His name is Mr. Bingley."

"Mr. Bingley. Where is he?"

"Mr. Hatcher, what is this madness? We both know why you are here," Darcy said, but Bingley, having heard his name, did appear with his rifle.

"Finally," Hatcher said. "The doctor is too tall. And your huntsman is too stocky. Well, that is that." He wiped more blood off with an already rag. "I have decided, given the current conditions, that a revision to my earlier demands may be required."

"I   agree."

"Not a severe revision but – I understand this matter of entail and all of that nonsense, so you may keep your precious castle on a hill. The lands being farmed will still go to their proper owners."

"My tenants, you mean."

"You do not own them, Mr. Darcy."

"It is a turn of a phrase. You know very well that I have every respect for them."

Hatcher laughed again and removed a flask, taking a drink from it. He was still breathing heavily. "Fine. Keep on with your nonsense. You keep Pemberley, and they get the land that is owed to them by the rights of men."

"You know my land is entailed away as much as Pemberley itself is."

"And I know you could employ many expensive lawyers to unravel that entail, should you be so inclined. And considering your son's condition, I would say you would need to hand me the paperwork ... I will give you a day. Meet me tomorrow, at eight o'clock. I trust you own a pocket watch. And I have already given you the list of names and the appropriate deed notifications."

"Yes," Darcy seethed. "Though it's not legally possible – "

" – I will deliver your son to you, once you have given me the deeds, and I have dispersed them to the people. Then my men will bring him here." He paused. "Oh, and I would like a rifle."

"What?"

"My pistol – it won't do. I have a wolf to kill, if I see him again. You wouldn't want me dying on the way home? Then your precious 'young master' would be dead, and all because I won't be able to defend myself from an animal attack."

Darcy sighed. "I don't know what you're about, Hatcher." He turned to Bingley. "The rifle."

With only the briefest of questioning glances, Bingley handed Hatcher the rifle. The man shouldered it, clearly with no intentions to fire it at present. "It is loaded, I trust. After all, you were planning on using it on me if you could manage it, so I imagine it would be."

"How intuitive of you," Darcy said. "And where is this meeting to take place, if I produce all of said deeds?"

"Signed with the Darcy seal."

"Signed and ready."

"Then – you may meet me at the place called Potter's Field. You must know it."

"I do," Darcy said. It was now overgrown and bordered the woods, some four miles from Pemberley, but it was said that it had once been plowed until the ground gave no more crops. "I have no intentions of coming unarmed and alone."

"Neither do I. You bring two men, and I'll bring two of mine. I think that would be fair. After all, this is just a trade of documents. And if you attempt to fill the area with your men first – well, I will do the same. So you understand the terms?"

"Yes."

"And you agree to them?"

"If you agree to return Geoffrey alive, then yes, I agree."

"I will not ask you to shake on it." Hatcher looked down at his hand. It was filthy and bloody. "I will just take your word." He bowed extravagantly and turned away, back down towards the road, where his horse waited for him.

Bingley scratched his head. "What in the world happened to him?"

"I've no idea," Darcy said, "but if it was good for us, I'll toss a ham to every wolf in Derbyshire."

~~~

Pemberley was bursting with activity as they made preparations for the next day. Dr. Maddox wanted another surgeon on hand should one be needed, but he was unlikely to arrive by the next day. Brian Maddox immediately offered to accompany Darcy, who was grateful for it, but to Bingley's offer, less so.

"Have you ever killed a man, Bingley?" Darcy said to him aside in his study.

"For Geoffrey, I would."

"I can't ask you to give up your life for my son. You realize it may come to that. Hatcher may ambush us. And even with Brian there – I'm not as young as I used to be, and neither are you."

"But I'm still a better shot than you are."

"True. But I must hear it from Mrs. Bingley that you have her permission."

"And I must hear it from Mrs. Darcy that you have her permission."

"You may ask," he said, "but I already do."

Bingley rushed off to find his wife, but in the wing of Pemberley the Bingleys had taken over, he first found his eldest daughter, wrapped in a shawl and sitting on the floor, rubbing Gawain's back. "Papa!"

"Georgiana. Have you seen your mother?"

"She's with Aunt Maddox," she said as she rose, readjusting the shawl around her arms. "You're not going are you?"

"How did you already hear?" Bingley shook his head. "Forget I even asked. Yes, I am going."

"Papa!"

"I thought you would forever brand me a coward if I didn't."

"I would rather have a cowardly father than a dead one," she blurted, covering her mouth. "Papa, Mr. Hatcher, he's not a good – "

"I know. But – " Further reassurance was halted by his daughter breaking out into tears, so unusual that he broke his sentence off. He imagined she might have cried when they heard Geoffrey was missing, but he had not witnessed her reaction himself, concerned as he was for Darcy. She ran to him and he welcomed her embrace. "I will be all right. Darcy has faced worse foes and lived, and Brian is coming, and he's the mighty warrior."

But she just buried her head into his shoulder and sobbed. He put a hand over her hair, so much like his in both color and length. Edmund was the only other redhead of the Bingley children. "I'll be all right. We all will. But we have to do this for Geoffrey."

"I know he's hurt. But he's strong – and he can't die. That's what the locket means. I know what it means and if he dies then it means nothing."

He managed to smile. "So you figured it out, did you?"

"You think you're so clever," she snickered, trying to wipe her tears away with the edge of her shawl.

"And you are your father's daughter. Which I'm not particularly proud of, if you're planning something foolish. And I know you are planning something for his return. Am I wrong?"

She said nothing.

"See? I'm not wrong. I am very clever." He kissed her on her head. "The shaman in India set that locket. I didn't know the name – just what it was set to. Though I wasn't very surprised." He squeezed her hand, which was more calloused than it should have been, for a proper lady. But Georgiana was not really a proper lady except when she wanted to pretend to be. She was something special, and he loved her for it. (That said, it was nice to have a

202

more conventional daughter like Eliza to balance it out) "Geoffrey will get through this. We all will. I promise you that."

"Well, then you'd better keep your promise," she said, and hugged him once more.

~~~

Darcy was briefly called away from his office to the Maddox chambers, where he found Brian and Nadezhda Maddox with a vast amount of Oriental gear lying about, much of it some kind of strange armor. "I assume Pemberley is lacking a suit of armor?" Brian said.

"Nor would I know how to manage in one."

Nadezhda presented him with a small square plate, with a small bend to it, and a looped buckle. "Put it over your heart, Mr. Darcy."

"Thank you, Your Highness," he said. "Do you have a spare one for Bingley?"

"Of course."

"Do you have a spare one for my kidneys? Because I feel that one spot is particularly unlucky," he said, remembering keenly the location of a near fatal wound caused by Wickham.

Brian smiled and sorted through the bag to produce some plated armor sewn together with bright orange threads. "It'll be a bit awkward under your coat if they see you from the back."

"I've no intention of showing them my back, or fighting them at all. These are merely precautions."

"Speaking of precautions," Nadezhda said, "we made fireworks for you."

"For your rifles," Brian said, producing a brown package. "You load one in and fire it into the sky. It sets off a small bit of fireworks that can be seen for miles away. The colors will indicate if we're in distress, and where to find us."

"Brilliant. What else?"

"Oh, I'm your samurai and I'll kill them all without hesitation if need be."

Darcy smiled. "I've never been happier to have you as a cousin, Mr. Maddox."

"And I've never been happier to be a collector of Oriental armor and military knick-knacks, Mr. Darcy."

~~~

That night, Darcy's steward took great care to streamline everything so that Darcy was finished at a reasonable hour, whereupon he kissed each of his nephews, nieces, and daughters goodnight in turn. He inquired after his wife, and to his surprise, was told she was in the chapel.

"Elizabeth?" he called out, not finding a particularly good place for knocking on the stone walls. She was seated in the second of the three tiny rows of pews. "Am I interrupting?"

"No," she said quickly. "I was just – thinking."

He sat down beside her and put his arm around her shoulder. "I know."

"Do you think Grégoire's gotten our letter by now?"

"I'm sure Georgiana has. Grégoire, maybe. But I like to think he continually keeps us in his thoughts, busy as he may be with his own family and his writing." He looked at his pocket watch. "He'll be up in a few hours to pray, anyway, while sensible people are sleeping."

"I heard about the armor."

"It's only a precaution. I have no intention of fighting Hatcher and his men."

She tightened her grip on his hand.

"I'm not going to put myself in danger if nothing will come of it. I promise." He kissed her. "But I will do anything to save our son."

She squeezed tighter. "We have three other children."

"I know. And I would do the same for them. With that said, I would prefer if Robert Kincaid did not have to inherit Pemberley." Realizing it was too terrible to even imagine, not because of the qualities of the toddler but because of the implication of the death of the first heir, he said, "Geoffrey will be all right. Who knows? Perhaps he will be safe at home tomorrow night and wake in his own bed, having no idea that any of this occurred."

That at least put a smile on her face. "Perhaps."

But until then, they could only hope.

~~~

The last to retire and the first to rise, Brian Maddox and his wife Nadezhda, Princess of Transylvania, began his preparations. He sat on a stool as she ritually shaved the front of his head. "Did you swear to protect Darcy?"

"Yes."

"And if you fail?"

"I didn't say it, but I will commit seppuku." He looked down as she took the back of his hair and tied it up before applying the layers of wax that would be needed to keep it in place on the top of his head in the perfect topknot. The fact that his hair was curly didn't help at all. "But only if you promise not to follow me."

"I can't leave Georgiana. I promised Mugin I would watch over her," she said, "until she has proven herself."

He could not move because of the application of the wax, but he tensed and said, "Did he say what he meant by that?"

"I know what he meant."

"Did you tell Bingley?"

"It's none of his business. Or yours." She pulled away, and wiped her hands off before draping the first layer of kimono over his shoulders. "I only told you because I had to. Otherwise I would follow you."

"I would dispute that, but since you won't be doing it anyway, I'll save my breath." He tied up his kimono and took the chest gear, layers of metal plates laced together with alternating green, white, and orange cords, against his chest so she could tie it in the back. "You could have a life without me, though."

"I'll decide whether I want to follow you or not when I can," she said. "And you won't be around to stop me. But do try not to die."

He smiled, breaking from tying up his shoulder pads to lean over and kiss her.   "I   love   you. You know that?"

She responded with a kiss. Beyond that, there were many layers to apply in his complicated uniform, complete with the back flag. She only had time to sew the Maddox crest onto a white linen sheet that would flutter in the breeze behind him. "This will make you a moving target, you realize."

"Death is supposed to be the first thing a samurai accepts."

Last, he thrust his short sword into his obi, and she handed him his long katana, bowing to him as she offered it as he bowed to accept it, "Don't accept it so easily."

His smile was his best way of telling her he agreed.

CHAPTER 15

The Wolf of Derbyshire

"I'M JUST saying, is – "

"What are you saying, Mr. Blackwood?"

Geoffrey could barely distinguish their voices at first. Hatcher and Jenkins he knew, and it seemed as if Dr. Maddox was talking to him about his dog, but how was that possible? It hurt just to think about it. But sometimes there was only sound, and he listened.

"Do you want out?" Hatcher said. Some noises in the background. "Are you going to run away like a coward?"

"I didn't come here to attack a kid and then shoot Mr. Darcy."

"Do you want him to rule over these poor people?"

"Doesn't mean I want ta kill him!"

Kill ... Darcy? His father? *If I could move!* But even understanding what was happening was beyond him. Was he just dreaming? If so, did his dream really have to hurt so much?

"Let 'im go," Wallace said. "He doesn't want to do it, he's just gonna hold us back."

There was another sound. A gun cocking? Were they getting ready to shoot someone? Why was he wet?

"It'll be all right, Master Geoffrey," Jenkins said, closer now. Maybe it was Jenkins who was caring for him. Why did his mouth taste like syrup? For a long time now, he had only been barely conscious of many unfamiliar sounds and nothing else but slight sensations of feeling that he usually just forgot about them and gave in to the blackness.

"Go, then," Hatcher said, and there was some more ruffling, and no more.

"Don't blame him," said the third man, with a voice Geoffrey didn't know. "He's just gun shy. What the feck are those?"

"Silver bullets," Hatcher said. He had a very distinct middle class voice, almost proper sounding. It made him easier to tell apart from the others.

"Yer serious about this wolf crap."

"It wasn't a wolf. It was – I don't know."

Howling.

"*Feck.*"

"I know. Let's be done with this."

"What if he just gives us the deeds and the money? Can't we let him go?"

"When he sees his son, he'll never let us go. We'll be the most hunted men in Britain. Don't you know that?"

There was some more talking, but it was too soft and Geoffrey was so tired. It was hard to strain to hear them. It seemed like he had less and less energy. The blackness was overwhelming.

"Let's go. Jenkins, let him get some air if you want. Otherwise, you know what to do."

"Yes, sir. Of course, sir. Mr. Hatcher, sir."

"Shut the feck up."

"Yes, sir."

Poor Mr. Jenkins. Did he have enough coal? *Did I remember to bring him the coal? Wait? Why am I worrying about that?*

But the noise was too rattling. He decided to let the blackness come for him again, and not to fight it, until all those noisy people that made his head ache so much worse were gone.

~~~

"Be careful," Elizabeth said as she kissed her husband good-bye.

"You know I will." He took one look at Brian, emerging from the house, his armor making a *ching-ching* sound as he walked, his back flag flapping in the early morning wind. "I have that maniac to protect me."

She clutched at his vest. Beneath it lay a small plate of armor. "Be careful anyway. I think Nadezhda wants her husband back in one piece, too."

"I think he lost his last piece years ago," Bingley said, and gave a nervous smile to his wife before embracing her. "I said good-bye to the children."

"Don't do anything too stupid," Caroline said to her brother.

"You were always the most supportive sister," Charles replied, and kissed her on the cheek.

"Do as Caroline said," Nadezhda said to Brian, handing him his black metal triangular hat.

211

"You're the best, Nady," he said before mounting his horse, and with many final good-byes from servants, children, and Dr. and Lady Maddox, the three of them were off. There was no reason to rush, and they didn't want to tire their horses, or themselves. Along with two pistols and a rifle, Darcy carried a satchel full of legal documents that wouldn't hold up in any court. In the other satchel was fifty thousand pounds in bank notes.

"Darcy, do you realize something?" Bingley said after some time.

"I realize a lot of things, Bingley. You'll have to be more specific."

"Potter's Field is not very far from that mine that collapsed. The one you sold to the Duke of Devonshire?"

Darcy frowned. "No. It isn't." He shook his head as he made the connection Bingley just had. "Idiot! Why didn't we think to search that area?"

"The   mine?"

"Yes! And then we could've found Geoffrey and not had this nonsense with Hatcher!"

"What's done is done," Brian said. "It might have been another false lead. We did the best we could to get to this point, Darcy. Let's not waste the chance we have."

~~~

From the beginning, Mark Blackwood hadn't liked the whole business.

Sure, there were the injustices that Michael Hatcher talked about. And Mark wouldn't mind a piece of land for himself, not rented or anything – not that he had one that he rented currently. He did look up at the dandy lords passing by in their fancy carriages and snort, thinking 'What gives them the right to be more comfortable than him?'

He was a smart man. He liked to think he was, anyway, before involving himself in this, but by the time he realized how bad this was, it was too late. Hatcher had royally messed it all up in one move by hitting the Darcy's son hard enough to almost kill him. "We'll hang for this," Mr. Graham had said, and Graham was right. They couldn't cover it up, not without killing Jenkins as the witness. At first Hatcher's ransom plan seemed good, almost like he had planned it, even though he hadn't. It was the best idea. As much as Mark Blackwood had little good to say of the rich, he couldn't stand the thought of killing old Mr. Jenkins just because that damned kid came by while they happened to be at his house to talk with him about joining them. And with a donation of coal, too! Made him seem almost noble – and in the good way. Not in the fancy "nobility" way that Hatcher always talked about it.

Mark was used to hiding in the woods. That wasn't a problem. But when the fancy London doctor came and said how bad it was, he knew right then they were fecked, and Hatcher knew it too. They all knew it. Maybe Hatcher would have made a deal the next day, had he not gotten attacked by some animal that he then imagined to be a werewolf.

A werewolf! Got silver bullets and everything! The man wasn't just suicidal – he was mad! Mark didn't care how many riots and mobs Hatcher had escaped from without being caught and marked as a Radical – he was boggy in the head and that was that, and now he was going to kill a bunch of people just to get away. Well, Mark Blackwood would have none of that. If Hatcher would let him go, he would walk away. He would walk to the tip of Scotland if he had to, but he would manage. He'd done it before, and it was better than killing someone.

Mark had stopped to rest and wash his face in a stream when the arrow came. It grazed his ear, landing soundly in the ground next to him.

"That was a warning," came the muffled voice from behind. "Where's Geoffrey Darcy?"

He spun around, but the pistol was knocked out of his hand with a kick, and a second knocked him right against a tree. He fell, looking down at wooden shoes and furry feet. "Holy feck – "

But his attacker was not in the mood for games. "Geoffrey Darcy," he said, his long metal claws protruding ominously from the paws.

"Jus' let me go," he said. "'e's – by the mine. Down that way."

The wolf-man paused only to retrieve his arrow, and turned in the direction indicated, and left with a leap that took him into the stream. How did he move like that? And in those shoes?

He wasn't interested in questioning the most bizarre thing he had seen in his life. Once in a lifetime was enough. He had the rest of his life to ponder it, so he got up and kept running, in the opposite direction.

~~~

"Come now, Master Darcy – maybe the sun will warm you a little."

Jenkins removed the tent flap. He might as well take it down – he had a feeling Hatcher would not be returning, whether he was successful in any scenario or not. Jenkins prayed that he wasn't. He crossed himself and focused on Geoffrey, laying down a blanket across the dry patch of leaves and setting the boy gently down.

He was used to the howling, but suddenly a wolf howled from close by, and he was immediately terrified. Used to talking to his silent companion, Jenkins said, "You don't think - ?"

The wolf landed with a thud on the ground, not a foot before him, and pushed him up against the tree. Jenkins could see that this was no wolf, the face barely visible behind the jaw mask, but it was painted red in two stripes as if his eyes had been bleeding. Maybe they had. It had long metal claws, one set of which were pressed against his throat. "Mr. Darcy," the wolf said. So it was real – and human, despite Hatcher's vivid imagination.

"I don't – I don't even want to be here – "

"Geoffrey Darcy! Where is he?" Now up close, and not in a shout but in a forceful whisper, the voice seemed to be female. He looked down, but saw only loose leggings and a pair of wooden stilt shoes. But the matter of the claws was more pressing, literally.

"He's – over – " He tried to point without moving his body. "Please. Over there. I've been watchin' 'im – "

She pulled back her metal claws and scraped something. It was only after a few moments that he had the courage to open his eyes and see that she'd merely stabbed his shirt into the bark behind him, not piercing his flesh.

The wolf moved over to the covering, under which Geoffrey Darcy silently lay. "Knife," she said, holding her hand out. Clearly she had no fear that Jenkins would disobey her as soon as he unpinned himself from the tree, and she was right. Taking the offered knife, Georgiana cut the rope tying his hands behind him, rolled him onto his back, and checked his pulse. "How long has he been like this?"

"Since they hit him," he said. "I swear, I didn't want ta get involved, and nobody thought it'd go this far – "

"He hasn't woken at all?"

"No, Miss."

She picked up the rag beside him and wiped his head wound tenderly.

"He doesn't respond to anyone?"

"Nothin.'"

"We'll see." She pulled back her wolf headdress and leaned over him, whispering something into Geoffrey's ear. Jenkins could have sworn she kissed him quickly on the side before hastily rising to her feet and turning to face him.

216

Despite the face paint, the masculine clothing, the sandals, and the wolf skin, she was unmistakable. No less intimidating, but unmistakable, especially with that very distinctive cut of wild red hair jutting out on both sides. "Miss Bingley – " he stuttered.

Georgiana Bingley held up the metal bracer claws again. "Do you want to live or die?"

"Miss, I'm sorry – "

"*I asked you a question, Mr. Jenkins.*"

"Live, Miss, please – "

"Then you must make this right," she said. "Seeing as how you claim to have no interest in the matter in the first place, it shouldn't be hard to help bring it to a close. Take Mr. Darcy – *carefully*, so not to kill him – and bring him back to Pemberley. We both know his father, and he won't harm you if you bring him his son."

"Mr. Hatcher – "

" – will surely be back soon, so you'd best hurry," she said, handing the knife back to him. "And if you whisper a word of me or anything involving a wolf, there will be repercussions. *Understood?*"

"Yes, Miss Bingley."

She sneered at him, replaced her terrible hood, and ran off. How she was able to run in stilt sandals, he had no idea, but that was about the last thing he would question at the moment. Instead he picked up young master Darcy, somehow finding the strength to bear him in his arms just one more time.

~~~

Some distance away from the edge of the woods, where the road seemed to end, the three men dismounted and continued their walk. Only Brian Maddox did not have a rifle ready, but he did have a pistol tucked into the back of his obi belt.

Darcy instinctively scouted the area. It had been a while since he was here last, but it was basically the same. There was a cliff up ahead, and beyond that a stream that originated back at the waterfall with the shelter, but that was some distance away. He looked up but could not see a sniper on the cliff. Nor was there anyone else to worry about from any other directions. Besides, Maddox was more of a walking target than he was.

"Darcy."

Hatcher had two men with him, Mr. Wallace and another man Darcy recognized as Mr. Graham, and the two groups each spotted each other at the same time.. "Mr. Hatcher. Mr. Wallace. Mr. Graham." They all bowed politely. They would do this like gentlemen, not madmen. "I have the deeds for you. Every single one, excepting Pemberley itself." Darcy readily produced them, a giant stack of papers that barely fit into his hand. He took a step beyond his companions, but not another. Hatcher would have to meet him halfway.

"Every man must have his castle," Hatcher said, and did step up, waving for his men to stay back. They looked nervous. Hatcher took the stack, and flipped through it. "Very official looking. I don't suppose they'll hold up in court."

"Not a one. You know that's not possible."

"Of course."

Darcy removed the other satchel and held it opened to show there was nothing but bank notes in it. "Tell me where Geoffrey is and it's yours. I won't chase."

"I want the money and the wolf."

"The what?"

"Don't be daft. We've come too far for this," Hatcher said, raising his rifle ominously. "Who's the wolf-man?"

"Mr. Hatcher, I've come for my son and my son alone. If I could supply you with this information, I would happily do it, but as I have not the slightest idea of what you're – "

Hatcher aimed his rifle at Darcy's chest. "The wolf-man. He must be one of your men. *Which one?*"

Bingley raised his rifle. "Take the money and go."

"No! Not with this face! Look what he did to me!" Hatcher said, gesturing as best he could to his scarred face with his rifle still raised. "How am I supposed to blend into a feckin crowd with this – "

"Hatcher!" Wallace screamed to get his attention.

Only Mr. Hatcher's swerve to respond to the interruption kept the arrow from his face. It whizzed past him instead, planting itself firmly in the ground.

"Shite!" Hatcher made no pretense of caring for conversation with Darcy anymore, turning in the direction of the arrow's source and raising his rifle to take aim at the figure up on the cliff overlooking them.

Brian stared up in wonder at the figure readying another arrow. "... M-Mugin?" It could be him, slim, and wearing those distinctive wooden geta shoes, but the upper part, aside from the high sleeves, was obscured by a wolf skin, which included the jaw as a mask obscuring the entire face.

Everyone had frozen in shock. The only two people to react were the Wolf and Hatcher, but the rifle was quicker to aim, fire, and hit, striking the Wolf quite obviously in the side. It cried out – more accurately, shrieked – and fell back in a spray of blood, disappearing from sight.

"We'll settle this later!" Hatcher shouted sideways, running off in the direction of the woods, leaving his two men. One of them made a move to raise his gun, but Brian drew his sword faster, and with a spray of blood his head came neatly off. Mr. Wallace gaped and stepped back before being knocked to his feet as Brian turned and hit him with the hilt of his long sword.

Wallace looked up to see a blade in his face, one sandaled foot on his chest. "Where is Geoffrey?" Brian Maddox demanded.

"I swear – he's back at the camp – shite, I didn't think that thing was real!"

"Where exactly is my son, Mr. Wallace?" Darcy said, readying his pistol, as if having an armored samurai bracing him down was not incentive enough for Wallace to talk. "Is he alive?"

"He's – yes, he's alive! But he's in a real bad way – but I'll show you to him, I swear! Please, Mr. Darcy!" Wallace was apparently not above begging for his life, especially now that his leader had abandoned him to pursue a costumed bandit. "We didn't mean to 'urt him! It just all got out of control, I swear on me life! Hatcher was so mad when he fought the wolf and nearly lost – "

"I thought his wolf story was all rubbish," Bingley admitted.

"As did I," Darcy said. "It certainly had nothing to do with us."

"But he thought it did. He was checkin' ye all fer wounds on your left arm – 'swhere he cut it – "

"He was wrong," Darcy said. "Maddox, can you bind him?"

"Yes." Maddox replaced his sword and grabbed Wallace by the hair. "Get up. Bingley, do you have the – "

"Darcy," Bingley interrupted, his voice quiet.

"*What?*" Darcy had lost whatever patience he had days ago. But when he turned and looked at Bingley, he had never seen the man pale, and regretted snapping at him.

"I – I need to go—Georgiana –." He stepped back. "I'm going after them."

"What?"

Bingley swallowed, steadying himself. "Send the signal for a doctor. I-I'll be back – "

"Bingley! Georgie?"

"She had a cut – on her arm. Under the shawl," he said, and broke into a full run into the woods.

That was when Darcy, in the moments afforded to him by being stunned, realized that the shriek of that wolf person had sounded rather feminine. But he didn't have the time to put the pieces together. "Maddox. Signal." Maddox picked up his gun, and they each fired two shots in rapid succession into the air. "Wait for the others. I'm going after Bingley."

"He's daft. It can't be – "

"I know," Darcy said, and holstered his pistol before darting across the field and into the woods in Bingley's wake. The cliff broke off on the other side, its hill dissolved over time by the flow of water from a stream that pooled against the rock wall. Hatcher was long gone, but Bingley was kneeling in the mud, holding a wolf skin in his arms.

"Do you remember?" he said, his voice barely above a whisper. He didn't turn to Darcy as he spoke, turning over the skin. The other side was layered with cloth that had been stained with blood. "We hunted for wolves that one winter. They were eating the cattle. Mugin killed more than all of us combined and he didn't even have a gun."

Darcy looked around desperately. He hadn't put any stock into Hatcher's wolf story at all, especially with Geoffrey's disappearance, when his mind had been consumed with parental concerns. Now it seemed to be extremely relevant, even though it was clearly not a wolf, but a person. "There's no body." He looked more carefully at the stream, only about ankle-deep. "Look, up there." He pointed to the arrow sack chucked to one side. Someone had been relieving themselves of baggage. "Following the river to hide the tracks." But there were tracks in the river – fresh enough and deep enough in the mud to still be visible before the current wore them down. "Bingley, I can't possibly imagine – "

But Bingley didn't seem to care what Darcy was able to imagine. He took off down the path alongside the stream. Darcy hesitated for only a moment before following him.

Bingley could imagine it, but he clung to the desperate hope that he was wrong.

~~~

As if it couldn't get any worse for old Jenkins, Master Geoffrey woke only halfway home. So far he'd been taking a quiet and slow amble, on account of the boy's injuries, but then he felt him stirring. "Now hold on, Master Darcy, and we'll get yeh home – "

"Jenkins." Geoffrey's voice was a hoarse whisper. "Waterfall."

"What?"

"The ... waterfall. You ... know it?"

"Now, Master Darcy, I promised I would take you to home straight away – " From his vantage, with Geoffrey slung over his shoulders, he couldn't see the boy's face, obscured by his hair, matted by his own blood.

"She ... said ..."

"If yeh'll 'scuse me, Master Darcy, the lady's obviously batty."

"Don't you ... dare ... speak of - ," he stopped to cough. " – Georgie ... that way ... Now, waterfall."

Jenkins had no real reason to listen to him, other than an overwhelming sense of guilt and pity. "'suppose you need a rest anyway."

He did know where the waterfall was, over the edge of a rock cliff that fed into a large pool of water that remained fairly deep even in the heat of summer, and several tiny streams poured out from it, going in all directions. Jenkins sped up his course a bit, finally coming into the clearing and setting young Master Darcy down carefully against a tree so he was sitting up. "'ere yeh go," he said, wiping the boy's forehead again. The bleeding had been intermittent, but had never completely stopped. The boy was trying desperately to open his eyes, but only succeeded with one, the other remaining half-closed as if his wound was pressing down on it. What the hell had Hatcher been thinking? No good would come of him, or any of this, especially if the young master didn't live.

"Rifle," young Master Darcy whispered.

"Sir?"

"Your ... rifle."

Surely he didn't intend to shoot him? Not that he probably didn't deserve it, but – something compelled him to pass over his rifle into Darcy's hands, which were basically a step above being limp. The boy held it for a long time before he could even tilt his head down to look at it. "Shoulder."

"Sir?"

"My shoulder ... I need it on ... my shoulder," he said, rather insistently for someone who can't open one eye properly or talk in a normal voice. "To ... steady it."

"Yeh can't do that, yeh'll hurt yer – " but he was distracted by the sounds of splashing in the stream beside them, and the calls from far behind. Suddenly Georgiana Bingley, now very recognizable without her wolf skin but still wearing the face and arm paint, came crashing down the path she was making through the water, holding her side. She leapt aside, ducking behind a tree so she was in full view of Jenkins and Geoffrey, but not of Hatcher, who appeared shortly afterwards, stopping just where the pool began.

"Wolf!" Hatcher screamed, his face flushed with frustration. He apparently didn't seen Geoffrey, who was on the ground and wearing dark colors anyway, and Jenkins had hidden the moment that Georgie had appeared. Geoffrey had made eye contact with her in that same moment. "We'll end this now! Here!" Hatcher tossed down his rifle and then his pistol, drawing his knife instead. "Come out, little puppy ..."

Georgiana braced herself against the tree. The side of her tunic was red, and not from paint.

"I gave up Darcy to kill you, you know. You should be honored – "

Georgiana nodded to Geoffrey, who raised the rifle with shaking hands and settled the handle on his shoulder. Jenkins said nothing. He couldn't without revealing his presence.

"I promise I won't – "

As quickly as she had ducked in, Georgiana swung her claws and weaved out, putting herself between him and the pool. Her swing was blocked by his own weapon, the clash of steel making a horrible clang.

"Holy feck," he said. "You're – a girl - ?"

Because all of a sudden, to Hatcher, the figure he'd been chasing was obviously, despite her masculine clothing, a girl. Maybe she had short hair and was wearing a baggy tunic and war paint, but that made it no less deniable. *"Woman,"* she growled.

Apparently Hatcher had no real issue with fighting a girl, because he swung for her, but she sidestepped him, dropping down and meeting his blade with the metal reinforcements to the sole of her clog sandals. With a groan of discomfort she managed to actually push him down, taking the time afforded to her to get back on her feet.

"You're injured," Hatcher said. "You've lost."

"Ore, tatteiru aidani, sorewa nai!" she said. "Not while I'm standing!"

But she wasn't, for long. He kicked one of her thin legs, and maybe on another day, when she could move more quickly, she could have avoided it, but injured and exhausted now, she did not. She lost her footing and he tackled her, but her metal claws were ready.

It might have ended that way, with them both going backwards into a watery grave together, or perhaps Hatcher would recover, but it was not to be,

226

either way. The gunshot was loud enough to make Jenkins cover his ears, and he was not alone in reacting. Hatcher was knocked back, his grip released in his final moments, and the two opponents fell in separate directions. Georgiana crashed on her back into the pool and sunk. Hatcher landed on the ground beside the stream, the remains of what had been his face spraying everywhere in front of him.

The last noise was the sound of the gun dropping to the ground and rolling away from a slumped over Geoffrey. "Master Darcy," Jenkins said, running back to his side. Gunpowder colored the boy's ear and shoulder, and his eyelids were still half-open but his eyes were rolled back into his head. The kick from a shotgun held so close to the ear could deafen a man easily, which was why Jenkins had advised against such a positioning of it. What it would do to a man with a serious head wound, he could not bear to wonder.

He was not to be spared a moment's peace for his sorrow. The sounds of pursuit made him drop Geoffrey's hand before he could find the pulse, as he put his hands up in surrender.

~~~

Darcy had a difficult time keeping up with Bingley, who was running like a man possessed. He was fairly sure where they were, even though Bingley probably wasn't. There was a watering hole somewhere down this way, from a waterfall. He used to swim there as a child. It fed this stream, and now the stream was polluted by blood, its waters turned as red as the Nile.

Yes, they were headed toward the waterfall there. He heard it before he saw it, and saw the carnage in front of him as the water went red again. Hatcher, or what remained of him, unrecognizable for a shot to the head, slumped in their way.

"Oh, Mr. Darcy, please, I didn't mean – "

Darcy immediately pointed his gun to the figure that seemed to be old Jenkins. So it began and ended with the same person. The man seemed legitimately terrified. Darcy's attention was not very long with him when he spotted Geoffrey, slumped against a tree, a gun beside him. "Geoffrey!"

"Jenkins – " Bingley said.

"The water," he said, pointing. No explanation was needed.

Darcy ignored it. Part of his heart did go out to Bingley, who immediately began stripping himself of his coat and waistcoat, but Darcy's concern was his son, who did not respond to his call. He knelt beside him, dropping his weapon. "Please God," he said, his voice wavering on a cry. "Please God." He reached for a pulse. Geoffrey's neck was cold and clammy, but there was a beat there, slow but steady. "Thank you," Darcy whispered, but he was not entirely relieved. Geoffrey's forehead was colored by bruising and blood, both wet and dried. He checked under the eyelids, but his pupils were rolled back into his head. "Geoffrey," he whispered. "I'm here." There was some kind of dust, like powder, in his ear, and when he probed it, blood came out. "I'm here," he repeated, cupping a wavering hand on the boy's face as he heard a splash. Surely Bingley wasn't –

- Surely they weren't losing *both* of their children in this?

"Mr. Darcy," Jenkins said quietly behind him. "He only woke long enough to talk me into coming here and to shoot Hatcher."

"And besides that?"

"Nothin.'"

As reluctant as he was to take his hand away, Darcy had to stand up and take his bearings. Bingley was somewhere under the water, his white shirt barely visible. Everyone else could have no idea that Geoffrey was here, and was looking for him elsewhere. Darcy pulled the fireworks out of his pocket and loaded them into his gun, and fired them up into the sky through the hole in the foliage. On any other day, he might have appreciated the beautiful red display, even if it was daylight.

Bingley surfaced in the center of the pool with a heavy gasp. In his arms was an unconscious Georgiana, and Darcy's heart sank at the sight. Her face was marred by war paint, which held up considerably well to the water and still formed what looked like two bars down her cheeks. He realized, nearly laughing with some hysteria and with some guilty humor, that with both of them soaked, Bingley and his daughter had almost identical hairstyles.

"Bingley," he said as calmly as he could, which considering his mental exhaustion, was considerably calm. He offered his hand, and Bingley took it and together they brought Georgiana to shore as Bingley regained his breath.

"She's not breathing," Bingley said, still heaving. "God, Darcy, she's not breathing!"

Ignoring the wound on her side for the moment, Darcy knelt beside her and pushed down on her stomach. Water gushed out her mouth. "It's the water in her lungs," he said, and held up her arms. "When I say, push down on her chest." Bingley nodded in mute understand. "All right. One, two – "

He hadn't done this since university, since he'd resuscitated his fencing team captain after a drinking bout his middle year at Cambridge. Still, it came easily enough, as he tried to force water out and life back into his niece. It took a few tries and some desperate pushes, but she finally started coughing on her own.

"Flip her over," he said, removing his coat. When she was kneeling, a semi-conscious Georgiana began hacking up all the water she'd swallowed, and some blood as well. It seemed endless, and Darcy covered her back with his dry coat as they held her up. When she finally finished, and was coughing only air, she shuddered and went limp. Bingley took her into his arms, and with her thin, exposed limbs she suddenly seemed tiny, and certainly was, in comparison to any of them. He cradled her, kissing her on her very wet head.

"My darling," Bingley said quietly, and seeing his job was temporarily finished, Darcy went to his own child. Geoffrey still would not stir, but his condition had not worsened. Darcy pried him a bit,

230

with no response, and steadied himself by touching his chest and feeling his heart beating. Despite everything, his son was alive. Georgiana was alive. Hatcher and his right hand man were dead. The situation could be salvaged. "Is he all right?" Bingley asked from behind.

"I've no idea," Darcy admitted. "But he's alive." *So there's hope.* "I'm not sure he can be moved without the doctor."

"I carried 'im here, Mr. Darcy," said Jenkins reverently, only to be rewarded with a cold stare.

"Perhaps you shouldn't have," Darcy said. "But – I suppose ..." He found no words to finish his sentence. He found no strength to lay judgment on Jenkins. Instead he turned to Bingley. "We should – clean her up."

"What?" Charles Bingley was in a similar mood; that of a slightly incoherent parent distracted by his desire to protect his child.

"If we can," Darcy said, his words slightly slurred by a sudden exhaustion, "the others shouldn't see – this." He added for emphasis. "Her mother shouldn't see her like this."

"Her mother is going to see her – "

"I mean," he said patiently, trying to remember they were both extremely distressed, "that it would be better if we kept this wolf business as quiet as possible. For her sake."

This idea seemed to take time to settle into Bingley's thoroughly distracted brain, but he did eventually agree. Though they had not the collective thought power to concoct a story, they did remove most of the paint with water and force, but could not remove the blue stripes on her arms and ankles, which had apparently been inked into the skin. Darcy removed her necklace of what looked like wolf claws and was about to toss it in the water before Bingley grabbed it from him. "She'll want it." Darcy had not the strength to argue, and it was stuffed in a pocket before he returned to his son.

"It is done," he said. "Geoffrey, you can wake up now." He stroked his hair, so lightly as to not bother his head, watching the blood pour out of his son's right ear. "*You can wake up now.*" But still there was no response. "Your mother's going to be so happy to see you." He knelt beside him, grasping his hand to elicit a response, and yet there was none. "She'll be so happy." His son was alive, Georgiana was alive, Hatcher was dead, and he had so much to be happy for. And yet, he was weeping.

Still Geoffrey did not respond.

CHAPTER 16

The Non-Magic Bullet

ALL THE WOMEN AND CHILDREN at Pemberley had been watching all morning for any new arrivals. So when Constable Morris walked up the path to the door, he was taken aback by the sight of them. The greeting was a little awkward, furthered by the fact that when he questioned Mrs. Darcy as to why her husband had taken the matter into his own hands instead of waiting for the authorities, she disregarded him as an officer of the law and treated him more like a man who had shown up to the ball after dinner had been served. He tried to make some headway by speaking to Dr. Maddox, but was interrupted by two successive displays of fireworks in the distance, which set off a chain of timed responses. The first one – blue – meant there had been fighting. The second, further away, was red, and meant someone had been injured.

Despite whatever objections the constable had, as he continued to be ignored, Nadezhda Maddox was the one who led the party with the stretchers and guns. The display was miles away, and the wait intolerable, so much so that Mrs. Darcy distracted herself by shooing the smaller children back inside.

"Charlie," Jane said to her son, "fetch your sister." Since Eliza was standing beside him, she clearly meant Georgie.

"She's in the chapel," Charlie replied nervously, showing signed his mother might have noticed had she not had other things on her mind.

"You told me that already. Go fetch her now! She ought to be with the rest of her family."

Not really knowing what else to do, Charlie Bingley headed inside and into the chapel, which of course was empty.

"I knew it," George Wickham said, startling his cousin, who hadn't realized George had followed. "I knew she was up to something. She told you to lie for her?"

"She said Aunt Nady would do it, but she left with the group. What am I going to tell – "

The side door of the chapel swung open, which prevented any further conversation, and suddenly Georgiana Bingley was in the chapel, held in the arms of her very wet and distressed-looking father. "Get the doctor."

"How did – "

"*Now*, Charles!"

That was all the incentive his son needed. Bingley laid his daughter on one of the pews. She was small enough to fit, even sideways. George looked over her in shock; she was barefoot, wearing some kind of tunic, and half of her shirt was stained with blood. Like her father, she was also soaking wet, and wrapped in what looked like Mr. Darcy's jacket.

"You're going to be fine," Bingley whispered, but she just coughed and spit blood onto the stone floor. "Just fine. Look – George is here."

Georgiana's eyes were shut tight, her body twisted and her arm holding on to what was obviously a wound on her side. "Hello, Georgie," he ventured, but she didn't respond to his presence.

"I didn't want to cause a scene," Bingley said. "She's been shot. There's no exit wound, so the bullet must still be in her." He added, "Geoffrey's alive, but unconscious."

"Hatcher?"

"Dead."

"Uncle Darcy?"

"Everyone else is fine. Except one of Hatcher's men. Brian took his head off." He turned away from his daughter to glare at George with an intensity that George had never seen in him before. "Did you know she was running about the countryside being a wolf?"

"What?"

"The wolf that attacked Hatcher yesterday; it was no animal, it was Georgiana in costume. Did you have the least of suspicions that she might be doing something that would in endanger her own life like that?"

"No," George replied. "My imagination did not extend that far." He was going to say she would never do something so wild and stupid, but clearly it was within her capabilities. Fortunately the arrival of Dr. Maddox and Aunt Bingley meant he did not have to speak.

"She was shot," Bingley said to his wife as the color went out of her. Dr. Maddox, despite all his experience, didn't look his best either. "She found Geoffrey and she saved us from Hatcher and his men, but he shot her." He motioned for the doctor to come over so he could embrace his wife. "She'll be all right. It's just a flesh wound."

She didn't believe him. "Our daughter – Charlie said – *He was lying to me!*" Jane cried. "What happened to her? Where are her clothes? Where are her *shoes?*" She pulled free of Bingley and ran to Georgiana as her daughter gave a cry at Maddox's prying hand. "What happened to my baby girl?"

"She was shot in the chest," Dr. Maddox said, "but the bullet seems to have missed her vital organs. She'll be all right."

Mrs. Bingley grabbed her daughter's hand, which was bare and covered in blood. Her arm was stained with blue ink. "Mama," Georgie said. Her voice was barely distinguishable.

"We need to move her," Dr. Maddox said.

"I carried her here," Bingley said.

"Then you're relieved of your duties, Mr. Bingley. George?"

Georgiana was not very heavy. George had never carried a person her size, but he was capable of it, as Dr. Maddox led the way past some very confused servants to a room where she could be set down on a bed. The doctor called for his surgical tools, and when they arrived, he threw everyone out to make his assessment.

236

There was a commotion in the hallway on the other side. One crying sister greeted another, as Geoffrey Darcy was brought in on a stretcher, his head bandaged, with his father by his side. Concerned as he was about his own son, he still had the wherewithal to inquire, "Where's Georgiana?"

"She – she's inside with Dr. Maddox," Bingley said, gesturing to the door. "How is he?"

"The same as he was when you left. Nadezhda and Brian are dealing with the constable – Mr. Wallace is under arrest." Aside from missing his coat, Darcy appeared much as he had when he left, except for considerable emotional duress that he didn't bother to hide as Geoffrey was taken upstairs. Elizabeth went with him, leaving the others in the hallway until Dr. Maddox emerged.

"Mrs. Bingley," the doctor said calmly. "Your daughter needs a surgeon."

"To state the obvious – "

"It's very delicate work," Doctor Maddox said. "I – I can't do it. We need someone else. Now if we stop the bleeding she'll hold until someone arrives from Cambridge - "

"We don't want someone from Cambridge!" Jane, in her over-agitated state, was literally shaking him by his coat. "We need you!"

Dr. Maddox shamefully lowered his head. "I'm sorry."

"For God's sake, leave my husband alone!" Caroline Maddox broke in, and her voice was so demanding that it silenced the room.

"It's that bad?" Darcy said quietly. "Your sight."

"As I said," the doctor mumbled, "I can't do this kind of work. It's too delicate. The shot is too close to her lung. I can't – I-I can't focus my sight *and* work at the same time." He added, "I'm sorry; I really am. I didn't know there would be a need for such a surgeon."

No one quite knew what to say. Doctor Maddox's sight was not a subject anyone normally dared to broach.

The first person to speak was the only one besides the doctor himself who had any real knowledge and comfort with the situation. "You could supervise someone, though?" his wife asked.

"Yes, I suppose. But it's very complicated – "

"It's an extraction and stitching, I assume," she said, her voice steadier than any of theirs. "What kind of stitch?"

"Uhm, a surgical suture, like tying a knot at the end of a cross stitch, maybe. It depends on where the bullet is and the complexity of the extraction."

"And you have all of your equipment?"

"Of course."

"Well, then," Caroline said, "I know a cross stitch. I'm an *accomplished woman*, after all. The rest can't be much harder than embroidery."

He blinked. "You will never fail to astonish me."

"Lady Maddox," Darcy said. "If he says she can wait for a surgeon..."

"Why risk it? If Daniel thinks I can do it, then I certainly can. And if you don't think I haven't seen or assisted in an operation before, then you have no idea how much trouble Frederick has gotten into over the course of his life."

"That is regrettably true," the doctor said. "They were all rather minor incidents in comparison, but I don't see anyone else here jumping up to do the job – anyone with knowledge of needlepoint, that is," he said, silencing Bingley's attempted protest. "This may be the best option."

"*Doctor –* "

"If she's willing to do it, I'm certainly not one to stand in Caroline's way," he said. "My bag is already in there. We need a lot of water and towels, and Darcy, you should send for the surgeon anyway, for Geoffrey. There's a Professor Fergus who is also an auditory specialist. Tell him I'll owe him a favor and he'll come. And don't try to rouse Geoffrey with smelling salts or anything. But if he does wake, get me." He felt for the handle and opened the door behind him. "No family during the procedure, excepting us, who will be working."

"I want to see my daughter first," Jane insisted. "If there's time."

He looked at her softly. Obviously, he was not completely blind. "I need to check on Geoffrey in the meantime. Yes, there is time."

~~~

Bingley was somewhat used to the anxiety of waiting on the other side of the door for a woman in distress, but this pain was far different from childbirth. It was his child, his daughter, and she was not giving birth. She could be dying. This time, though, he had Jane in his arms, though he was mostly comforting her. Darcy disappeared up the stairs for a bit and then returned. "The same," he said to Bingley's look of inquiry as Jane cried into his shoulder. "Elizabeth and his sisters are staying with him. But he *was* awake, earlier – long enough to fire a gun. So, that must be a good sign."

They fell into silence as Darcy collapsed on the settee. Only the appearance of Brian Maddox, very loudly announced by all of the metal he was wearing, alerted them at all to the world beyond their suffering. His headgear and shoulder pads had been removed, and he was soaked with sweat from running around in armor. "Where's Danny? In surgery?"

"Caroline's doing it."

"*Caroline?*"

Bingley nodded. "Your brother is supervising, but he said he can't do it himself."

"It must have been serious, for him to admit it," he said, and then realizing the gravity of it, added, "but Georgiana will be fine. She is clearly the toughest woman in England."

"We thoroughly blame you for this," Darcy said, not looking at him.

"*Me?*"

"Yes, you, you crazy Japanese whatever you call yourself – "

"*Samurai.*"

"Yes, that," Darcy said dismissively. "You brought this into our family. I suppose you trained her as well."

"No!"

"Don't deny it," Bingley said.

"No, I didn't!" Brian said, a little alarmed by the sudden need to take the defensive. "I swear; I've never once given Miss Bingley any sort of ... instruction of the sort. Yes, I do let my nephew play around in the garden with bokken. But he's a boy, and it's not so different from the fencing and such nonsense that we all teach our children. Bingley, doesn't your son know how to fence?"

"Not well," he said, "but yes. But this is *entirely* different."

"And I am entirely uninvolved in ... whatever Georgiana's been up to. How would I even be? I don't live in Derbyshire and she hardly strays from it. Yes, I brought Mugin into our lives, but that was years ago! She was a child when she last saw him! Besides, what does it matter?"

"What does it matter?" Jane spoke up, barely more than a whisper at first, but gaining in strength. "What does it matter? Mr. Maddox, my daughter – who is of an age where she should be a mature and polished young lady– has been running around in the woods, fighting and nearly getting herself killed! She's ... – " But she sobbed, leaning into her husband again. "What are we going to do?"

Seeing that he needed to try to salvage the situation and prevent Jane from making any more connections between her daughter and the mess with

Hatcher, Darcy said, "Mr. Hatcher shot a wolf, if it was even real to begin with, or just one of his hallucinations. Obviously the man was crazy."

"Obviously," Bingley chimed in.

"So The Wolf died. Or never existed. Who knows? England is full of such legends. I imagine they'll be telling it some years from now in a tavern somewhere and one us will overhear and try not to laugh." Even if he didn't feel like doing so in his heart, he offered them a weak smile at the idea.

They decided it was a good one.

~~~

Georgiana's surgery began, unfortunately, with the cold pliers waking her from her exhausted sleep enough to cry out.

"I'll hold her," Daniel said, pressing down on the wound to stop the bleeding as much as possible. "Make the opiate." Measuring things was easier for Caroline than it was for him, so he had taught her the recipe. "Quickly."

"I'm going as fast as I can," she said. "We should have told them."

"Yes. I did insist they have another surgeon ready when I heard about Geoffrey being missing, but I didn't tell them why. And when we appeared for support, they just assumed." Georgiana squirmed and he stroked her hair with his free hand. "Shhh. You're going to be all right. And you're going to feel much better in a few minutes, I promise." He could hear the clinking as his wife stirred up the potion. "You've been very brave."

"*Exceptionally* brave," Caroline said, oddly with none of her usual sarcasm. "Open up." She served up a spoonful of the green concoction and Georgiana managed to swallow it. "One or two?"

"Considering her height and weight – probably one. We'll start with one. Georgiana, you'll tell us if you're in too much pain, won't you?" He took her hand. It was so incredibly small in his own. "Just squeeze my hand. All right?"

Somehow, she managed to nod into the pillow.

Caroline took up her position on his other side again, and they waited a few minutes for Georgiana's body to slacken before pulling away the towel to expose the wound again. It was on her side, very close to her breast. Maddox put on his spectacles and peered in for a very close look.

"Does your profession normally have you gazing at a woman's breasts?"

"Not nearly enough," he said. "Now, the trick is to find the bullet without harming her lung. I believe it's buried in muscle. If we have to cut her side, that's all right. There are no organs there." He looked up at his wife. "Are you sure you're up to this?"

"Are you sure you are?"

"It was my damned pride that got us into this position. If I had told them how blind I was – "

"Daniel, you're not blind," she said as she pried open the entrance wound with the forceps. Georgiana did not move. "Your vision is suffering

243

but you could still make a diagnosis. And you treated Geoffrey in that camp."

"It wasn't hard. His injuries are mainly internal, and there was little I could do in any case."

"How serious is it?" she said as he leaned in to guide her hand, searching for the bullet.

"I'd rather let Doctor Fergus make the formal assessment, but at the very least, he's blown out one of his ears and his head is seriously concussed. The fact that he was captive while injured certainly didn't help." He pointed. "There. Do you see it?"

"I see something moving."

"That's her lung. It goes in and out when she breathes. But – there's something there, between the muscles. I think it's – silver. Instead of lead. So it's not black."

"Is that normal?"

"For hunting werewolves, I suppose," he said. "Hatcher must have really been bothered to get silver bullets for his rifle. There, you see it?"

"Yes."

"I'll hold the wound open – you extract it. It's not buried in bone, so it shouldn't be hard." His wife didn't immediately answer, and he looked up to see her face was slightly green. "Do you need to be ill?"

"No," she said with a very definitive swallow.

"Because it's best not to vomit *on* the patient."

"Now you're trying to make me laugh. This is serious."

"All the more reason for us to pass the time in this sort of conversation. It eases the mind."

"Then why do you work alone?"

"I haven't found an assistant with a decent sense of humor. Or one willing to put up with mine. And I think you've got it."

"I just pull it out?"

"Slowly, yes."

At last the bullet was freed from its fleshy prison and Caroline held it up for a moment, incredulous of her own accomplishment, before dropping it in the pan next to her. "She'll probably want to keep it or something."

"Victims of gunshots usually treasure the bullet or want nothing to do with even the sight of it. It's one or the other. Makes no sense."

She stole a glance at him as he passed her the sewing thread and needle. "You are a wholly different person when talking to your patients and when they are unconscious."

"Levity is the only way to get through this sort of business, my dear. I once had a professor – in France of course – who insisted on having a man sit and play the violin during important surgeries, so he would have a musical accompaniment."

"You're serious?"

"Aren't I always?" he said with a smile. "Let's take one last look at the muscle – " He ducked in again. "Torn, but muscles heal. The point is, he missed organs and arteries, which don't heal so easily." He held the flesh together so she could begin sewing to his instructions.

"What doesn't heal so easily is her mind, which she's obviously lost," Caroline said.

"Well, you can't blame my brother for that. Not her blood relation."

"*Your* brother? I blame *my* brother and his stupid obsession with the east. And her cutting her hair – that should have been a warning sign. I would have sent her straight to school."

"It would be torture for her," he said. "Worse than what we're doing now."

"Are you presuming to know my niece better than I do?" Caroline was, as she had said, a very accomplished woman and sewing came easy to her, even if it was flesh instead of fabric.

"Hardly. But surely you don't imagine she would enjoy a girl's school."

"Of course not," she conceded. "But she *needs* it. Am I making too many stitches?"

"Better too many than too few," he said. "Not too tight. There, I think you have it. Georgiana?" There was no response from the girl. "Wash up. I'm going to turn her a bit." As Caroline washed her hands, he bandaged the site and positioned the pillows so she was on her back but partially propped up on her side, pulling pressure and blood away from the wound. He called for a clean shirt – Georgiana could hardly be expected to be maneuvered into a dress in her condition – and upon receiving it, redressed her.

"Was I a good surgeon?" Caroline asked.

"Very good," he said, kissing her on the cheek. "I've never seen stitches that were quite so pretty."

~~~

246

Bingley and Jane had initially decided they would sit by her side in shifts, but quickly relented, as neither was willing to give the first shift to the other. They sat together instead, Jane holding her daughter's hand as she slept on. Considering the pain she was going to be in when she woke, Doctor Maddox encouraged that she be allowed her peace for as long as it lasted.

"Charles," Jane said, leaning into his shoulder. "What are we going to do?"

"I don't know."

"We should send her to seminary."

"I couldn't bear to send my daughter away to a place she would despise," he said.

"Neither would I," Jane said softly.

"We could bring Eliza out and send them both to Town for a bit, even move the family there. Charlie is in Eton most of the year anyway," he said. "And, certainly, we must hire a better governess for Eliza. If anyone is truly to blame, it is us for our hiring practices. The next one should keep out a better eye for what our daughters are doing and which type of animal they choose to dress up as."

Jane laughed into his shoulder. "You're driving me to distraction."

"Certainly my intention. We could all use some distraction."

Eventually, they were both falling asleep in their chairs, a very uncomfortable situation indeed, and after being startled awake by almost toppling over, Jane convinced Bingley to finally clean himself up and go to sleep while she kept watch.

It was early dawn when he was awoken. He kissed his wife, said hello to a tired Darcy in the hallway, and took up the vigil. He was nearly asleep again when he noticed Georgiana's eyes were open, and probably had been for some time. He sat up, more alert.

"Is Geoffrey alive?"

For some reason, the question stunned him. Her voice was ragged, but still carried an amount of her usual cool composure, as if nothing bizarre had happened. Bingley stuttered, "Yes."

"Oh." She closed her eyes again. "Good."

He thought maybe she would sleep again, and leaned in and kissed her head. He was surprised when she took a tighter grip on his hand and said, "Can I see him?"

"Who? Oh," he said. "No, I'm afraid Doctor Maddox said it's best for you not to move for a bit, in case you've forgotten about your own injuries."

"No," she said. "I have not."

"Georgiana," he said, "are you in pain?"

She said nothing.

"*You can tell me*," he said desperately. "I'm your *father*." Georgiana had always been secretive, even as a small child, but now it went beyond all reason. "Well, I'm not waiting for you to announce it." He got up, retrieved the bottle of opiate, and poured her a spoonful, forcing it into her mouth. "And he said you should drink something. You lost – " He stammered. "You lost a lot of blood yesterday." He helped her sit up enough to drink a full glass of juice.

When he went to put it back, she grabbed the end of his waistcoat, "Papa," she said, her voice softer. "I never meant to hurt you."

"I'm not hurt. Worried, but not hurt. Your father is stronger than you believe him to be."

"You're crying."

He was beginning to do so. The exhaustion from the events of the day before, the trial of comforting his wife, and the pain of what seemed to be an endless chasm between him and his eldest daughter – it was too much. He could talk so easily to Charlie or Eliza or even Edmund, but not Georgiana. Granted, she did speak to him more than her own mother, but there was always a distance. She was distant from everybody.

Except, of course, Geoffrey Darcy.

"I think I'm allowed to be a little upset when my daughter has been shot," he said, returning to his seat. "Just like you're allowed to admit when you feel discomfort."

"Did he take out the bullet or did it go through?"

"*She*, actually," Bingley said. "You know your uncle is going blind, correct?"

"Yes."

"Well, the work was too difficult for him, and we had no one else. So your Aunt Caroline did it." This time, the expression on her face was not a mask. "Yes, I know. Our family is prone to strange obsessions and acts of courage, it seems. She took out the bullet – a *silver* bullet."

"Really?"

"Yes," Bingley said. "Really."

"Where in the world did he get a silver rifle bullet?"

"I've no idea."

"Well..." Weak as she was, her face was lit by a smile. "Good thing I'm not a *real* werewolf, then, I suppose."

"Yes," he laughed, taking her hand and holding it until she fell back to sleep.

CHAPTER 17

Anger and Accusations

FORTUNATELY FOR the Darcys, Constable Morris escorted Mr. Wallace to the gaol in Lambton and was busy interrogating him there for the remainder of the day. As soon as Dr. Maddox reappeared from Georgiana's surgery, he checked on Geoffrey's condition. By then the Darcy sisters had seen their brother, who, aside from the bandage around his head, had been cleaned up and put into cleaner bedclothes, and looked like he was sleeping. When the doctor returned, he put on his heavy spectacles, which looked more like goggles, and turned Geoffrey's head to the side to look in his right ear. Though they had cleaned the outside, he made a further inspection. Elizabeth gave a little shriek when he withdrew blood.

Dr. Maddox had Geoffrey's manservant help him turn his head carefully to the other side, and held a mirror to get the candlelight precisely right. The doctor sighed again and set the boy's head aright. "The bad news is that his right ear is most likely blown."

"From the rifle blast?"

"Combined with his concussion, most likely. I'm not an expert, but it appears his eardrum has burst. The good news is that the other side is merely

251

inflamed. In time, the inflammation should go down. But again ..." The doctor shifted uncomfortably.

"I understand." Darcy only wanted the best for his son anyway, and Dr. Maddox was willing to admit where he was not the best and had sent for Dr. Fergus.

"It will take several days for Dr. Fergus to get here. As long as the canal doesn't close, Geoffrey should recover his hearing."

"And the rest of him?"

Again, Dr. Maddox did not look so comfortable. "He needs to wake up soon, Mr. Darcy."

"He was awake, just hours ago."

"I know. But there was damage after that. Still, his pulse is strong and there are no other injuries to him, so he is under the best conditions to begin to heal. And he was in excellent health to begin with." Dr. Maddox said, "I think there is good reason to be hopeful."

Darcy knew he did not need to have a private word with Maddox; Dr. Maddox knew Elizabeth well enough to tell the whole truth in front of her. "And Georgiana?"

"She will mend. The bullet didn't strike anything vital," he said. "She was extremely lucky."

Darcy withheld commentary. He felt for the Bingleys, but Geoffrey took precedence, and Geoffrey was half-deaf and in a coma – but he was home. He was home in his bed, and they didn't have to worry where he was anymore, or what he was thinking, because he was so peacefully asleep. In fact, Darcy fell asleep in the very chair he sat in, watching his son's breathing.

~~~

The morning sun was very cruel on the Darcys. It was a reminder that they were the master and mistress of Pemberley, and that a world existed behind that room, and beyond their son, and they would have guests to attend to, and doctors they to consult, and the constable to speak with. There would be an inquiry, of course.

"Sir?" Reed, Darcy's manservant, cautiously approached him as he wandered into the hallway, and subtly began to imply that he might want to wash up and have a change of clothes before dealing with what the day had to bring. Elizabeth's lady-maid approached for much the same purpose, and for the first time in her life (or as much as Darcy could recall), Elizabeth asked to be excused from all of her duties as mistress of Pemberley.

"Someone should stay with him," was all she said, and that was that. Geoffrey's condition had not changed.

Darcy reluctantly left his son for his own quarters, and eventually found Bingley at the bottom of the stairs, in a sorry state and still wearing the clothes from yesterday. Darcy tactfully ignored this and the fact that his eyes were red. "How is she?"

"She's been shot," Bingley snapped. "How do you think?" He rubbed his face. "I'm sorry – I should not have – "

"Bingley, I understand," Darcy said, because he did.

"She won't even talk to me. Have I been such a bad father?"

"My daughters don't talk to me," Darcy said.

"This is entirely different and you *know it*! What do *you* have to worry about? That Sarah is too withdrawn? That Anne is too eager to be out?"

"That my son is dying," Darcy replied before he could check himself.

Bingley had no response to that. His friend was as near to breaking as he had been when Geoffrey was missing. At least his son being home should bring him some level of peace.

"Mr. Darcy," Jane's very polite but tired voice sounded from behind, and Darcy turned and bowed to her. "How is Geoffrey?"

"The same. Dr. Maddox has called in a specialist for his ears."

"But he's still unconscious."

"Yes."

There was nothing else left in her to say. She instead embraced her husband. They were probably taking shifts, as Elizabeth was with Darcy. Georgiana was out of danger, but still very badly wounded.

"Mr. Darcy. Mr. Bingley. Mrs. Bingley," Brian Maddox said, announcing his presence. "I've just spoken to the constable."

"And what is the story?"

"The same as it was, except that the man dressed as a wolf was not recovered, and we have no interest in pursuing the matter further, considering Geoffrey's condition."

"Oh," Darcy said. Seeing the constable was really the last thing on his mind. "We will keep that in mind."

Nadezhda joined the group to inquire, "How is Georgiana?"

"Recovering," Bingley said, releasing his wife as she stepped away from him.

Jane wiped her eyes, and took a deep breath before looking up at the princess, in her Japanese silk robes and her golden circlet and her covered hair – "It was you."

"Mrs. Bingley?"

"It was you," Jane said, her shock laced with something else. Something meaner. "You taught my daughter these foreign things. You turned my little girl into ... whatever she is now."

"Mrs. Bingley," Brian said in a slightly harsher tone, "My wife did not – " But he suddenly realized that his wife was not denying the charges as he was. "Nady?"

"Georgiana is no longer a child," she said. "She can make her own choices."

"No, she cannot!" Bingley said. "In case you've forgotten or never noticed, Your Highness, this is England! She's an heiress and a respectable woman with a reputation that has to be maintained, if she's ever – ," he blinked away his tears, trying to focus on his anger instead of his pain. Darcy could see it, but he wasn't used to Bingley being angry, or Jane, for that matter. He didn't know what to do. He was too drained, too tired of being angry, as Bingley continued. "She has to at least be *sane* to be presentable in society. Any society! And I know I've been a bit permissive – I let her have that friendship with Mugin – "

"I sent Mugin away," Brian said. "He didn't leave of his own will."

"What?"

"It was nothing inappropriate, Nady was there. But he was – encouraging her. When I found out, I sent him back to Japan. That is probably why he ended his friendship with me," Brian said. "But that was years ago. Five years, to be precise, since he was in England."

Darcy had to state the obvious. "Then it was Nadezhda."

All eyes turned to Nadezhda, who only said, "She asked me and I did train her to know how to defend herself. That she would take it to this extreme – "

"You turned my daughter into a lunatic! Just because – "

But as he stepped forward towards Nadezhda, Brian Maddox drew his sword, and Bingley stopped just in time to save his head.. *Please step back from my wife.*"

"Mr. Maddox!" Darcy said, his voice calm but unquestionable. "This is Pemberley, not the Orient! You will not draw your sword in my house!"

Darcy had been pushed to the brink of physical and mental exhaustion, but he was still perfectly capable of slapping a man with his voice – especially within the great halls of Pemberley. Brian immediately replaced his sword, and bowed to Darcy, "My apologies, but he did threaten my wife."

"I am allowed to accuse her of what should be a crime! I am a free man and you are not actually a samurai! You are English, not Japanese! You cannot take my head for insulting someone, you *madman!*" Bingley shouted, and turned to Nadezhda, though he did step away from her this time. "Your Highness, with all due respect, you brought this madness into my house and influenced my daughter so much that now she almost got herself killed – "

" – in order to save all of you incompetent Englishmen!" Nadezhda exclaimed. "Talking about contracts and bribes while Geoffrey was dying!"

"We should all be praising her," Brian interrupted. "Incognito, she managed to spook the enemy, find Geoffrey, *save* Geoffrey, and eliminate Hatcher. She's done more in the past twelve hours than we've done in three days! Since she was wholly responsible for salvaging the situation while we were drinking tea and worrying, I'm not inclined to care one bit how she was dressed while doing so!" He met their stares, his own indignation building. "You are all thinking she belongs in Bedlam, but as far as I can tell, she's not insane at all. Everything she did was perfectly calculated and a lot better planned than anything *we* did. If I were the king and I knew about this, I would knight her for her courageous actions! So you may be dismissive of your own daughter, but I will not be!

"Your Highness, Mr. Maddox," Darcy said, unable to disguise the anger in his own tone, "while we have established that her actions were successful, that is not the issue here. She has a larger reputation at   stake!"

"We all know about reputations and we've heard enough of it!" Brian shouted back.

"What do you know about reputation?" Jane said. Her voice had a higher pitch, so it was heard above them all, even though it was softer. "You ruined yours and then your brother's, ran from all of your responsibilities, and kept running at every opportunity! And now you try to redeem yourself by drawing a sword on my husband for *daring* to question your wife!"

"You're a fake and a liar," Bingley seethed. "You never told me about Mugin."

"And you're a coward. All you did while your own nephew was missing was pat Darcy on the shoulder! And then, when it did come time for action, you failed to notice that one of your own children was missing! What kind of father is that?"

"At least I *am* a father!"

Darcy had spent years negotiating tenant disputes. He had spent his childhood watching how his cousin Richard separated him from Wickham during their infamous brawls. His competitive fencing team at Cambridge often got drunk with their opponents afterwards, to very negative results. All of that led to the instincts that saved the situation, now. He grabbed Nadezhda's arm as she lifted it to strike Bingley, and Brian's as he went for his sword, stepping between them and the Bingleys. "Your Highness and Mr. Maddox," Darcy said authoritatively, "I am going to have to ask you to leave."

"What?"

"I would ask the Bingleys to leave as well," Darcy said, his voice so steady that it betrayed no emotion, not even sympathy, "but their daughter is lodged in my home and so is the doctor treating her. We are all very, *very* upset at all that has happened, but I will not tolerate violence in Pemberley under any circumstances, least of all between family." With that, he released them, pushing so hard they stumbled. "I am truly sorry." He bowed. "Please leave."

"Of all the – "

"Brian," Nadezhda said, and said something to him in Romanian, or some other of the tongues they knew that everyone else did not. She curtseyed to Darcy – and a Princess of Transylvania did not curtsey to anyone. "We apologize for our actions to you, Mr. Darcy, for abusing your hospitality." And with that, she dragged her husband out of Pemberley, so quietly it was shocking. She said nothing to the Bingleys, who Darcy knew he now had to face.

"I really would do it," Darcy said. "I would send you home to calm down – with all due respect, Mrs. Bingley, your husband knows he cannot even appear to attack Nadezhda in front of Brian without suffering the consequences, however misplaced." To her stunned silence, he added, "I am very sorry for all that has occurred under my roof, but I think your daughter needs you now. Being shot is not a pleasant experience." That was Jane's order to go to Georgiana's room – and Darcy had never ordered Jane around before. Darcy turned to Bingley, and after she was gone, said, "Shake yourself out of this state, man."

"Darcy, she – ," but Bingley was not in a condition to form a sentence. "I don't know – "

"My son is upstairs," Darcy said. "If he does not wake in the next few days, he will most likely die. If he does wake, he could be deaf for the rest of his life. And now I have thrown out the beloved brother and sister of the doctor who is treating him, who hardly needs any distractions right now. I will remind you that your daughter, who did save all of our lives, no matter how improper the manner, is also suffering and requires that same doctor. So I will not stand for anything *else* happening under Pemberley's roof." That was, of course, ignoring the fact that something had just happened, and he had not the slightest idea of how to resolve it, short of setting them apart and hoping tempers cooled on their own. "I can't take it, Bingley. I can't take anything else right now."

Bingley nodded numbly.

"I must go speak to the constable and hope my story is coherent enough to match up with Mr. Maddox's. Take care of your wife and your daughter – and let everything else cool."

Bingley nodded again, and Darcy turned on his heels and headed to where the constable was waiting for him.

~~~

As he sat down with Constable Morris, Darcy did something else unprecedented – he had a drink. The constable would think nothing of it, an Englishman having a stiff drink like brandy so early in the morning, but for Darcy, it was exceptional, and his manservant knew it and so stayed in the room until the constable forced him out. Darcy sat back in the chair of his study and told, as best he could, all of the events that had passed, beginning with his selling of the land to the Duke of Devonshire and the mining disaster, and ending with the doctor's assessment the night before. It was so distant to him, as he told it so quietly, as if he were recounting a story that had happened to another man in another lifetime. That was comforting, in its own way. The constable was not too interested in the wolf, and anyway he knew it was not worth pursuing – Hatcher was dead, and that was the point.

"Michael Hatcher," he said, "was a Radical. A Spencean."

"So I gathered," Darcy said, leaving alone the implication that he'd only just found that out, even though he had actually gathered that information weeks ago.

"He escaped the noose because his name isn't Michael Hatcher. His name is Michael Amsted, or so I've been told, which is one of the names that appears on the list of Spenceans who confessed to a membership roll while under investigation. He had escaped, and they stopped looking after Peterloo, when they were concerned with other things. The Spenceans didn't seem to exist anymore."

"These were the people that believed that land should be communal?"

"Yes. Anyway, we have little on Mr. Amsted, or Mr. Hatcher if you will, but if he's survived this long and he's the man you described – he was likely very good at getting away. They caught most of them – almost everyone on that list, which was kept secret. The only reason they sent me was because I was a junior member of the investigation, and when you wrote to London about your son and mentioned a Spencean, they sent me."

Hence the delay, of course. "Why do you think he came here?" Darcy said.

"He was probably heading north anyway, and came across the mining disaster. You said that was Darcy land for a long time?"

"Since at least my grandfather's generation, yes. It had only recently changed ownership, and only because of the mine."

"Mines are worth a lot of money."

"Lives are worth more. And land is always a steady investment, especially in Derbyshire," Darcy said. "Hence the trade between Duke Devonshire and myself."

"And had he turned up in the county, would most of the people still have felt you were responsible?"

"Unlikely, but the connection could be made. I sent care packages to the families, but Mr. Hatcher seems to have overlooked that."

"Yes," the constable said, looking over his notes. "And you provided free coal in the winter."

"To the truly needy, yes."

"And His Grace did not?"

"The Duke has many holdings. The man is worth ten times what I am and is hardly ever this far north. I have no idea of his doings here, which are all carried out by one of his many stewards."

The constable scribbled more notes. The sound was loud against the quiet of the room, especially after all of the shouting outside, but the warm fuzz in Darcy's head helped him weather it and all of the questions. "So I think we can safely reconstruct what happened, or might have happened, based on your testimony, Mr. Maddox's, Mr. Jenkins's, and of course, Mr. Wallace's."

"How is he?"

"He'll likely face deportation; he can claim he was an accessory and he did not actually attack any of you. So – Mr. Hatcher comes into the general Lambton area and begins his own little people's rebellion, or so he thinks. Gets a crowd worked up about their land, alters his philosophy by what they want to hear. He even develops a little gang, but he realizes he's in heady waters so he gets himself a hideout near a place no one would dare to go – the mines. Tells no one about this. Then one day, his gang is out to talk to Mr. Jenkins about contributing to their cause, and your son shows up. According to Mr. Wallace, your son's dog – "

"Gawain."

"What?"

"His name," Darcy said, "is Sir Gawain. After the Arthurian myth."

The constable went on, "So the dog attacked Mr. Hatcher, and Wallace instinctively shot him. Mr. Geoffrey reacted as any boy would to his dog being shot, which was by taking a swing at Mr. Hatcher, or so both Jenkins and Wallace testify. Hatcher responds but he hits him too hard, and suddenly he's got the landlord's son on the ground, wounded. And he has a witness, Mr. Jenkins. So he decided to make off with both of them and hope for the best."

"I offered him money," Darcy said, "for Geoffrey's return. He did not even want to hear of it. He brought up this land nonsense."

"He had to. He had promised Mr. Wallace and the late Mr. Graham the deeds to their land for going through with the mess and not turning him in, as they were initially inclined to do. The young Mr. Blackwood, still missing, was a transient and Hatcher promised him treasures from Pemberley, or something. Apparently Mr. Hatcher was a persuasive talker, but he talked himself into a corner, when Mr. Geoffrey couldn't wake to sign the papers."

"Yes," Darcy replied.

"His last chance was to cut and run. He couldn't leave witnesses, so he planned to take your money and kill the three of you – until this wolf-man showed up. Mr. Jenkins said he was – some man with a grudge against Hatcher.

As Mr. Jenkins had been told to say. "Mr. Hatcher was the sort of man who attracted enemies – even in animals."

"That's the part I really can't figure out – but again, we can't account for this man's whereabouts for years, so unless you want to pursue something beyond pressing charges against Mr. Wallace – "

"Nothing beyond that, no."

"And Mr. Jenkins?"

"Nothing. He was as much a victim as my son in many ways." And they needed him to tow the line. He knew about Georgiana.

"As you like, Mr. Darcy."

But Mr. Darcy still didn't like it very much.

~~~

Georgiana eyed George as he entered to visit her bedside. She was still not allowed to see Geoffrey, who had not woken in the two days since his return. She was still badly hurt, and in more pain than she would admit, and she didn't like the way the drugs dulled her mind, but it was still sharp enough to know when something was wrong – and something *was* wrong, from the look on George's face. "What did they say?"

"Who?"

"Don't play with me. Doctor Maddox and the other one. What did they say?"

George sighed uncomfortably and took the seat beside her bed. "You're not even supposed to be sitting up."

"I'm not supposed to sock you either, but I will if you don't tell me." It was an empty threat and they both knew it, but she could, and probably would, at least injure herself trying.

"They're not – telling anyone. Or, I don't know who they're telling. I just overheard it, so don't say anything." He glanced up and seemed to shrivel at her intense gaze of impatience. "He's – his heartbeat is slowing down. His breathing is shallow. He needs sustenance or he'll whither away."

"Is there any way to make him drink?"

He shook his head. "We can't make him swallow, or he'll just choke on it."

She frowned, "Will you tell him something for me?"

"He can't hear us. Even if he was awake, I don't think he could."

"You don't know that."

"It's ... unlikely. Especially because of his ears. One is completely blown. The other is inflamed. Doctor Fergus put a tube in to keep it open." He looked at his cousin with concern and swallowed. "Georgiana – "

"What?" Then she noticed George's eyes were red and watery.

" – I'm sorry. I don't really have anything to say beyond that."

"Then will you just tell him something? Even if he can't hear?"

He sighed. "All right. What?"

"If he dies, I'll kill him. I don't know how, but I'll find a way. I promise him that."

George managed a smile. "I'll tell him you said that."

CHAPTER 18

Geoffrey's World

IF NOT FOR the pain, he would not have remembered.

He was asleep in his bed, wrapped in clean sheets, with his faithful hound asleep at his side. He could feel a weight– not large enough to be human, but sizable none the less – on his bed, and knew it was Gawain . It was a normal morning, except for all of the ringing, not of multiple church bells but of one, piercing, long ring. He waited, in what he thought was a patient manner, for it to subside, but it did not. Beyond that, there was only pain and silence.

Pain sapped his energy and prevented him from opening his eyes. He managed only one fully, the other pressed down by an impossible weight, and there was not much to look at; his room was lit by candles, so it was night. He was not hung over – this was much worse. He remembered being cold, and wet, something about a wolf, a gun, and that man named Hatchet or Hatching, and old man Jenkins. The coal! Did he deliver the coal?

It took him some time to realize the movement was Dr. Maddox speaking to him. His lips were moving but no sound was coming out. There was something plugging his left ear, and he raised his hand to move it, only to have the doctor grab it, and hold it down. Lips moving again, another explanation lost in the air between the doctor and him. Geoffrey couldn't read the expression – it was too blurry. He could only feel the hand pressing his back down, and his faithful hound moving on the bed, licking his face. Gawain hadn't done that since he was a puppy. Geoffrey opened his mouth to talk but his throat was too dry to speak.

The doctor provided him with a glass and made him drink. It was tea, very sweet, with lots of honey and sugar. Swallowing took the last of his energy. He was happy to close his eyes again.

~~~

Since he could feel without opening his eyes, he felt first when there was more than pain and darkness, and he felt most keenly the thing in his ear. Had he been stabbed and they had forgotten to remove the knife? He reached for it again, and a hand stopped him. It was gentle but firm, hard like a man's hand, squeezing his.

He opened his eyes (more accurately, one and a half) to the sight of his father. It was his father's hand, and when Geoffrey focused, it was his father telling him something, very insistently, without words. There was just ringing. Didn't he know he couldn't hear him with the thing in his ear? With that infernal sound in his head?

The activity around him was disorienting, because the ringing made it hard for him to focus.

His mother had the cup this time and made him drink. *Mother would take care of everything.* She would take the thing out of his ear that hurt him so badly. She squeezed his other hand and kissed it. Why wouldn't she stop talking? He felt so guilty; she was talking and he wasn't listening.

"I can't hear you," he said. Or, it was what he intended to say. Maybe he didn't say it, because he couldn't hear it. Maybe what came out of his mouth was nonsense, but he wasn't sure of anything, except that his mother started crying. He turned to his father, who looked dismayed and didn't bother to hide it. His father usually tried to hide his emotions, but Geoffrey always saw through that mask, because it had been there all his life and he was familiar with it. Now his father wasn't even trying. He just held his hand until Geoffrey fell asleep again, which as far as he could tell, wasn't very long. He closed his eyes because he didn't want to see his mother cry, and once they were closed, he couldn't open them again.

~~~

Every time he awoke the ringing was a little weaker, and he was a little stronger, and could focus more, but there was also more activity around him. They made him drink again. It was Reynolds, his manservant, with a very concerned and emotional look on his face. He liked James Reynolds a lot, being much the same age, but he had never seen him so openly upset.

269

Geoffrey wasn't tied down, but every time he reached for his ear, they grabbed his hand and spoke to him again, even though he couldn't hear and they must have known that. "It hurts," he tried to say, hoping that was what he actually said.

His father, again at his side, just nodded, but still held his hand.

The other ear was all right. There was nothing there. There were bandages around his head, but nothing around his other ear, the right one, where the ringing originated. Why didn't they do something? He wouldn't ask; then they would just put the spike in that ear and then it would be in both ears and the pain would be unbearable. No one (and he could not for the life of him keep track of who was in the room) stopped him from inspecting that ear. But that was where he'd held the gun –

He remembered now. He'd fired the gun to shoot Hatcher. Maybe he'd shot him and maybe he hadn't, because he didn't remember anything after the gun fired. The sound was tremendous. The vibrations knocked him out cold and now he was safe in his bed at Pemberley. Where was Hatcher? Had his shot hit or missed? Where was Georgiana?

"Someone tell me something," he demanded, and his parents expressed concerned glances. Had he said something odd? Had the words not come out right?

Maybe he slept a little bit before they produced the cards and maybe he didn't; he really couldn't tell. His mother held up two cards – one that read "yes" and the other "no", written in bold strokes of a brush on crème paper.

"Did I shoot Hatcher?"

Yes, she held up.

"Is he dead?"

Yes.

"Is – Georgiana – I don't remember." He realized he was confined to the cards.

Yes.

"Georgiana – is she all right?" Mother hesitated, and held up, *No*.

"Is ... is she dead?"

No.

Hatcher attacked her. He threw her into the water. She was bleeding. In what order that all happened, he couldn't quite process. "Will she be all right?"

Yes.

He nodded, then immediately blacked out.

~~~

He would not nod again. That had been stupid; his head was hurt too badly. When he awoke his parents were still there, in similar positions, but someone else was there as well. It was an old man, not too old, in very nice clothes, who started giving orders to the servants. Where was Dr. Maddox? But he didn't have time to ask as they flipped him on his side and the old man pulled out the spike. It was just a bar, made of glass, which Geoffrey saw only briefly when he was finished screaming, so tiny and covered in blood.

His mother was there, kneeling under the doctor, squeezing his hand and speaking to him. He could tell what she was saying by instinct. *It's all right.* Or something like that. She was trying to reassure him as they placed a pan under him.

"Dr. Maddox," Geoffrey said. He didn't want this doctor. He wanted Dr. Maddox. He was feeling ominous about the pan and all the instruments the doctor was sorting through. Eventually Dr. Maddox did appear, and smiled reassuringly, but did not stop the other doctor from taking a needle and putting it in his ear.

He must have been screaming very hard. His throat hurt from it. They were ready to hold him down as he felt the liquid drain from his ear. It smelled bad. The doctor had hurt his ear something awful and wiped him up, removing the pan, which was now filled with a yellow gunk. Then he reproduced the glass rod.

"No. Please, no." He prayed to God they heard what he said. Dr. Maddox shook his head sadly; his mother held his hand, but they got the rod back in, and it was worse than everything previous, even the gunshot, but somehow he stayed awake. By the time they had him on his back again, he was able to take only a sip of broth before closing his eyes.

~~~

It was the first time he'd managed to keep his instinct in check. Geoffrey reached for the rod that was in his ear and then put his hand back down. He turned his eyes and Dr. Maddox held up a card. *We have to keep the ear open.* He held up another one. *I'm sorry.*

"I can't hear," Geoffrey said.

A stand was there now, and not only a pen, but a brush and a jar of black ink. Dr. Maddox made large strokes, normally an unthinkable waste of paper. He had to blow it dry before he could hold it up. *We are trying to save your hearing.*

But he couldn't hear, and his right ear felt fine. "My ear – " Geoffrey lifted his hand and grabbed his right ear.

Dr. Maddox shook his head.

Geoffrey sighed. Even with the ringing going down, and the pain subsiding, his dread was increasing. *We are trying to save your hearing*, the card had read. They were *trying*. He had blown out his right ear. The left was their last hope.

"How's   Georgie?"

Dr. Maddox, ever the attentive doctor to his patient, wrote and held up, *Better*.

"Can I see her?"

No.

"Why not? Is she too hurt to be moved?"

Yes.

"Is it permanent?" Like his ear.

No.

Dr. Maddox did not allow for more questions until Geoffrey drank something. This time it was not just tea, but also a salty meat broth. His manservant attended to him, giving the best smile he could.

Geoffrey tried to understand on his own, because it was easier for them to answer questions with yes and no. "Is the other man a doctor?"

Yes.

"Is he some kind of ear specialist?"

Yes.

It must have taken time to get him. Of course, he had no idea of the passage of time. Sometimes he woke and it was clearly day, and sometimes he woke and it was clearly night. Every time he was tired, regardless of the actual hour.

"Do you have any medicine? For pain?"

Dr. Maddox sighed. There had to be a reason, and he actually sat down to write it, producing one card as the other dried. *You slept for a long time*, he wrote. *You were in a coma.*

"So?"

The medicine makes you sleepy. We are afraid to use it. The doctor held up the card, *I'm sorry.*

"I understand."

The doctor must have understood him, because he nodded. Geoffrey couldn't hear his own voice so he was never sure, but apparently he was saying actual words and they could understand him. That was a small comfort to pass the time before he fell asleep again.

~~~

He woke to find them changing the bandages on his head. The ear specialist had used a mirror to get the candlelight right into his eye, the one that he had only just succeeded in opening all the way. The feeling of something pressing down on his head was not as bad, and the ringing was fading. He wished other sounds replaced it, but they did not.

The first face he saw was George Wickham, who must have said something like "Hello." It sort of looked like it on his lips. George sat on the bed and petted Gawain. Usually George was not particularly affectionate with the dog, but he was now. He touched the area with the little scar from the healing wound.

That was right. They shot his dog. Mr. Wallace shot his dog, and then Hatcher hit him. It was coming back to him. But Gawain was all right, and he was getting better, and Hatcher was dead.

There was a white-haired man at the far end of his bed, next to his father. For a second Geoffrey was frightened it was the awful doctor, but it was not. It was old man Jenkins, nervously playing with his worn hat, talking to him. Finally someone handed him a card and he held it up. He probably couldn't even read it. It was the '*I'm sorry*' card.

"It's all right," Geoffrey said. He wasn't sure what Jenkins had done. Surely if it was serious, he would be arrested, not free and apologizing. His father would never let a man of that sort into Pemberley. He didn't want to forgive him because there was probably nothing to forgive. "I feel better," he said.

Mr. Jenkins smiled hesitantly and bowed. Then his father shooed the visitors away, including George, leaving Gawain on the bed as Dr. Maddox appeared with a new pile of papers. *Answer these questions*, said the first.

"All right."

What year is it?

"1823."

Who is the king of England?

"His Majesty King George the Fourth."

What is your name?

He felt a little insulted, but he hid it. They were testing his memory; he could tell that much. "Geoffrey Darcy, son of Fitzwilliam Darcy, heir to Pemberley and Derbyshire."

Dr. Maddox and his father both smiled, and it made Geoffrey feel warm inside. Still, he was thankful they didn't ask the month, because he honestly did not know if it was still March, or if he had lost time and it was April – or worse, it had been even longer than that.

~~~

The next day (or time he was awake; he wasn't sure), Reynolds came and shaved him, as he had the beginnings of a beard, and when he was done and perhaps somewhat presentable, Geoffrey saw his sisters. They all talked a lot to him, and his mother said something that was undoubtedly to mention he couldn't hear them, but Cassandra and Sarah were ready, and held up a crayon sign that said, *We love you. Get better soon.*

"I am trying."

The doctors entered – Maddox and the one he didn't like, and he immediately tensed. This time, however, Dr. Maddox produced a vial of green medicine, and made him swallow a spoonful of the awful stuff before they turned him over to empty his ear again. It was not as bad this time, either because he was better or because he was drugged, but as the doctor took his time looking into his ear with a gigantic lens before reinserting the rod, Geoffrey felt sleepy. He still screamed, but it was all a little distant, and when it was over, his ear was not as painful, just quite uncomfortable. They asked no more of him. He could rest.

~~~

When he woke, George was there, reading a book. Apparently he wanted to do more than just wile away the hours staring at an unconscious cousin. "George," Geoffrey said, startling him.

George had a letter all ready to go and handed it to him. It took some time for Geoffrey's eyes to focus, but he could read it.

I'm leaving, George had written. *Term starts at Cambridge in a few days. Charlie and Frederick left for Eton but you were much sicker and we didn't want to wake you.*

"You're saying goodbye?"

George nodded.

He would miss Eton. Geoffrey would not finish there, in this condition. It wouldn't affect his entrance into Cambridge, and to be perfectly honest he had never cared much for school, but he had been preparing for that sense of accomplishment, and now he would miss it. Even though there were things to feel worse about – like being deaf – he was struck by the sudden sadness of it. Gawain somehow sensed his mood, sitting up next to him and licking him until he was shooed back into position with a good scratching behind his ears. "Good dog." He looked back at George. "Can you understand what I'm saying? I can't hear myself."

George nodded.

"Can you tell me what happened? Do you have time?"

George held up the *Yes* card, and sat down most studiously at the desk, drawing a fresh sheet of paper and a pen, and began to write. Geoffrey dozed. He could feel Gawain's breathing as the hound's stomach moved in and out, but he couldn't hear him growling softly with content. He just knew that he was.

George shook Geoffrey's hand to wake him, and handed him the letter. The lettering was large but not exceptionally so, and as much as it was a strain to read the writing, much less the several pages George had produced, Geoffrey did – all of it, even the unbelievable bits. Hatcher and his demands. His father trying to break the entail. Dr. Maddox *had* visited him and *had* told him about Gawain. So had Georgiana – unbelievable, but George was not the type to lie, especially in writing. If it had been anyone else, except maybe his father, Geoffrey would have questioned the validity of what he read, but he couldn't. "Is Georgie in trouble? I mean, because of this."

George nodded.

"And they're all not speaking to each other."

Yes.

"I want to see her."

George quickly scribbled, *I will see what I can do.*

~~~

Their first real attempt to sit him up was a monstrous disaster. First, the rod in his ear fell out and rolled away. By then he was so dizzy he was nauseous, and he lost the soup they had just forced down his throat. His head was still spinning when they laid him back down, propping his head up at his harried demand, which he was almost too blindsided to say. Added to the embarrassment of throwing up on his father (of *all* people) was the sudden appearance of the other doctor, and he just thought, *I'm done for.*

But his father wasn't upset – he was only concerned. So concerned that he started talking to Geoffrey, as if forgetting that his son couldn't hear him. Although he might have caught a word or two if he could have focused his eyes, but he couldn't. When the doctor came at him as well, Geoffrey said, "Leave me alone!" It was probably a lot louder and angrier than he meant it to be. He just wanted to be left alone and close his eyes until the room stopped spinning.

It was lucky that he was too weak to be violent, because it took his father, Dr. Maddox, and Reynolds to hold him down as the other doctor put the needle in again, turned him over, and put something in his ear that made it burn, then over again so it could pour out. "Stop it! Stop it! I'm going to be ill!"

He could see his father saying something over and over as he held him down, and he liked to think it was, 'You will be all right.' But Geoffrey just wished he could pass out or go to sleep and the burning would end and they wouldn't put the rod back in. Maybe he was sick again and maybe he wasn't; either way, they had to clean him up and set him aright, and suddenly it was all over.

But he didn't sleep. His head was spinning and he felt as though he were moving and so he couldn't sleep. His father shed his waistcoat and sat down beside him as the others talked in the background. They still hadn't put the tube in yet. That was coming. He was dreading it. His father's grip on his own hand said it all – *You're going to be all right.* That was what he was trying to say, even if it wasn't true.

Geoffrey swallowed. At least he wasn't really moving and at least he wasn't ill again, and when the doctors came back into his vision, Dr. Maddox held up a card. Geoffrey had to concentrate to stop his head from spinning long enough to focus on it. *The inflammation has gone down.*

"Oh, good." Actually, he had no idea what that meant.

His father asked him something, maybe to him, maybe to the others. Geoffrey was tired but couldn't rest, which was the worst kind of tired there could be.

Can you hear anything? Read the next card.

"No."

They had reverted to using a charcoal pencil to make the words big enough for him to read. *It will come back.*

He wished he could believe it.

~~~

Geoffrey was confined to his bed, even though he was slowly recovering his strength, and was contemplating moving about. Dr. Fergus – that was the name of the other doctor, Geoffrey had discovered – wrote that his inner ear was irritated. Whatever that meant, it didn't sound good. But they didn't put the rod back in and the ringing had gone down, so he was better, and able to stay awake for long periods of intensely boring time. He couldn't focus on a book for very long, and he could hardly make conversation with his guest without wasting a lot of paper, but regardless, someone was always there when he woke.

Finally, George, who had long gone off to Cambridge, delivered on his promise, because Georgie was there when he woke. She was not the same Georgiana Bingley he remembered. Something about her was inexplicably changed, even though there was no sign of injury on her, and she was dressed properly, aside from the blue ink lines that were fading on her arms. He reached out his palm, but instead of taking his hand, she put something in it. He looked intently at his signet ring – he hadn't realized he'd lost it. When had he lost it? Hatcher must have taken it from him. "Thank you." It was the first time he remembered smiling in a while. He had sometimes smiled falsely, to reassure his mother when she looked at him with eyes that couldn't hide her worry, but this was different. Genuine.

This was Georgie, his Georgie, so he knew he could ask, "Where were you shot?"

She pointed to a spot on her side.

"Does it still hurt?"

No.

He could tell she was lying, but he withheld comment. "George wrote that you saved me."

Yes.

"Thank you."

She grabbed the charcoal pencil and scribbled, *You saved me, too.*

"I shot Hatcher. Right?"

Yes. She giggled. He couldn't hear it, but he could see it.

"What's so funny?"

Her bemused look at his question made it worse. Again she wrote, and held up her question. *Are you aware that you are shouting?*

"*What?*"

Now she was outright laughing. Eventually she paused to hold up, *Yes.*

282

He had no ability to temper his voice. He had only assumed that he was speaking in a normal tone. "No one said anything."

She wrote, *Well, you are.*

"Stop it. It's not funny."

Yes it is.

It hurt to laugh, but it was the kind of pain that was worth the struggle.

CHAPTER 19

The Knight's Tale

DOCTOR MADDOX was thankful for the Darcy's constant vigil over their son, because someone would need to be there when the boy woke, and the doctor needed to think. He had seen Geoffrey's condition in the camp and when he was brought back, and he knew it was beyond his abilities to repair.

He had no time, as a doctor, to question his own actions. He was used to the difficult rhythm of surgery, which allowed for no mistakes and no regrets, even if a few deaths still haunted him. He had worked with people who were beyond hope. He had deferred authority in cases where someone else was better. But he had never had to do it for a relative, and more importantly, never because of his sight. It didn't affect Geoffrey's case much, but there was the matter of Georgiana. She could have held out for the local surgeon, but his wife insisted. As the sun went down on that dreadful day, and both children were being watched by their parents, he had time to think, and his mind was filled with medical ruminations on what to do with Geoffrey.

"Daniel." His wife, of course, found his hiding spot in the library, where he strained to read the

285

words in the French medical tome he always carried in his trunk.

"Does someone need me?"

"You need to sleep," she said, shutting the book in front of him. "There is nothing in there you don't already know, and you are only straining your eyes to read it."

He had to cede to her authority, mainly because he was too tired to do otherwise. He wasn't sure what had been so exhausting – he'd dealt with longer hours and more medical trauma before. Maybe he was getting old. Pemberley's halls were too dark for him to see properly at this hour, but he had memorized them long ago. He checked on his patients once more before finally following Caroline to their chambers.

"I should have told them," he said.

"You told them you needed assistance."

"I obviously was not perfectly clear."

"Darcy was in no mood to hear reason with Geoffrey missing. You can hardly blame him for that."

He dismissed the servant and stumbled his way to the bed. "It was my damned pride and I know it."

"You are perhaps the last person on Earth I would accuse of being too proud," she said. He could hear her move about the room before she joined him on the bed.

"I am allowed to have my moments."

"No harm was done. Georgie will be fine, and Geoffrey – well, we all have no idea, but your 'pride,' as you call it, could have made no difference."

"If he wakes, he'll most likely be deaf," he said. "And if Professor Fergus does not arrive soon, it is almost certain."

"Quite a pair you will make, then."

She could still make him laugh. That was a good sign. He would not give in to total melancholia quite yet.

~~~

Geoffrey did wake, after what seemed like a lifetime, even though only two days had actually passed. Dr. Maddox was not sure if he was grateful or sorry that he missed the fight between Bingley and Brian. But with two critical patients in Pemberley, he could not attend to his brother and sister-in-law's wounded pride in Lambton, and Brian knew that. In case he didn't realize it, Dr. Maddox composed a brief letter, and when he asked Darcy to have it sent, the master of Pemberley just looked surprised that he was not angrier that Darcy had tossed his brother from Pemberley.

"If it hadn't been for Georgiana, I would have sent Bingley off, too, for the way they were acting," Darcy said. "Not that that's a comfort."

"Mr. and Mrs. Bingley have a lot to be angry about and nowhere to direct it," Dr. Maddox said. "And Brian does bear some of the responsibility. As does Nadezhda, who does not walk on water as he

287

thinks she does. But that shall all be sorted out in time."

"You are very logical about it."

"Am I ever anything else?"

Darcy probably would have given one of his little smiles at that, if he had it in him. The exhausted father did not. Dr. Fergus did arrive, in time to diagnose Geoffrey's left ear, declaring it able to be saved, with some luck and a tube to force the canal open. Fortunately he was asleep when it occurred, though even then, the boy did not seem pleased about the tube, as one of his first conscious actions was to try to remove it. But he was awake and that was what was important. The swelling on his head was going down, so that his eye opened more with further tries, and he had not been whacked dumb, as Dr. Maddox secretly worried he'd been. His other senses were intact.

As Geoffrey rested between brief periods of consciousness, Dr. Maddox checked on his other patient. Georgiana had not been awake much either, and when she was, the medicine obviously dulled her senses. No matter how mighty a warrior she was, her height and weight dictated that even the smallest dose either put her out cold or into such a daze that she spoke in a slurred voice and was slow to understand others. In a way he was grateful; it spared her from the realities that the rest of them faced, and if anyone needed a rest, it was Georgiana Bingley.

"How is my patient today?" Dr. Maddox said as he entered, finding her mother at her side.

"She needs her medicine," Mrs. Bingley said, her voice ragged. "She won't admit it, but she does."

"Mama!" Georgiana whispered in protest.

Jane Bingley just looked up to the doctor with pleading eyes, to which he responded, "I have many obstinate patients. Some of them are even my cousins and dear friends."

She nodded and took her leave, as he sat beside Georgiana, who was trying to make it look like she was not holding her side.

"I need to see the site, if you don't mind, Miss Bingley." He pulled aside the robe, and some of the bandages, enough to look at the wound. "You're healing quite nicely."

"Stunning."

"Wounds like that can be dangerous, even at this stage," he said as he went to mix a fresh batch of medicine with the opium he kept on his person and not on the tray.

"I want to see him." She did not need to specify who she meant.

"I know you do, but you can't be moved, and neither can he. That puts us in a precarious predicament, doesn't it?" he said, as he measured out the dosage. "He asked about you."

"He did?"

"He was relieved that you had survived. Apparently he does retain some memory of the incident, though perhaps not the whole of it. That is a very good sign." Talk about Geoffrey was one of the few topics that seemed to animate her. Her brother Charlie was confined to his room for lying about her whereabouts, and she was not able to see Brian and Nadezhda, perhaps the only people who were truly proud of everything she had done. "How are you feeling in comparison to yesterday?"

"Why won't I just heal?"

In other word, she felt the same. "Patience is something generally acquired by age, sadly. Your body needs time. You were shot with a rifle."

"What happened to the bullet?"

He had thought she would ask, and immediately produced it from the medical bag on the stand. Her eyes lit up at the sight. "I always found it strange that patients either want nothing to do with the item or treasure it forever. I assume you will do the latter." He dropped it into her awaiting hands. "Your Uncle Darcy, for example, had little interest in making a keepsake of his wound."

"From when he hurt his hand fighting Uncle Wickham?"

"No, the only thing that hit him then was a sword hilt and a fist. I mean from the time Lord Kincaid shot him."

"Lord Kincaid?"

"Oh, yes. You were practically an infant at the time," he said with self-amusement as he stirred. "I mean the present Lord Kincaid's older brother, the late James Kincaid, who was once my wife's suitor, until Mr. and Mrs. Darcy discovered he was a lying scoundrel, only after her inheritance. James Kincaid didn't take well to this discovery and shot Darcy in the back."

"Where were you?"

290

"I was Mr. Hurst's foot doctor at the time, and Mr. Bingley called me to save Darcy. The first time we were formally introduced was, I believe, when he was barely conscious. But that was a long time ago." He presented her with the spoon. "Open up."

"It tastes awful."

"You can have lemonade afterwards. Now *open*, Miss Bingley."

She obeyed, and he didn't remove the spoon until she swallowed, and he handed her the lemonade, which she gladly finished off. "It makes my head funny. Not really in a bad way, but I don't like to feel off."

"I assume you would not prefer the alternative."

She played with the bullet in her hands.

"It is real silver, you know. Your father looked at it. It must have cost the man a fortune."

"Really?"

"Someone *did* appreciate your lupine antics, Miss Bingley. And by appreciate, I mean that you scared him to death."

"It was sort of my intention."

"Well then ... good work."

Georgiana giggled. Yes, the drug was taking effect. At least he could comfort *someone*.

~~~

Hearing Geoffrey scream when they removed the tube and cleaned his ear stung Dr. Maddox in a particular way. He wasn't ready for it – no one was, only Dr. Fergus, because he had no particular attachment to the boy, and he was accustomed to this. "A normal reaction," the doctor said when he was finished. "In fact, it shows how alert he's become in the last day."

"Thank you," Dr. Maddox said, but could not bring himself to be entirely relieved. This was Geoffrey Darcy, the boy who fenced with his son, the son of one of his best friends and relatives – and to see them all devastated by it only made it worse. It had taken both Darcy and the manservant, with some of Dr. Fergus's own strength, to hold the boy down, especially when he was screaming, shouting specifically for Dr. Maddox, who he couldn't see sitting at his other side. *As if I could do something to help him.* To see Darcy, looking so old and grey, stroking his son's hair after he had passed out, whispering things to him that he knew the boy couldn't hear. Wisely he had shut the door, but of course Elizabeth heard it through the walls. He doubted there was anyone in Pemberley who hadn't. "Mrs. Darcy," he said politely as she entered. "It was a normal procedure. He's past it now." He said it because he knew she wanted to hear it from him, not the other doctor, no matter how kind Dr. Fergus actually was. But giving that news did not require him to stick around, watching her cry again. In fact, he avoided almost everyone and made a stealthy exit, leaving a note behind that he was (finally) going to Lambton.

The carriage always felt ostentatious, but he could no longer ride, and hadn't been much of a rider in his younger years, anyway. He arrived midday at the best inn of Lambton, where his brother and sister-in-law were lodged. By then he had regained some of his composure. But he couldn't yell at his brother – not yet, anyway. Instead he just embraced him, and greeted them neutrally.

They did not make him endure sitting on the floor for tea, as the inn was not set up that way. They did, however, serve it very exquisitely, and then Nadezhda excused herself.

"I can't help Geoffrey," he said after a long silence as Brian separated the leaves himself. "The treatments for his condition are not within my abilities."

"But that doctor came? Professor Fergus?"

"Yes. And he's doing his best to save Geoffrey's hearing, but we still won't know – maybe not for weeks. I don't know how we'll stand it." He took the offered tea, which was green, and sipped it. The taste was very mild and soothing. "Georgiana is recovering more slowly than she would like. She's asked for you, but she's too drugged to be truly insistent."

"What does her father say?"

Dr. Maddox frowned. "He is doing everything he can to comfort her, his wife, and his family. They're devastated – by everything, but at the moment, mainly her condition. Do you know what it's like to have a child in pain and not be able to do anything about it?"

Brian looked down, his eyes distant. "I do."

"How could you – " But then it came to him, in a flash – all of those awful memories of his cataract surgeries, especially the one when it had become infected. They had been in Scotland, just the two of them.

"My ability to empathize doesn't excuse our part in the situation," Brian said. "I should have – well, I should have stopped my wife. Or even noticed. I thought sending Mugin away -"

"Yes. Everyone's quite confused about this business about sending Mugin away. As far as we knew, he simply left all of the sudden, but that was typical for him. At least that was what you told me."

It was strange, when Brian was so serious, because he rarely was. "The last time he was here, about a week before he left, Mugin and I got drunk together and he told me that he had been teaching Georgie how to fight. And being the Englishman that I am despite all my denials, I immediately questioned him about it and he confessed that not only had Nadezhda known, but she sanctioned it and went to every one of their practices. When Georgie came to visit us, she wasn't coming to see her crazy aunt and uncle – she was coming to learn from Mugin."

"Why would he do that?"

"He said – quite honestly – she had a natural talent and she had begged him to teach her, so he saw no reason not to. Nady told him that it wasn't proper, now that she was older, so she would also be at all of the practices. It was Mugin who taught Nady how to fight in Japan, while Miyoshi taught me. I know he seems like a drunken convict to you, but he takes survival very seriously." Brian shrugged.

"Nonetheless I couldn't sanction it. I told him to pack his bags, and he was gone the next week."

"But you didn't tell Bingley."

"Nothing improper had occurred. Georgie was only thirteen. It had all been chaperoned. I thought that what Bingley didn't know, wouldn't kill him." He added, "In fact, it saved his life. Hatcher meant to kill us there, and he might have succeeded in shooting at least one us before I got to him, had Georgie not been there."

"But you still couldn't expect Bingley to not be devastated – by her injuries alone. And Jane – "

"He called my wife barren," Brian said. "I don't care if it's true. He did. What am I supposed to say to that?"

"Did he open with that accusation or was it at the end of a long and frustrating argument?"

To this, Brian had no response.

"Even if Nadezhda had the right to do what she did – and I can't even begin to fathom what propriety calls for here – she had the responsibility to tell Miss Bingley's parents. Or at least *you*."

Again, Brian said nothing, not in indignation, but in defeat.

"I've never known her to be unreasonable. In fact, she's possibly the most reasonable woman I know – and I am including my wife in that. Will you please look at your actions and realize they were just done in anger and from frustration, and make your peace with Bingley?"

"I'll speak with her," Brian said, and downed his tea in one swallow. It seemed as though he was not looking forward to the conversation. "She loves Georgie."

"I know. But Georgie is not her daughter. She's not even her proper niece. She's a second cousin by marriage."

"I know, I know," his brother responded. "It's just hard to say that to Nadezhda."

"But you have to say it. You want to be the responsible samurai? Protect your family from disaster."

Brian nodded. They were both too tired to continue the conversation, and Dr. Maddox was due back, so he rose and Brian saw him out.

"I'm just a crazy man with too many swords, Danny," he said as Dr. Maddox climbed into the carriage. "You're the real knight."

~~~

Brian Maddox watched the carriage disappear from his sight before he turned back inside and climbed up the steps. Entering his quarters, he found the main room empty, and deposited both his swords on the table before stepping into the bedchamber.

"You just take the wind out of my argument when you do that," he said to Nadezhda's sobbing. He had tried to prepare himself, but of course, like most things in life, he had failed. "I really did have an argument. I was going to say something valid, and now I can't." He pulled her into his arms and they sat together on the mattress they'd pulled on to the floor. "Should I be a good husband or a good brother? What do you want me to do?"

"How can I apologize for something I don't think is wrong?" she asked him in Romanian. "I never told her to put her life in danger. I taught her how to defend herself. I made her happy. She's such a lonely child."

"But she's not ours."

Nadezhda tore off her head covering. "I will never understand England."

"In all fairness, I think you understand it perfectly well. There are customs everywhere that just don't make sense sometimes," he said. "We have to apologize because it makes people feel better when they're hurt. And Bingley and Jane, seeing their daughter suffering – that hurt them." He added, "Georgie made her own choices, but I think it would help *her* if we took some of the responsibility for them. And at the moment, she needs all the help she can get."

"I want to say she made me proud," she said.

"They won't understand that. It's beyond their comprehension."

"I want them to understand her. I want her to be loved by her parents."

He felt her trembling, and some ancient ghost of a memory haunted him in passing. "She *is* loved by her parents. She's not understood, but she is loved. There is a difference; we just haven't noticed it."

Nadezhda had ample sleeves to wipe her tears, no matter how many of them there were. "I don't want them to suffer – I don't mean to inflict this on them. But I still love her."

"And I still love you, and I won't think of not demanding an apology from Bingley and Jane for what they said to you. Somewhere, there has to be a middle ground."

"The Middle Way," she said.

"Are you a Buddhist now?"

"No, I still have my heretical Papist beliefs, thank you very much," she said. "But I am willing to consider the options."

For the moment, that would do.

CHAPTER 20

The Wife of Bath's Tale

LADY GEORGIANA KINCAID was able to arrive before her half brother Grégoire. "Brother!" she said, and embraced Darcy.

"We came as soon as we received your message," Lord Kincaid said, shaking Darcy's hand. "Fortunately our worry has already been relieved. While the horses were resting, a local told us of Master Geoffrey's rescue."

"Yes," Darcy said, unsure exactly what the locals knew, beyond that the heir to Pemberley had been recovered, the gang killed, and its remaining member scheduled to be sent to Australia.

"I'm sorry we live so far away," she said. "How is he?"

Darcy tried to smile. "He's recovering. His hearing is – temporarily diminished. Nonetheless he will be very happy to see you. As will Elizabeth – she is with him now." He turned to the young Viscount Kincaid, now old enough to walk on his own. "And how is my nephew?"

"Hungry!" Robert said – not rudely, but very insistently.

"Tired from a long journey," his father said, "if a little fussy. Robert, be polite."

Robert Kincaid bowed and was carried off by his nurse to be cared for. Lord Kincaid turned back to Darcy. "We did come as fast as possible. Too late to be of any good, I'm afraid."

"Anything that puts a smile on my wife's face will be good," Darcy said.

"It's serious, then."

"We won't know the finality of his condition for days. Maybe weeks. And if that were the only thing, it would be enough." He took Lord Kincaid aside and told him the whole of the story, including the part that they were making a point not to make public, or even known to the servants.

"It seems Miss Bingley has outdone me," was the earl's response. "In terms of costumed antics." His swinging from a chandelier in full tartan was still a not-so-fond memory for Darcy, at least for the sake of Pemberley's lighting.

"I suppose there is ... some humor in that," Darcy said. Yes, he could admit that there was. Maybe shock was giving way to perspective. "Her parents might not be so appreciative of it, though."

"I will keep that in mind."

~~~

Geoffrey was suitably distracted by his aunt and small cousin for some time, but it left them both secretly frustrated, having to resort to paper and pen for any kind of detailed responses. He also hated not being able to hear young Robert's babble. But

Elizabeth was thrilled to see Georgiana, and Darcy was relieved for that alone.

His son was becoming a fussier patient with each passing day. In a way it was a relief; the doctor was encouraged that his senses were not lost. Geoffrey could fully open both eyes now, and even read for prolonged periods of time. But if being unable to make conversation wasn't annoying enough, he was still confined to his bed, and as the young man recovered his strength, he was more inclined to do otherwise.

He was home for nearly a week before he could stay fully upright for a few minutes, although still with his father holding him up. "Are you all right? Do you need to be ill?" It was hard to break the instinct to ask him something, and Geoffrey was concentrating too hard on keeping his head up to be able to read lips or facial expressions.

"I'm all right," Geoffrey said, though it didn't sound much like it. Reynolds was standing over him, ready for anything. "I'm all right," he repeated. He swallowed. "I need to lie down."

He had lasted almost two minutes. Darcy held up two fingers as his son was eased back onto the pillow. "God damn it," Geoffrey said, and Darcy had not the heart (or the ability) to remind him about his language. "I want to be better."

"I know," Darcy said, and held up the card that said that.

"You're not – upset that I'm not to finish Eton?"

Darcy shook his head. "No."

"I must be truly ill, if I want to go back to school."

Darcy smiled and patted his son on the hand before letting him rest.

"It is an improvement," Dr. Maddox said to Darcy as encouragement.

Darcy was not encouraged.

"Mr. Darcy," said the servant at the door, "Mr. and Mrs. Bellamont have arrived."

Now *that* was encouraging.

~~~

Married life was good to Grégoire Bellamont-Darcy. He still had his bald spot, but the rest of his hair stayed in place, with only a few grey streaks in the brown and as wild as ever. When not otherwise employed, he was usually wrestling his wild son, a toddler with the deadly combination of his father's tireless energy and his mother's stubbornness. Sometimes they traveled with a proper nurse, and sometimes they did not, depending on the length of their stay. Caitlin was mostly responsible for him, mainly because she was the best person at catching him.

When Darcy made it down the stairs, Elizabeth was already greeting them. That gave it a certain formality despite her best intentions, and Darcy bowed to his guests. "Grégoire. Mrs. Bellamont." He looked down at the boy who had suddenly grabbed his leg. "Patrick."

"Uncle Darcy!"

"Patrick!" Caitlin said. "One of t'ese days yer gonna trip someone!" She scooped him up. "'e's wound up from the trip."

"Well, then he's welcome to be wound up together with Viscount Robert," Elizabeth said. "Maybe they will tire themselves out."

"One can only hope," Darcy said. Robert Kincaid and Patrick Bellamont were only two years apart in age and got on fabulously with each other to the exclusion of anyone nearby, mainly because they both had somewhat similar impenetrable accents, and could run circles around Danny Maddox as he tried to figure out for the life of him what they were saying. "Geoffrey's resting now, so perhaps Patrick can see his cousin later."

"How is he?" Elizabeth asked.

"Aggravated," was all Darcy said, which was enough, and turned to his brother. "We're so relieved you've come."

That was putting it mildly.

By the time their new guests were settled, Geoffrey was ready to receive his aunt and uncle as best he could. Grégoire was very quick with the pen, but it still made for an exhaustive experience. Their physical presence – that they were here for him – was more to the point.

"Uncle Grégoire," Geoffrey shouted, either quite unaware that he was doing it or unable to control it, "thank you for coming."

Grégoire nodded. "Of course."

"My father – is he in the room? I can't see around that corner."

303

He shook his head.

Geoffrey took his uncle's hand. "I've never seen my father like this. I believe he needs you more than I need you. Though, if you wish to work a miracle on my eardrum, I would be forever grateful."

Grégoire smiled and nodded.

"I'm old enough to understand that you can't grant wishes, but you'll have a hard time convincing Father of that." Geoffrey frowned. "And I always thought he was the most sensible person in Derbyshire."

Grégoire wrote and handed him the paper. *He is not the only one who thinks I can work miracles. I wish that I could, but it is only by God's grace that wonders happen, and He is not to be bought or bargained with.* He took the paper back when Geoffrey had read it, and scribbled on the other side, *With that said, His grace is not to be underestimated.*

"I don't regret it," Geoffrey said. "Shooting the rifle, I mean. Even if I am deaf, I still would do it over again, to save Georgie."

Grégoire wrote, *If I am wrong and the Lord God can be bargained with, you are a very good bargainer.*

"That's not what I meant," Geoffrey said, and blushed.

~~~

Even though he had heard the story once from Darcy, Grégoire cornered Elizabeth in the chapel

304

after Compline to discuss Georgie, as he had been warned to tiptoe around the Bingleys, who were still frightened and confused.

"Yes, it's all true," Elizabeth said. "I wish I had been there when they argued with the Maddoxes – and yet, I'm glad I wasn't." She was exhausted, and looked it. "I cannot tell them what they did wrong or even if they did anything wrong, as parents. She did save my husband and my son, and now she's just suffering for it."

"They are not supporting her?"

"They are supporting her within their abilities, but they cannot condone her actions. If Anne or Sarah were to put themselves in danger like that – " She looked down at her hands. "Georgie has always been distant and reserved. It seems the only one who understood her was Nadezhda, and she was wise enough not to share."

"Not everyone adheres to the same mold of society," he said. "And as devastating as it seems within your circle – somehow, room is always made. You accepted Caitlin."

"Caitlin is a wonderful woman who loves you to pieces."

"That does not qualify her for a Season in London, though."

"I hardly think she would enjoy a Season in London, or you would have endured one for her years ago."

"Of course. But who knows? Patrick might one day parade around with the dandies of Dublin for all

305

I know." He chuckled at that. "I can only hope not, but anything that makes him happy."

"He's so much like Geoffrey was. Do you remember? He was a little troublemaker." Elizabeth smiled at the memory. "Though Geoffrey we could understand when he tried to explain himself later."

"I can understand him."

"Can I confess something to you?"

"As long as it is not a formal confession."

She laughed. "I find myself not always comprehending your wife's words."

"That is probably for the best," he said. "When I don't understand her, I assume she is swearing. There is *my* confession."

Elizabeth giggled. "You will talk to the Bingleys?"

"If they can understand my accent."

~~~

"'Oh, have you slain me, you false thief?' I said, 'And for my land have you thus murdered me? Kiss me before I die, and let me be.' He came to me and near me he knelt down, and said: 'O my dear sister Alison, so help me God, I'll never strike you more –'"

"Grandpapa!"

Mr. Bennet looked up from his book at his convalescing granddaughter, peering at her over his spectacles. "What is it?"

"I thought her sister's name was Alison. How can the Wife of Bath also be named Alison?" Georgie asked.

"On this, I do not believe Chaucer was ever clear. After all, he never quite finished his famous Tales. Now, do you want me to finish before someone comes in and finds me reading you this bawdy tale?"

"Yes, Grandpapa."

"Good, then," he said, and cleared his throat. "'What I have done, you are to blame therefore. But all the same forgiveness now I seek!' And thereupon I hit him on the cheek, and said: 'Thief, so much vengeance do I wreak! Now will I die; I can no longer speak!' But at the last, and with much care and woe, we made it up between ourselves...'" (1)

"He *made up* with her? After she punched him?"

"Well, to be fair, he punched her as well, so I believe it was even," Mr. Bennet said, and he was about to continue when the door opened and Mr. Bingley entered. "Ah, the prodigal son returns."

"Mr. Bennet. What are you reading to my daughter?"

"A good, old, proper English tale of marital felicity," he said, closing the book. "Only something I would have allowed any of my daughters to read – Oh, wait. Did not one of them run off with a scoundrel? Perhaps I *should* have stuck to Fordyce's sermons." He sighed. "But then again, it all turned out all right in the end, didn't it? A rich man rented Netherfield and it was all happiness and wonder - "

"And you can stop before we get to the embarrassing part of *that* story," Bingley said. "Georgie, have you had your medicine?"

"I'm all right, Papa," she said, "as long as I don't move much."

"Well, you had better take it, because you are about to."

"What?"

"Precisely what I said," Bingley said, passing Mr. Bennet in the armchair and pouring a spoonful of Dr. Maddox's concoction for Georgiana, who reluctantly swallowed. "There. Now I can let him in."

"Who?"

Bingley opened the door, "*Kinasi!*" and Monkey came bounding into the room, first climbing onto Mr. Bennet's knee, and then into Georgie's awaiting arms, sniffing her side, where the bandages were. "Monkey, you behave yourself, because I had to get special permission from someone. And you will need special permission from me to not be in a pen forever if you hurt my daughter just when she is recovering."

"Do you really think he can understand you?" Mr. Bennet said.

"He can sense when another creature is injured," he said. "Though my daughter is not a creature."

"I missed you," Georgie said to the monkey, scratching his soft fur so he squealed with delight. He did position himself in such a way that his weight rested away from her injured area. "Papa, thank you. How long can he stay?"

"Until you recover or he misbehaves. Whichever comes first," Bingley said. "And now I owe Darcy a *massive* favor. Monkey, sleep!" But Monkey of course would not sleep on command. "Well, *stay!*" This the animal did do, even though he still chirped in protest as Mr. Bennet rose and Bingley tucked his daughter in. "If he keeps you up, toss him out. Physically, if you must."

"He won't. I promise."

Bingley kissed his daughter on her forehead. "Good night, Georgie." Monkey squealed. "Good night, Monkey."

By the time Mr. Bennet was up and at the door and the servants had extinguished most of the candles, Georgie was already asleep, Monkey curled up beside her like a doll. "Well, I've finally done something right, perhaps," Bingley said, and escorted his father-in-law to his own chambers.

~~~

The next day, not one, but two people (well, creatures, as Bingley had called them) were carried back up the stairs in an armchair. It was Georgie's second visit to Geoffrey and Monkey's first. Fortunately the animal got on fabulously well with Gawain, who was more overprotective than usual. "Good dog. Good Monkey," Geoffrey said. Someone had to make sure neither patient tired themselves out, and Grégoire offered, taking a seat at the writing table moved up next to the bed.

309

"How are you?" Geoffrey said, and Georgie shrugged. "Well, you look better."

"Thank you," she said, and he seemed to understand her. He was a fast learner and they didn't always need the cards for common words if the person speaking was looking at him straight on.

"So we're both fine, as long as we never move."

Georgie quickly wrote, *Apparently, that is the plan.*

"Did they all decide?"

She whispered to Grégoire, who wrote and handed him, *They're still not speaking to each other.*

"What? Still?"

She nodded. "The room was very tense."

"Is that why I haven't seen Uncle Brian and Aunt Nady?"

They both nodded solemnly.

"What is this nonsense?" Geoffrey shouted, louder even than his regular shouting, since this was intentional. "Why are they still angry? How long has it been?"

Georgie held up two fingers. "Two weeks."

"Two *weeks?* And what has my father done?"

Grégoire wrote out a response. *He is busy with you, Nephew.*

"That's ridiculous! I don't care how worried he is, he should still – what are you doing? Let me speak." While he talked, he was inadvertently sitting up, and Grégoire quickly came to hold him back down.

"I don't want you to hurt yourself," Grégoire said, his hands occupied.

Whatever part of that Geoffrey understood was enough. He fell back on the pillow, frowning and scratching Monkey's back as he stared out the window. They waited patiently – as there was little else for them to do – until he turned and said, "I'll need paper. And my seal. Reynolds knows where it is."

"What – "

"I won't sit here and wait for them to stop being angry about whatever silly thing they're angry over. I can't walk, but I can write." He turned to his uncle. "What are you standing there for? You wanted to help, right?"

Grégoire nodded. "Yes."

"Then help me now."

As per his instructions, they called Reynolds and shut the door to everyone else. Even with a proper stand made out of a breakfast tray set up before him and all of his materials at the ready, Geoffrey was still visibly struggling to put the words on the page, either because he couldn't focus his sight or couldn't concentrate. It was grueling to watch him pass out or be ill each time he sat up, the ink staining the rest of the page where he stopped writing, but he would not relent. It took almost the course of the entire day between rest periods and his limited faculties, but he intended to write, and write he did. As the sun began to set, Reynolds lit the wax and an exhausted Geoffrey stamped his seal on all eight letters. He ordered them addressed and delivered accordingly, but would not settle down until Georgie held his hand and spoke to him. Even though he could not hear the words, they succeeded in lulling him into sleep.

CHAPTER 21

To Whom It May Concern

> *LET me begin by apologizing for my uneven hand and possible impenetrability. This letter was written to the best of my abilities at this time...*

From there it varied, but even the opening lines made some eyes begin to water, braced for the inevitable with the shaky text, the ink blots of abnormal size, and the words scratched out and written again. With a heavy heart Darcy read his son's letter. Geoffrey had been raised to have remarkable penmanship, like his mother and father, so the very appearance of the letter indicated the level of his disability, temporary or not.

> *Father, I am grateful that you have let Miss Bingley recuperate here, where the best doctors are available, even when you may feel that other members of the family have given you cause to ask them to leave. I am glad I am not Master of Pemberley now, and forced to face an argument between various segments of the*

> *family. That said, I will admit to you*
> *now that I know Georgie is greatly*
> *distressed. Her Highness, Princess*
> *Nadezhda, has always been her*
> *closest ally, and I cannot help but*
> *wonder (when I have little else to do*
> *because of my infirmity) who else has*
> *stepped up to support her? Am I the*
> *only one who has personally thanked*
> *her for my rescue?*

Darcy frowned. The answer was yes.

~~~

In her own study, Elizabeth was already crying. She wished so much to embrace him, but he had written instead of speaking to her, and that had to be respected. She had to at least complete the letter.

> *Aunt Bingley is confused and I*
> *imagine you have sought to comfort*
> *her, but there is no need to comfort*
> *her about having a mad daughter.*
> *Georgie is not mad. Her actions to*
> *save me were strange but perfectly*
> *comprehensible, perhaps the only way*
> *she could have acted and she would*
> *quite possibly have escaped with her*
> *identity intact, were it not for her*
> *injuries. I do not think anything she*
> *did held a hint of impropriety.*

Did he not understand the gravity of it, or was he right? Georgie had not run off with a man. She had fought one, and to protect her identity as a woman, done so in disguise. That, Elizabeth could not deny.

~~~

> *Sir Daniel, I have no doubt that you understand that there is an emotional component to physical suffering, and that even the most distracted patient has some awareness of their surroundings and how they are perceived by others. My parents have not said it, but I know they are terrified. First they were terrified that I would die; now they are terrified that I will never hear again, and though I can have a reasonable life without proper hearing, they only wish the best for me. I must conjecture, then, (thus proving that patients are indeed aware, no matter how dizzy and ill they may feel, or how silent the world is to them) that even if Aunt and Uncle Bingley have not said a word to Georgie about her actions on said day, or her previous attack on Mr. Hatcher to try to discover my location, she knows very*

well that they disapprove, or are even scared for her sanity...

Dr. Maddox paused in his reading. His eyes were bothering him again, from a combination of things, and Geoffrey's letter was not easy for anyone to read. He knew his wife had gotten her own letter, and he heard murmurs from the servants that at least four had gone out. When he was ready to read again, he entered the guest bedchambers, where his wife was sitting in bed, her hand over her mouth. "What does he say? Or is it private?"

"Has he scolded you for being a poor physician?"

"In a way. You?"

"Geoffrey is more observant than we give him credit for. He thinks me a woman who puts so much emphasis on the good behavior of young ladies in proper society that I would therefore not comfort my brother and Jane about Georgiana's ... you know."

"Yes, I know. Because we all can't speak of it."

Caroline sat up. "Well, maybe we should."

~~~

"What did he say to you?" Brian asked his wife. His voice was gentle, but protective, mainly because she was openly weeping as she held the letter before her, reading and rereading the scrawled words.

"I should have told them," she said. "He's right." She leaned into her husband's robe. "I'm not Georgie's mother. Jane is. She deserved to know."

316

"He said that?"

"He implied it. I don't know if he fully understood the implications –maybe he did." She clutched the letter as she wrapped her arm around her husband, who kissed it. "He's not a child. And he knew someone was helping Georgiana along."

"He's a Darcy. They're very intuitive." He held up his letter and let her read from it.

> *You know very well that my father has a distaste for violence, especially since the death of Uncle Wickham, so for you to draw your sword on Uncle Bingley – I cannot imagine the turmoil that must have put him through, while he was still readying himself to grieve for me as I lay in my coma.*

"He goes on," Brian said, and read the next sentence aloud.

> *Forgive me for saying it, but your system of honor is nonsense if it leads you to be so dishonorable. And is there no room for forgiveness when the family – especially your own brother – has granted you so much?*

"How could he know this?"

317

"Maybe he was listening to all those jokes you've been making about being the scoundrel of the family," she suggested, and they read on.

~~~

From his own notes and reading many different languages (or attempting to do so), Charles Bingley was accustomed to near-illegible handwriting – but not from a Darcy.

It must pain you to think that you understand your daughter so little. I do not think any man can claim a full understanding of his daughters, otherwise they would never be surprised by their actions. Our own family history has proven that Mr. Bennet was surprised many times in many well-repeated stories, some good and some bad, that I have heard or overheard over the years.

You should know this: I do not understand Georgie. I have never understood her, nor have I attempted the feat. I like to think I know when I am beaten, and therefore have never tried to fully comprehend her actions or her intentions. Perhaps that is why she has opened up to me in ways that apparently she has not with her other

*cousins or her own siblings, because
she has no fear of a reaction beyond
amusement. That she would take
action to rescue me does not surprise
me; how she did it does. In truth, if
she had been completely conventional
about it, I would have been a bit
disappointed in her!*

Somehow, while blinking back his tears, Bingley
succeeded in smiling at that.

~~~

Aunt Bingley,

*I have no understanding of a
woman's proper place in society. I
have been told, most prodigiously,
how to expect women to act, and to be
disappointed when they do not act
appropriately within our social circle.
Please do not tell my father I've told
you, but he has lectured me on how to
spot a flirt or a fortune-hunter, now
that I've come of age, he would be
most displeased if I did not attend
Cambridge because I was no longer a
bachelor. I know women are to be
modest but some are not. They are to
present themselves as pleasing to the
eye but not too much, and without the*

*use of scandalous things like makeup
or perfumes. They are to wear gloves
when appropriate, and keep their hair
up and sometimes covered, and I am
never to be fooled into what could be
misconstrued as a compromising
position with anyone I do not wish to
marry.*

*Georgie is perfectly capable of being
all of those good things I have just
mentioned, and many others I am
forgetting because I admit I am
having trouble concentrating, and
cannot write as fast as I can think. I
wish I had my father's patience, but
then again if I did, between that and
my illness, I fear this letter would not
be produced before midsummer.*

*But I have lost the topic. Georgie is
capable of being modest and shy and
demure. She has her wits about her
and is honorable and polite in every
way, and she has always adhered to
the rules of society when they were
demanded of her (her hair is one
admissible exception). That she broke
those rules to save my life is of no
consequence to me and I do not
understand why it would be of
consequence to anyone else. The rules*

*of polite society are not meant for a
situation involving a violent man who
kidnaps sons and attempts to murder
their fathers. They are meant for
ballrooms and afternoon calls and
dinner parties, none of which
occurred (to my knowledge) from the
moment I disappeared.*

*Nor is she mad; you must know
everything was perfectly calculated,
even reasonable. Much of it was to
save her own reputation by extensive
disguise, and it would have worked
and in essence, did work, if the wolf
rumor is left to tavern tales. She never
revealed her plans to me, and has
never had cause to since I have begun
my recovery. I do not require an
explanation. She did what she had to
do to save me and to save her father,
mine, and Uncle Brian. There is
nothing simpler than that.*

*Though she is obviously, right now as
I write this, in great physical pain, I
know it would be lessened if her
family supported her. I will not go so
far as to accuse you of casting her out
in any way, and I have no doubt you
have cried by her side when she slept
and held her hand when she was*

awake. But there is a chasm between you and it pains her, even though she won't admit it. Her Highness, Princess Nadezhda, supported her and probably still does, but she is not Georgie's mother, and no amount of willpower on either side can change that.

Georgie once told me – and do not tell her I said this! – that her earliest memory is of speaking to you and watching you fainting in shock, and how concerned she was for you then. In her own way she has always been concerned for you, because she is afraid that she has always been a disappointment to you. But she is who she is and it pains her too much to deny it. And I think we would both agree she is in enough pain already.

Jane's sobbing must have attracted some attention, because her husband appeared at her side when he had previously been in his own chamber, his own letter still in his hand. Without words he embraced her.

"I failed my own daughter," she said. "She needed me and she could not bring herself to say it."

"You did your best," he said. "And thank God, there is time to try again."

~~~

Darcy was not entirely surprised when it was announced that the Maddoxes – Brian and Nadezhda – were at the door. Everyone seemed to have retreated to their own quarters, so he received them alone. They stood on the front steps, waiting for his pronouncement, which was a cool but perfectly polite greeting by name.

They bowed. "I would prostrate myself on the ground," Brian said, his usual ebullience gone, lost in humility, "but you would probably think me a wild savage."

"I already do," Darcy said, "but that is no reason to get your head dusty. Welcome to Pemberley."

"How is your son, Mr. Darcy?" the princess said as they entered the main hallway.

"An accomplished writer, it seems. Much like his uncle," Darcy said. "He is on the mend. As is Miss Bingley." He turned his head at the sound of footsteps. "And speaking of, it seems – "

Mr. Bingley, looking a bit worse for the wear, stepped up to the little party. "Darcy." He bowed, and turned to the Maddoxes. "Your Highness. Mr. Maddox, I apologize for my implications. I was so distraught – "

"I should never have drawn live steel. Not in Darcy's house, not anywhere on a relative," Brian interrupted. "We were suffering and you were suffering. A lot of bad things were said."

"On both sides."

"I deceived you," Nadezhda said. *"Gomen nasai."* (I'm sorry)

"W*akarimasu,"* Bingley replied. (I understand)

Brian, with less formality, embraced Bingley, who eagerly returned it as the more reserved Darcy and Nadezhda watched on. These men were partners in business and in travel, and cousins more distantly by marriage. They both seemed delighted to have some semblance of relations restored. But this meeting still left one person unaccounted for.

"Where is Mrs. Bingley?" Brian immediately asked.

"She is, at the moment, occupied," he replied.

~~~

When Jane finally had regained enough of her composure to enter her daughter's chambers, Dr. Maddox was there. He bowed. "Mrs. Bingley."

"Dr. Maddox. How is my daughter today?"

"Better. I am lowering the dose. But she is very tired from being up all day yesterday, assisting Geoffrey."

"I'm all right," Georgiana insisted from her bed. She was beginning to recover her strength now, two weeks after the actual damage had been done. With that, Dr. Maddox nodded and excused himself, and Jane seated herself beside her daughter.

"You've been crying," Georgie said.

"I never get anything past you," Jane said. "Or so you think."

"I know you've been worried about my psychical health."

Jane looked down, and took her daughter's hand. It was so small and she had such fair skin, like her father. "It took me – some time to understand it. Or not understand it, so much. I won't tell you everything Geoffrey wrote to me, but he is – well, the Darcys have always been exceptionally wise, except when it comes to matters of courtship. There they need a little help." She smiled briefly. "Geoffrey seems to enjoy being pleasantly surprised by your behavior. He has a certain appreciation of it." She said, "He knows you better than I do."

Georgie's tone softened. "Mama, he's my age. We were raised together, and grew up as the best of friends. Though I did beat him at being born."

"Yes. And your father won five pounds off of it." But she did not explain this, even when Georgiana raised her eyebrows in surprise. "I always thought – my mother loved me and I loved her, even though sometimes she was embarrassing, and she was so anxious about us being married that she almost drove men away – but I always knew what she was about. She wanted me to be safely settled. She always said I was the most beautiful of us and had the best chance of a good marriage." Jane swallowed. "When you were born, I told myself that I would never be the fretful mother and make a fool of myself, trying to interfere in everything to my daughter's advantage and pushing her to balls and to make herself look pretty. You were like Lizzy in a way, so much smarter than I am and so observant, and quiet when

325

you wished to be, and assertive when you did not. And I thought, 'Oh dear, I have to raise Lizzy.' But you were someone else entirely. I didn't know what to do. No one taught me how to be a mother. They taught me how to raise a *proper* daughter and all that nonsense, but it never made you happy. After a while it seemed like nothing I could do or say could make you happy – "

"*Mama.*"

"And you got rid of all of the governesses – some of them by sheer strokes of brilliance – even though you didn't truly hate your lessons. Except pianoforte."

"Except pianoforte," Georgie agreed, tightening her grip on her mother's hand as Jane's voice trembled.

"I discussed it with your father, but it was my responsibility. You were my daughter and my mother raised me, so I was responsible for you, and I tried everything, and I never knew if I was doing too much or too little, to mold you into…something. Now I don't even know what that something is." She looked up at her daughter through watery eyes. "All I know is that my daughter somehow saved the life of her cousin, her father, and two of her uncles by the most extraordinary means possible. Why was I so afraid to be proud of *that?*"

Georgie had no response. She looked stunned, but Jane could barely look at her, so ashamed. "My nerves," Jane said. "Oh dear, I'm turning into my mother."

"As long as you don't start making me go to balls, and interfering on my behalf to a ridiculous extent to make me a fortuitous match – "

"Oh, I hardly doubt that – " But then she realized Georgie was joking. Georgiana Bingley was smiling, and she was joking. She could hardly sit up with the wound on her side, but somehow she managed to embrace her mother, with a lot of maneuvering on Jane's end. "My baby girl."

"Someday, some hardy dismissed soldiers will be telling legends about your baby girl," Georgie said. "Only they won't know it was her."

"No," Jane said, "but I'll be proud anyway."

CHAPTER 22

Blessed Equilibrium

DESPITE having restored balance in the family, and all from his sickbed, Geoffrey Darcy could not restore his own.

Leaving aside his lack of hearing, the major thing that stood between him and returning to some semblance of normal life was his inability to stand, or even sit up for very long. Most his body was strong enough to be up and about, and sitting in bed all day because of his head was frustrating to him. Unfortunately, Dr. Fergus was the best ear doctor in Britain (by Dr. Maddox's very high standards) and all he could recommend was time.

"His inner ear needs to settle," he said to the Darcys, "like the inflammation in the canal. We waited and it went down."

"How long do we have to wait?" Darcy demanded.

But Dr. Fergus could not give him a solid answer. Neither could Dr. Maddox. And none of this, when explained to Geoffrey, made the boy very happy. What did put a smile on his face was seeing his Uncle Brian, even if he couldn't hear what he said.

"There's my boy," Brian said as he entered with Bingley. "The big hero. How is he today?"

"Not happy," Darcy said, intentionally facing away from Geoffrey. "The blasted doctor can't do anything for his inner ear."

"I did not know we had one," Bingley said. "Why would you need an ear inside you?"

"Apparently, for balance."

"If we were in China," Brian said, "we could try acupuncture. I'm sure he would love that."

"It did work," Bingley said. "It worked very well. Just a bit unnerving."

"What is this?" Darcy said.

"Chinese medicine. They put little needles on your skin – just piercing the upper layer. It's supposed to affect energy lines, some Oriental superstition," Brian answered. "There's – I believe there's a man who does it in Brighton. He's Indian, but he knows the therapy. Not very popular, though. People can't get past looking like a porcupine."

"But it did work," Bingley repeated. "It worked in Hong Kong."

Darcy paused for only a second before saying, "Can you get him?"

"Will you at least *try* to let me in on the conversation?" Geoffrey shouted.

Startled, Darcy held up the, *I'm sorry* card.

Brian sat down and wrote out, *We are considering a Chinese treatment.*

"Why am I not surprised?" Geoffrey said. "Georgie's always going on about some abstract theory about perfect balance. I never understood it."

That gave the gentlemen good reason to pause. Brian quickly wrote, *Did Mugin tell her about it?*

"Yes. He told her if she mastered it, no one would ever be able to defeat her." He swallowed. "I probably shouldn't be saying this, should I? Since that's the cause of all this?"

Darcy shook his head. "No, you should." It hadn't been true a day ago, but it was true now.

"Well, you didn't hear it from me. I didn't even think to ask her – I always thought it was nonsense, to be honest."

Darcy took the pen from Brian's hands and wrote, *I would rather consider talking to my niece before allowing an Indian put needles in your head.*

"*WHAT?*" Geoffrey said, this time *really* shouting, now that he'd heard the details of this Chinese treatment they'd mentioned.

~~~

"Slowly, slowly..."

"If I go any slower, I won't be moving at all," Georgie protested as she took a few steps across the room, her mother holding her arm in case she lost her strength. Dr. Maddox watched her carefully. She was clearly strong enough to move around, but she kept one hand pressed on her side.

"Does it hurt?" he asked very patiently.

"It is a little uncomfortable," Georgie said. "Nothing more."

"Like lying on a hard pillow, or is it sharp?"

"Sharp," she admitted. "But not all the time. Just when I move in certain ways." She let her mother guide her back to her bed. "I'm all right."

Jane looked up at the doctor, who nodded encouragingly. "The muscles on the side of your chest were bruised and torn. It is very important not to irritate them as they heal. With that said, I will sanction moving about a bit more. But no stairs." He was going to say more encouraging things about her progress, which was proceeding as expected, but there was a knock on the door.

"Come," Georgie said as she sat back down.

The servant entered and announced, "Her Highness, Princess Nadezhda to see you, Miss Bingley. Mrs. Bingley."

"Tell her to come," Jane said, and Dr. Maddox excused himself as the princess entered, curtseying quickly to him and then to the occupants.

"Mrs. Bingley. Miss Bingley," Nadezhda said, her hands behind her back.

"Your Highness," Jane said.

"Nadi-sama," Georgie said. "I'm so glad to see you. Mama, I'm sorry – "

"You do not have to be sorry," Nadezhda said. "I have to be sorry." She bowed to Jane. "I should not have concealed anything from you, Mrs. Bingley."

Between Nadezhda's royal pride and Jane's motherly defensiveness, it still made for an awkward moment, and they did not rush to embrace, but Jane did respond, "You make her happy when I cannot."

"*Mama* – "

"There's no need to deny it," Jane said. "I cannot imagine myself fighting, or even my husband. His own career is notoriously bad. And if that's what she wants..." Jane reached out and stroked her daughter's hair. "Even when you were a little baby, you were a handful. And considering all the good it's done, I wouldn't have it any other way."

Nadezhda held up what she had been hiding behind her back – Georgiana's geta shoes, still in reasonable condition despite the wear they had seen over the years.

"My sandals!" Georgie squealed with delight. "Where did you find them?"

"Because of the metal, they sunk," she said. "Brian is a very good swimmer. Or he was, because I made him."

Jane had seen them before. Georgiana never wore them in proper social situations, but she wore them when she was out 'walking' or playing. "They were a gift from Mugin, I always assumed."

"He left them for me," Georgie said. "They were too big for me until a few years ago. Mama, please – "

"Of course. They're yours," Jane said, and Nadezhda set the shoes down by the bed. They were still quite dirty.

"They're very hard to walk in," Nadezhda said. "Let alone run. I certainly cannot."

"Then who taught you?" Jane asked her daughter.

"She taught herself," Nadezhda said. "Your daughter has extremely good coordination."

"As long as she doesn't join the circus – "

"Mama!" Georgie tugged on her mother's gown, only to look up and see her mother smiling.

~~~

"Do you remember when we used to spin around so much, and got so dizzy, that we felt like we were still spinning when we'd stopped? It's like that."

Monkey was the first to respond, squealing and waving his tiny hands in Geoffrey's direction as Georgie held him in her lap. "Not now, Monkey."

"Georgie, you have to help me. They're going to get an Indian man from Brighton to put needles in my head."

Georgie looked over at her Aunt Darcy, who just shrugged. "I don't know precisely what I should do."

"Anything would suffice," Elizabeth replied.

She thought, and then requested paper, whereupon she wrote a long list of instructions, which took her some time, as Monkey tried to interrupt from his new place on Geoffrey's lap. Finally she passed it to him. "Do you think this will work?"

"I have no idea, Geoffrey."

He seemed to understand that. "I don't want needles in my head."

"Coward," Georgie said good-humoredly, and turned to Reynolds. "Sit him up."

"You are aware, Miss Bingley, that this tends to – "

" – make him ill, yes." She whispered out of her aunt's hearing, "I've seen him throw up before, thank you very much."

Reynolds had to hide his blush from Mrs. Darcy as he helped Geoffrey sit up with his legs over the side of the bed. Geoffrey looked ready to topple, but Georgie grabbed his arm. "Geoffrey," she said. "What did I tell you? You're supposed to breathe." If he couldn't hear her, he could at least *feel* her. "What did I say? Five seconds." She held up her fingers, and counted down with them as he breathed in, so he could watch the fingers. "Five, four, three, two, one – now hold it. Five, four –,"

Geoffrey swallowed ominously but was not sick. He sat across from her, clearly trying to focus on her hand and those fingers going up and down, as he was supposed to breathe in, hold it, and breathe out on a timer. She pulled away her other hand and he grabbed. "Don't," he said, his voice distant. He put her other hand back on his shoulder where it had been. "I – don't leave me." He closed his eyes.

"Five," interrupted Reynolds finally. "It has been five minutes."

It was obvious Geoffrey could no longer continue the exercise. He was so exhausted that he said nothing as Reynolds carefully set him back down, and lay halfway on his side, gazing at the little end table with the writing implements.

"It is a record," Elizabeth said, and kissed her son on the head. "Five minutes. You did so well."

Clearly, Geoffrey felt otherwise, but it was a triumph nonetheless.

~~~

"He's pushing himself too hard," Darcy said to his wife after Geoffrey endured three brutal days of

335

Georgie's breathing exercises. He was now able to sit up for nearly an hour, or until something set him off and he lost his concentration, whichever came first. But when he tried to stand, he fell and nearly banged his knee. He had not given warning that he was going to attempt this, and it was Georgie, of all people, who caught him before Mr. Reynolds or Dr. Maddox could step in.

"You scared him with the threat of the Indian doctor," Elizabeth said, trying to lighten her husband's mood. It was very hard to keep it afloat, even with Geoffrey so clearly progressing, because the boy's hearing had not returned. It was not as bad as a death knell – he could live a full life if he learned to read lips proficiently, and he had never been much for musical performances, but they both wanted their son to regain complete health. "There is still reason to hope. If Dr. Maddox and Dr. Fergus have not given up hope, then we certainly should not."

"Their patient is our only son. It is their responsibility to coddle us."

"That is nonsense and you know it," Elizabeth said. It actually wasn't – though she did trust Dr. Maddox to tell the truth, it would be understandable if he were just hoping for the best about something he could not change. She didn't like Darcy's words, and the way he said them, and she made that clear in her tone. She had dealt with his obsessive terror when their son was missing and it had been reasonable. For him to go into one of his strange moods again now would be nothing short of disaster.

"Dr. Maddox was honest to you about Geoffrey's condition from the start. He has always been perfectly honest to you. You are being unreasonably suspicious that the worst will happen."

This gave Darcy pause. In fact, he stopped entirely, gazing out the window of their sitting room. "You know me so well."

"I would hope so, sir."

He gave one of his little smiles and sat down next to her so she could lean on his shoulder and have a moment's peace. They did have many demands on their time and energy beyond Geoffrey's condition, some of them everyday estate business, and some of them still concerning the family. Good relations had been uneasily restored, and Georgie seemed on her best behavior for the moment. What passed between her and her parents, neither of the Darcys dared to question. All they knew was that at least a temporary understanding had been reached. It was one of the situations that they hoped would not be temporary.

~~~

In mid-April they received a letter from George Wickham, saying that he was doing well in Cambridge, and saw his sister on weekends at the Maddox house, where Lady Maddox and her daughter had reluctantly returned. Dr. Maddox would not leave his patient's side, and when asked about his standing at Cambridge, he laughed it off and said that professors coming and going was a long-standing problem in the University, anyway. Dr. Fergus said there was nothing more he could do at Pemberley and did return, leaving everyone a bit unnerved, because Geoffrey still sat in silence.

Although he still couldn't hear, he had made lots of progress. He could walk about Pemberley now, and even came to dinner, and they were slowly adjusting to his condition. The best way to get his attention was to stomp on the floor, because he felt the vibrations. He seemed to understand them, even beyond 'yes' and 'no,' or could at least nod along with the conversation as if he did. It was impressive to watch him take the reigns to his own recovering health, demanding that someone read to him as he followed along in a book, so he could watch his face. Mr. Bennet was only too happy to do so for his grandson. The only thing Geoffrey seemed to take badly was the departure of the Bingleys, when Georgiana was well enough to go. Chatton House was only three miles away but that was three miles too far for him to travel, and he expressed his annoyance in the typical Darcy fashion of not saying anything about it while it was clearly written on his face.

"At least that creature is gone," Darcy said to his son. "Monkey."

"Monkey?" Geoffrey asked, not clear on the word.

"Yes."

"You're the only one who doesn't like him, Father."

"I will not make excuses." Darcy added a shrug for emphasis. His son seemed to understand, or at least was good at pretending to do so.

~~~

The understanding Georgie had reached with her parents did not, unfortunately, extend to her sister, who seemed frightened whenever she entered the room. "I don't bite," she said. Charlie might understand, but he was at Eton.

Edmund, at least, seem to grasp some of the complexities of the Bingley household, and how it had been forever changed. He was still not old enough for Eton, but he was sharp as a tack. Georgie was willing to go as far as to say that while he was not as sympathetic, he had a cleverness that Charlie did not.

"Are you going to give it all up now?" Edmund asked as she sat in the drawing room, doing precisely that. Georgie looked up from her art at him with an expression that answered the question. "Apparently not."

"I don't have the costume, and I lack enemies to shoot, and yes, perhaps I shouldn't have been so dramatic about it," she said. "That does not mean I intend to sit on my bottom and paint china cups until the next ball."

"So, what? You can't pretend to hide it anymore."

"I've no intention of doing so. I told Mama and Papa that I would be on my best behavior in society,

339

and they said what I did on my walks was my business, provided they do not overlap – ever again."

"I don't know how many Hatchers there are in the universe."

"Too many, but not in Derbyshire, perhaps. Mama and Papa can only hope."

Edmund smiled. "I thought it was smart." He did not wait for her response. "You probably would have managed it without being hurt if Hatcher didn't have the rifle. You were too far away to be hit by a pistol."

"How do you know?"

"I know Potter's Field. And I've thought about it," he said. "If you had hit Hatcher and ran away as you intended, the only one who would have been any the wiser would have been Mr. Jenkins, and he would have kept it secret. You probably threatened him."

"I did," she said.

"And maybe Geoffrey, if he even remembered, but he wouldn't say anything. He would be the last person on earth to say anything. It could have gone differently and because you were dressed up, your identity would have been safe. In fact, because you were dressed up like a wolf, precisely the type of animal currently overpopulating our forests, no one took Hatcher seriously from the start and even if he'd lived, they wouldn't have begun to believe him. I bet he didn't even know you were a woman until the very end."

"He didn't," Georgie replied. "He was a bit surprised. You – thought this all out, did you?"

"I've had little else to do."

"What   about   your   lessons?"

"I always finish them too quickly."

Because Edmund was smart. In a way, it was good that he was the second son, because he was clever enough to make his way in the world. He showed no inclinations towards religion and was about as adverse to violence as everyone else in the family (with one obvious exclusion), but he would probably either take an interest in the shipping business or start one of his own. "Thank you," she said abruptly.

"For what?"

"No one's ever ... really said anything about it to that sort of extent. An appreciative extent." She had put her life on the line to save Geoffrey, and though she had never expected a congratulatory slap on the back, the appreciation of her plan was pleasant. "I really do intend to behave."

"I'm sure," he said with a smile.

~~~

April became May, and Geoffrey's health was restored enough to ensure that he could begin Cambridge in the fall, despite his disability. He did not, however, take to his own task of joining his father when he met with tenants. It was not that Geoffrey had lost interest in Pemberley, but he hated being questioned or stared at, at least when he could not formulate a decent reply. So he wandered and followed every trail in Pemberley with his faithful hound at his side. He made one attempt at fencing and found his balance was not restored enough for such rapid and often awkward motion, and he suspected it might never be. He kept mainly to himself, because that was so much easier to do, and read more than he was accustomed to doing, or played with his youngest sister, but was generally silent.

A hard tap on the ground brought his father's presence to his attention. 'We're leaving for church,' his father said, or Geoffrey was able to conjecture that he said. It was Sunday and they were dressed for it.

Geoffrey Darcy stayed behind when the rest of his family went to church. He did not want to go, not out of any existential crisis, but for more logical reasons. He knew he would be gawked at, being the Darcy heir who survived a kidnapping and defeated his own captors. He would have to watch everyone else just to follow the service, none of which he could hear. The crux of the service was the sermon, and unless he sat very close and tried to watch the preacher very hard, he would understand nothing of it, so he was released from attendance.

Geoffrey was hardly alone at Pemberley. The Bellamont family did not attend the local services and he had their company.

On this particular morning, he was trying to enjoy the good weather and sunlight by going for a walk. He did not stray beyond Pemberley's grounds and he took a rifle with him as a precaution, though little good it would do him if an attacker came from behind. So he sat in the shade overlooking the hills of Derbyshire, his back against a log. In the distance he could see the spire of the church where normal people were singing hymns whether they wanted to or not, no matter how off-key. Mr. Bennet was undoubtedly sleeping through whatever part of the service was not done standing. Anne and Eliza no doubt spent a lot of the time re-adjusting their bonnets to look just perfect as Georgie scowled at both of them. He could see it all in his mind, but if he'd been there, he would hear none of it.

There was a hard tap on the log, waking him from his reverie. He felt the vibrations and looked to his side. Uncle Grégoire, having finished his own private services, had walked up to find him, put his staff down and sat down on the fallen tree. 'How are you?' Geoffrey watched his lips closely to understand the words.

"Fine," Geoffrey lied.

Grégoire nodded and with a pleasant smile removed something from his bag. It was a few of the little wooden figures that he liked to carve, but someone had painted them so they were a bit more distinguishable. One was quite obviously a man on a cross. "I know that. That's Christ on the cross."

The next wooden man was a soldier, judging from his spear, and from his red cloak covering most of his body, probably a Roman. Grégoire set the soldier up next to Jesus and began poking him with the spear.

"Longinus, who stabbed Christ to make sure he was dead," Geoffrey said. "I did study my bible, you know."

Grégoire just smiled at him and took out another figure. This one was harder to make out, and Geoffrey had to peer closely to see it. It was another person with a sword and a red helmet – no, that was hair. This figure didn't stand very well because instead of feet he had little stubs of stilt sandals. "Georgiana?" But his uncle removed the final figure, that of a man in a brown cloak, holding up a rifle. Together the rifleman and the sandaled soldier struck down the Roman, knocking him over. Grégoire picked up the Jesus figurine and raised it into the sky. "This bible story I'm not so familiar with," Geoffrey said, picking up the rifleman that was obviously supposed to be him, "but I like it all the same." When Grégoire pressed the figurines into his hands and closed them, obviously meaning for him to keep them, Geoffrey bowed to his uncle. "Thank you."

His uncle embraced him, kissing him on the head. When all the world was falling apart, Grégoire Bellamont-Darcy still had that serene smile on his face that said – all would be right.

"Church is over," Geoffrey said at the sound of the bells in the distance. The residents of Lambton would slowly be shuffling out, making gossip and thanking the rector for a job well done no matter how much they disliked the sermon, and his parents would be –

- the bells. He *heard* them. The sound was very distant, but so clear, not muffled by anything else to be found in man or nature. "The bells." Geoffrey fell to his knees. "I can hear them!" In a fit of joy he grabbed his uncle and shook him by his tunic. "I can hear!"

Grégoire looked him full in the face and said something that was clearly, 'Praise God.'

CHAPTER 23

The Courtship

GEOFFREY COULD HEAR – mostly in higher tones. His overexcited sisters made a game of pressing the keys of the pianoforte from the top to the bottom of the range, and seeing how far he made it. At first, he could only hear the piercing of the first key. Patrick Bellamont and Robert Kincaid decided to make a game of squealing as loud as they could, but Darcy put a stop to this immediately for everyone *else's* sake. He couldn't stop Monkey, but the smile on his son's face made it worth it.

They had a feast of celebration after his hearing had returned enough to hear the murmur of conversation through his one good ear. He wrote to Dr. Maddox, who politely suggested an ear horn, an idea that Geoffrey did not take well to.

"You should do it," Georgie said.

"You say that only because you wish to make fun of me."

"Maybe. So?"

He just smiled at her.

His career at Cambridge for the fall now assured, Geoffrey began to resume his normal duties at Pemberley. If he couldn't always hear the tenant's voice, he could read their lips, and he was still just an observer. His father was in good health, all things considered, and barring accident or sudden illness, Fitzwilliam Darcy would live a good thirty or forty years more. And with the son and heir back in good health, a feeling of calm that had been missing was restored, even if no one had quite realized the disquiet.

Life for Geoffrey would have been perfect, if not for the fencing. His balance was still not totally restored, and could be set off easily by a fall or a spin. His various attempts with his coach failed and left him in bed for days, until a heavy-hearted Darcy persuaded him to give up the sport. Ironically, Geoffrey was permitted to shoot again, provided he covered his left ear to protect it with a special piece made for him by Dr. Fergus. His right ear was dead and would remain so for the rest of his life.

May provided him with plenty of distractions, when Charlie returned from Eton and they could shoot together, or play cards, or whatever other activities boys their age found to do.

In June, George Wickham made his triumphant return to Pemberley to visit his favorite uncle. Not only had he succeeded at Cambridge, but after much haranguing, he was permitted to retake his exams and have his credit restored at Oxford, so he had a year of University under his belt, and would continue at Cambridge in the fall.

"My sister is already in Town," George said. "Believe it or not, by my suggestion."

"I thought the Maddoxes extended the offer to host you this summer?"

"They did," he said to his uncle, "but I thought it might be a good idea to ... try to restore relations with my parents. She is not, however, going to any balls unless I escort her."

"As I am sure you are most eager to do."

George smiled shyly and took a drink.

~~~

When the adults had gone to sleep, George Wickham, nearly twenty and feeling very much the adult, knocked on his cousin's door and was welcomed in. Geoffrey poured him a drink, but not one for himself, to which his cousin raised his eyebrows.

"Drinking made me dizzy before," Geoffrey said. "I can't imagine what it would do to me now."

"So you're a temperance man, then?"

"Temporarily, I suppose."

"A shame. I enjoy watching you get drunk and moon over Georgie," George said, continuing before Geoffrey could reply with anything more than a blush, "Where is your faithful companion?"

"Gawain's right here," Geoffrey said, snapping his fingers for his hound to come loyally to his side.

"You know very well what I meant."

Geoffrey turned away, collapsing into his armchair. "Georgie is playing nice at the moment."

"She did give us all a bit of a shock."

Geoffrey just swallowed his tea.

"Are they thinking of sending her to Town?"

"I don't know."

"Haven't asked her?"

"No," Geoffrey snarled. "What is this? If you want to know Georgie's comings and goings, ask her. Or if you cannot bring yourself to do so because she's so intimidating, ask Charlie. Maybe she will go to London. Maybe they'll put her in a seminary – all for just trying to save my life. What am I supposed to do about it?" Geoffrey scratched his sideburn. "I am going to Cambridge, which I'll be lucky to get through without that blasted ear horn, and she will go to ... Town. And balls. And wherever they make her go."

"She is eighteen."

"She can be five and twenty. She has fifty thousand pounds. She can marry whenever she pleases," Geoffrey said. "What do you care?"

"I don't. You're the one yelling."

Realizing he was, Geoffrey tempered his voice. "Give me a drink."

George, sitting closer to the wine, poured his cousin a small glass. "Well, if I am to endure the social life of Town for my sister's sake, perhaps it would be nicer with Georgiana on my arm."

"You wouldn't dare."

"Of course not. You would ride to Town and put a bullet in my head before the second dance."

"Why are you doing this to me?"

"Because I'm trying not to state the obvious."

"Stop smirking! You look like my father when you do that." Geoffrey said, finishing his wine. "I am half-deaf, dizzy, and about to enter Cambridge. I

350

have enough to do without needing to decipher your riddles, Wickham."

"You certainly will, when you discover the first exams are all in Greek."

"What!"

George raised a glass. "To Cambridge, and my future roommate, gullible and lovesick as he is."

"You are lucky I had to give up fencing, Wickham. I am serious."

"Lucky indeed," George said with a cruel smile.

~~~

Good relations had been entirely restored between Bingley and Brian, and the Maddoxes in general. Brian and Nadezhda returned to their home outside of Town when business could no longer be avoided, and Bingley made a trip in June to check on things, and brought Georgie with him, perhaps as a sign of good faith between them.

It was only then that Georgie first got to speak with Nadezhda truly alone, even if her father was only a few rooms away, talking to Brian. Georgie knelt on the cushion across from Her Highness, who was in her most formal kimono, with her hair perfectly tied up. They sat on the tatami mat floor, with a long box resting on the floor between them.

With great ceremony, Nadezhda removed the cover, revealing a very familiar sword with jutte metal attachments to the hilt and a knitted shoulder strap.

"Mugin's sword!" Georgie was thrown off by seeing it. She knew she should have expected it, but it brought to the surfaces so many emotions.

"What Brian told you the note said," Nadezhda said, "was not precisely true."

Georgiana looked up as Nadezhda passed her the note. Of course, she could barely read kanji. "I only recognize – something about an ookami."

"Wolf. Correct. All it says is, '*For the next wolf,*'" she said. "Brian didn't know what it meant. I wasn't sure, until you proved it to me, but I had my suspicions. That said..." She closed the case. "The wolf has to go away for a while."

Georgie nodded, sitting very still, when all she wanted to do was grab the box and run.

"There will be a time for the wolf again," Nadezhda said, with a gleam in her eye. "I'm sure you will manage to get yourself in some kind of trouble. When you do, we will give it to you."

"You told Brian-san?"

"I did. And he agreed." She pressed her hand on the cover of the box. "When the time comes."

~~~

July was pleasantly hot after such a cold winter. The Darcy sisters made much use of Pemberley's lake, with their nurse and watchful brother to look after them. Derbyshire was quiet after the well-known death of Mr. Hatcher, but Darcy was playing it safe with all of his children. With all that had happened, there was a record low in tenant disputes brought to Mr. Darcy, and most afternoons he let his son go to enjoy the wilderness before he departed to Cambridge. Geoffrey was used to being at Eton, but University was different, and he would return not a boy, but a man. It was the lazy summer that no one at Pemberley really wanted to pass. The Kincaids retreated to the cooler north with many hugs and kisses for their nephew, who had aged more since their arrival than the few months that had passed.

Charlie babbled nervously with him, no doubt anxious about being the oldest family member at Eton. It would be his last year and Edmund's first, and until this point, Geoffrey had been the oldest. Still, Geoffrey was sure Charlie would assume the mantel with some grace.

There came a time when packing could not be delayed. Geoffrey spent as much time as possible playing with Gawain, who would be left behind. The old hound tired easily, never fully recovered from his wounds, and was resting on a mat in the library as Geoffrey went through the titles on his bookshelves, looking for anything he would need. He was alone when a servant said, "Miss Bingley to see you, sir."

He just nodded and Georgie entered. "When did you become an intellectual?"

"I'm not to turn into George, if that's what you mean," he said. "Hopefully not, anyway." Geoffrey opened the book to the title page. "I won't need this."

"What is it?" she said, approaching him.

"*Le Morte D'Arthur*," he said, and closed it, a little cloud of dust floating away from it. "Not exactly a Greek philosophic classic."

"Have you read it?"

"Some time ago. Or it was read to me. Honestly I cannot remember," he said, replacing it on the shelf. "I remember Sir Gawain does not come off too well."

"Poor Gawain," she said, glancing at the dog, who looked up at his name being called. She knelt beside him and scratched behind his ears. "Who will take care of you when Geoffrey is gone?"

"My father is rather fond of him, and more so when no one else is around, or so I am told," he said. He paused in what he was doing, distracted from his books. "He reminds him of his own hounds, though if either of them ever saved his life, it is not a story I've heard."

"Because they were not noble Sir Gawain," she said as the hound licked her face, "who was so rudely portrayed by Malory."

He stepped towards her. "If you really wish to take him – "

Georgie stood up, to Gawain's whine. "Monkey is enough, thank you. Though, I will be lonely."

He smiled. "Are you admitting to a weakness, Miss Bingley?"

"I am allowed to have my share. A refusal to act proper when I think it's ridiculous to do so, a lack of interest in dancing and singing and embroidery, never a proper Season in Town– "

"So, no going from assembly to assembly with Izzy?"

Georgie turned around to face him. "I am sorry to disappoint. Or surprise."

"You hardly surprise me," Geoffrey said, "and you never disappoint." He paused uncomfortably. "I don't believe I ever properly thanked you for ... what you did in March."

"Whatever do you mean, precisely? I did so many things in March. It was an entire month."

"You will make me speak of it?"

"If you won't, then no one will."

He grinned and looked down, rather bashful. "I am thankful that you dressed up like a wolf, tried to kill Hatcher, and rescued me from captivity. I could not be more grateful."

"And my methods?"

"I suppose sometimes you do still, after all these years, manage to surprise me."

"You would be the second person to thank me, you know. With all the appropriate references."

"I would? Who was the other? My father?"

"Edmund."

He lost his smile. "No one appreciates you. Except maybe Edmund, though I don't know precisely what he said -"

"It doesn't matter what he said," Georgie said. "What *you* say matters to me."

There was no real rhyme or reason behind what Geoffrey did next; it was all of his baser instincts rolled into one motion, one that he had been contemplating not as a rational thought but as something to be dismissed as impossible, ridiculous, and embarrassing. She was Georgie, his friend, his cousin, the girl who cut her hair short like a boy and could kick the snot out of anyone he knew.

And yet, he loved her. So he kissed her, and it was not the quick kiss of relative or friend. It lingered until neither of them could help it, and as he came to his senses, he panicked and pulled away.

"Oh God," he said, "I'm sorry."

"What?"

"I'm sorry." He turned away. "It shouldn't have happened."

Now she said it with less shock and more feeling, "*What?*"

"I said, it shouldn't have happened," Geoffrey said, frustrated that his backtracking wasn't helping. Why had he let himself go? The only other time he'd seriously considered what he'd just done, was when he'd been drinking heavily. Now he wasn't even drunk! "You're my best friend, Georgie. You really are."

"That is all I am to you?"

"No. No, no – you're my cousin, and my friend, and you're like a – "

"Don't you dare say I'm like a sister to you," Georgie interrupted. "Don't you *dare* lie to me. I'm not a sister to you. Maybe I was at some time when we were little children, but you do not treat me like a sister. Or a cousin. Or a friend."

"I said I was sorry," he stuttered. "It was a mistake."

"Don't say that!"

She was making him nervous. He was already exposed and he didn't want to feel nervous. "It was. I'm sorry – "

"You're not. You can't be." She nearly pushed him against the wall. He didn't like the physical contact; it had already gotten him into trouble enough today. "You're not sorry because it wasn't a mistake and you wanted it to happen and if you say otherwise, you're lying to yourself and you are lying to me."

But it had been a mistake! And yet he would be lying if he told her it meant nothing. Because it had meant something, been the culmination of something that he – No, he was a Darcy. He was in control of himself and he would do the responsible thing. "It was a mistake. It didn't mean anything. You know how boys are."

"I know how *you* are. I don't care about anyone else. I've never cared about anyone else in my life like I've cared about you."

"Georgie, please don't say it – "

"I love you!"

He closed his eyes. He had to focus, to push down all of his instincts, contradictory as they were. None of them were good. All of them would get him into trouble. "Just – leave me be."

"I tell you something I've been waiting to say for years and you tell me to get out? Open your fecking eyes."

Unfortunately he did, and saw that she was crying. And if he had been telling the truth – that there was truly nothing between them except

357

cousinly feelings and friendship -- he could hold her in his arms and comfort her and try to make her tears go away.

But he couldn't do that.

"You don't – understand," Geoffrey said, speaking more to himself than to her. "All the things I've gone through – "

"All the things that *you've* gone through! You slept through your little kidnapping and became the shire hero! Your parents don't look at you like you have some kind of brain fever. Your siblings aren't just wondering what you might do next whenever you walk in a room." She grabbed him by the trim of his waistcoat. "I fecking lined him up for you, so *you* could be the hero and kill the villain who hurt our family! I didn't care about all my secrets, because if you didn't survive, I didn't care if I lived or died, and no one else was going to save you. I did it all for you!"

"Georgie, you can't ask me – "

"Geoffrey Darcy, if you lie to me and tell me you don't love me, you are a lying shite of a man."

He swallowed, and just bowed his head. "I'm sorry. I know you sacrificed for me, and I didn't ask you to – "

"If you didn't need me for everything – "

"If you weren't such a freak – "

She didn't hit him. She did worse. She grabbed his arm and pulled on it just right so that he spun around all the way almost twice, very fast and hit the bookcase very hard, because he could no longer tell up from down. And then she left him without a word.

She stomped out of the room the way a jilted woman should, because that was what she was. He had time to process that, and plenty of it, before a servant found him. With his vertigo set off, he was helpless to do anything other than stay on the floor where he was, since he needed the ground and the wall to have some semblance of location. He had time to ponder all of the ways *that* had gone wrong before someone found him on the cold stone floor, half-covered in fallen books and helpless against the spinning sensation and whirling thoughts in his head.

~~~

When Georgie didn't return for dinner, Jane expressed concern. It was exactly the type of expression that her well-trained husband knew meant, 'Go find her.' He checked her room, of course, and her usual haunts, and was even considering heading to Pemberley when he decided, just in case, to check the grove in the back, beyond where he had planted all of the Indian flowers for whichever daughter was wed first. There he found her, not in costume or even in her wooden sandals, just in an ordinary, pretty dress and proper women's shoes, seated on a carved stone that might have been part of a church ruin at some point. She looked up at him with unapologetically red eyes.

"I am happy to report," Georgie said with a sad chuckle, "that I am weeping over a completely normal, ordinary thing that a girl my age should be upset over. If anything, I have every right to claim a headache and lie in bed for several days as if I am ill, because I have been jilted by the man I love."

"Who hurt you?" Bingley said, already knowing the answer.

"He called me a freak," she said, pulling at her hair. "He just said it in anger, but – he can't do that. It's not fair." Bingley sat beside her, putting his arm around her and letting her head rest on his shoulder. "Papa, tell him it's not fair."

"I never succeeded at policing you as children, and I doubt I could do it now," he said. "Georgiana – did I ever tell you how I met your mother?"

"At a country dance," she said. "Mama told me."

"I daresay the whole of our courtship was a bit more complicated than that," he said, managing a smile for his wide-eyed daughter. "From the moment I saw her I was in love with her, and yet somehow, it took a full year of heartbreak and failed expectations and deception before we made it to the altar. I suppose I've never told the whole story because – well, it does not reflect well on anyone involved, including your father, your Uncle Darcy, and your Aunt Maddox. *Especially* them."

It worked. She smiled, just a little bit. "Now I have to hear it. Even if it's disgusting."

"Courtship is not – Well, I suppose hearing about your parents might be, but we shall make an exception, and I shall tell you the very embarrassing story of how Darcy and Caroline conspired to muck up my courtship with your mother, and I spinelessly went along with them." He sighed. "It all started when I decided to lease a house in Hertfordshire, and was persuaded to attend one of the assemblies..."

CHAPTER 24

The Third Time

GEOFFREY DARCY completed his packing mainly in solitude. He informed everyone that he did not want celebrations to see him off, and his wishes were for the most part respected, except for the obligatory dinner with the nearby relatives. He had a drink and was at ease in company, because Geoffrey was always at ease in company, but he did not linger at Chatton House like he usually did.

Between the two families, everyone knew that something had occurred between Geoffrey and Georgie. Most assumed it was a disagreement over something or other, even though they were not known for their disagreements. Most of the blame was put on Georgiana, the mysterious one, who could be so cruel when she tried. The more intuitive members of the family realized that whatever happened, the blame probably went both ways. The effect was awkwardly seismic; they hardly said another word to each other. As was general policy with Georgiana, no one said much of anything about it, at least not in front of the two involved, and assumed it would blow over. If anything, Geoffrey's absence would speed along the resolution.

On the day he was to leave, Geoffrey sat down with his father in the study for a glass of brandy, and

Darcy dispensed with a surprising amount of advice about Cambridge, not all of it related to schoolwork. "And don't let them rob you. Decide on the price in advance."

"Father!"

Darcy smiled. "I am giving you the advice bestowed upon me by my father."

"Now you've made it worse."

Darcy chuckled. "And don't pick up any diseases."

"Really! Father, please!" Geoffrey's face was hot.

"While you're in such a befuddled mood, I suppose I will bestow upon you the news that you will not be alone in missing Miss Bingley's company this fall."

Geoffrey's demeanor changed. "What?"

"She is to go to France. To a seminary in the south."

Geoffrey played with the glass in his hands, no longer willing to raise his eyes to his father. "She agreed to it?"

"My understanding is that she specifically requested it."

Geoffrey said nothing. He wanted to scream *why?* But he already knew the answer.

"As to why she would do something so utterly contrary to her character, I suppose you might have some suggestions."

"N-No."

"Really? None whatsoever?"

Geoffrey shook his head. His dilemma was not whether he could hide it from his father, because he knew he couldn't. The only thing in question was whether his father would let him leave without the proper answer. "Can I ask you a completely unrelated question?"

"Of course."

"Totally unrelated."

His father rolled his eyes. "Yes, yes."

"Have you ever been unable to say something because you knew it would mean so much more, and instead said something awful?"

"On any number of occasions, yes. In fact, your mother has probably not only memorized, but counted and categorized the number of times and ways I have said something stupid, harsh or unintentionally insulting. You are fortunate to have inherited your mother's silver tongue." Darcy paused. "If you have, however, said something unintentionally insulting in fear of saying what you truly mean and now intend to run from it for as long as possible, then I will congratulate you in this respect: You are most thoroughly a Darcy."

Darcy stood up and gave his son a hardy pat on the shoulder, and Geoffrey did his best to look reassured.

~~~

When all his trunks were finally in the carriage, Geoffrey was nowhere to be found, and Reynolds said he had just gone out and would be back, but was rather evasive about where precisely he had gone. He didn't tell them that Geoffrey had sent a message to Georgie, through him and her lady-maid, that they should meet out behind Pemberley, on the edge of the woods.

Geoffrey arrived on time, but Georgie was already waiting, her expression best described as one of stone.

"I want to apologize," he said.

"Good."

"I shouldn't have – said just about everything I said. Afterwards. You know." He looked at his shoes. She didn't budge. "I'm sorry."

"Thank you," she said, without much emotion.

"Are you going to ..."

"Apologize? No," Georgiana said, leaning against the tree. "I refuse to apologize for something I'm not sorry for. It's like lying."

"I'm trying to restore some kind of relations – "

"I don't want a friendship with you," she said, "and you don't want a friendship with me. And until you can say that, there's nothing else to be said that won't hurt both of us. Despite everything, I don't want to hurt you again."

"You are doing a good job of it."

She said nothing, but she did look away.

"You don't have to go to France."

"I want to go. It was my decision."

"I'll miss you."

"What does it matter, if I'm in Derbyshire or some county in France? Either way, we won't see each other, but this way, I don't have to spend another year avoiding London. Don't I deserve to see something other than the same walls of my father's estate?"

"I will write."

"If you want to write something meaningful, by all means. If you want to chatter away about drinking and fooling around as a Cambridge boy, don't waste the paper." She stood up, and turned to walk away from him. "Goodbye, Geoffrey."

"Georgie."

She paused, and looked over her shoulder. Her eyes were red. "What?"

"I will miss you," Geoffrey said.

"I know." And she turned, and did not turn back.

He stood there, tongue-tied, watching her disappear across the hill. Yes, he was thoroughly a Darcy.

~~~

Geoffrey did write her. He wasted a great deal of paper, in fact, because not a single letter was mailed. Somehow everything he wrote ended up balled up and tossed into the waste bin. He tried to do it when George wasn't around, to avoid the snide comments, but they had stopped fairly quickly when George seemed to sense he was really hurt.

Not that there were no other demands on his time. Geoffrey discovered that though there were plenty of opportunities to indulge in pleasurable pursuits, more than he had imagined, most of his days were consumed with lectures and tutors, beginning with the awful bell for services and ending when they locked the gates at night. George, unsurprisingly, was a quiet roommate, often in the library, or "out." It took Geoffrey some time to figure out what George meant when he said he'd be "out", to the point where he was so confounded that he was tempted to ask Reynolds to follow him. But then he managed to piece together the picture, from watching George go out in the early evening and returned a few hours later with his hair tussled and his clothing obviously hastily redone.

"George Wickham! Of all people! Am I to have a rake for a roommate?"

George was unapologetic. "Rakes deflower maids and shopkeepers' daughters. Surely your father gave you the embarrassing lecture about gentlemanly ways to pursue your baser instincts?"

"He did but – " He did the math on his fingers. "How much are you paying?"

George just grinned. "Do you really want to know?"

"Not really, come to think of it."

~~~

The rhythm of Cambridge life was established by the University, and Geoffrey fell into it easily. His studies were not too imposing and between George and friends both new and from Eton, he was only alone when he wished to be. He could do without their snickering when he used his ear horn, but Professor Matheson was too old and his voice too much of a mumbled growl for *anyone* to really hear him. George, who was in other lectures anyway, never said a word about it.

Geoffrey's studies were primarily classics and mathematics, and like most students, he stayed far away from gruesome and complex medical lectures, so the only time he saw Dr. Maddox was in the hallways, and on Sundays when he was invited to dine with Dr. and Lady Maddox in Chesterton with Isabel and George. What made him the happiest was when he was fit enough to return to fencing, though he was not well enough to try for the team and likely would never be. He was limited in his movements and stamina; spending three days in bed with vertigo after a grueling session taught him that.

With some feeling of accomplishment he left Cambridge not for Derbyshire but for Kent, to attend the wedding of Amelia Collins and a Mr. Stevenson, a man who had inherited some small fortune from his uncle, who was heavily invested in the Bahamas. Amelia was a year older than Geoffrey, the oldest of the four Collins daughters. Her father had put up a surprising amount for her inheritance, and that had ensured the match, though from what everyone gathered, there was some genuine affection between the couple. The family had met when the man was investigating buying a home in the area. When asked more privately about his concerns, as he would need money to run Longbourn when Mr. Bennet died, Mr. Collins merely replied, "My daughters are more important than a building."

"That is perhaps the wisest thing the man has ever said," Darcy said to his wife.

"Though he has set a low bar," she added, and left his side to congratulate an ecstatic Charlotte.

Geoffrey, still being caught up on all of the family news, was surprised to encounter his Uncle Grégoire and Aunt Caitlin at Rosings. Actually he encountered Patrick first, as the boy came running in and nearly knocked him over on his way outside. "I want ta go out!"

"I'm sure you do, Patrick," Geoffrey said, "so much so that your cousin doesn't deserve a greeting."

Patrick frowned. "Hello!" And then in an overexcited scamper, left for the same tree that Geoffrey remembered climbing as a child.

"Yeh'll watch him, eh, what that 'e doesn' fall down?" Mrs. Bellamont asked him. "Jeff?"

"Aunt Bellamont. Of course I will." And with that, he followed his cousin outside. "Patrick! You come down from there before you hurt yourself!"

"No!"

"Well, then – at least try to fall into my arms!" Geoffrey said, and heard his aunt's laughter in the background.

~~~

"I was going to say hello to my nephew," Grégoire said, "but he seems otherwise occupied."

"You wouldn't want him to lose his concentration as he tries to prevent your son from

370

killing himself," Darcy said, and smiled at his brother. "How are you?"

"A bit surprised to be in Kent, but an invitation is an invitation."

"You are unfortunate enough to be an object of Mr. Collins's great respect."

"I do not find it so unfortunate." Grégoire added, "Most of the time." He bowed to Elizabeth, who was just entering the hallway. "Mrs. Darcy."

"Grégoire. If either an injury or a wedding will get you back to England, we shall have to arrange more marriages for the Collins daughters somehow."

He smiled and excused himself, and Elizabeth joined Darcy at the window as they watched their son run around the tree frantically as Patrick swung from the limbs.

"Something about this seems familiar," Darcy said.

"What? That our son, a tree, and disaster all deserve to be in the same sentence?"

"Not that," Darcy said. "Did this guest house not used to be the Collins' cottage? Before renovations?"

"It was. I remember the grounds quite well."

He looked around, apparently puzzled at something, and then turned to her and said out of nowhere, "So I am to understand our wayward niece is doing well?"

"According to her letters, yes. According to the school, she is a brilliant student in language arts and other more scholarly subjects, but a social nuisance to all of her teachers."

"But enough that they can tolerate."

"As long as Mr. Bingley keeps paying the bill, I suppose so."

Darcy looked out the window again, but said nothing.

"You're thinking of something," Elizabeth said, "and at this point in our long and thriving marriage, it is downright rude not to share it, if you're going to think it so publicly."

He smiled. "And, at this point in our long and thriving marriage, you have caught me. I was thinking that the Darcy men are particularly terrible at expressing their feelings. At least in their youth."

"Oh? And what brought this notion about?"

"A simpler thought than you realize. This was the room in which I proposed to you."

Elizabeth was taken aback. This was not the answer she had expected, nor did she expect the sly grin on his face as she looked around and assessed that, barring some refurbishments, it was. "Yes, you Darcy men are particularly terrible at expressing your feelings sometimes."

"Not all the time. I did get it right the second time."

"I started the conversation."

"I initiated the walk."

"No, I think that was Mama."

"Well, I offered to go with Bingley to Longbourn."

"With the express purpose of seeing me."

"True," he smiled. "I could not have been more motivated, or so terrified. Telling a woman you love her and wish to spend the entirety of your remaining days in her presence is quite a daunting task for a confirmed bachelor. Then mucking it up and having to do it a second time is even worse."

"I suppose it might eventually get easier."

Darcy paused, and turned about the room before facing her. "Elizabeth Bennet, will you spend the rest of your days as my wife?"

"Seeing as how I have but little options at this juncture – I believe I am required to say yes," she said, taking his hand. "Not that I need such a requirement."

He kissed her. He had not the first time, or the second time, but the third time, he kissed her.

"Yes," Darcy said. "Definitely easier the third time."

The End

Historical Notes

So, there are no wolves in England.

Of course you know this. You must know this obvious fact which is common knowledge to anyone who knows anything. Unfortunately, I didn't, until about book 8, when a reader said to me, "By the way, wolves are extinct in England." It turns out that medieval England was pretty serious about hunting them. At this point I was five books in to the wolf plotline and motif, so I wrote in a bit about some earl introducing them to Derbyshire for sport (like the one who introduced rabbits to Australia in this period) to explain away their presence. In other words, I cheated, but you may have noticed that it's a pretty important plotline.

English Radicals did exist and were very interested in communal property and against land enclosure, an issue so boring that I couldn't bear to have any of my characters discuss it at length in the book. If you want to read about the Land Enclosure Acts, see the bibliography, and I hope you have insomnia that needs curing.

The issue of entail is also a tremendously complicated one, and the breaking of an entail is not much written of because it rarely happened, so I may have had some particulars wrong due to lack of source material.

Bibliography

Chase, Malcolm. The People's Farm English Radical Agrarianism 1775-1840. London: Breviary Stuff Publications, 2010.

Clendening, Logan. Source book of Medical History. New York: Dover Publications, 1960.

Cole, G.D.H. The British Common People 1746-1946. London: Methuen & Co LTD, 1961.

Druett, Joan. Rough Medicine : Surgeons at Sea in the Age of Sail. New York: Routledge, 2000.

Hammond, J. The Village Labourer. Stroud: Nonsuch, 2005.

Perkin, Harold. Origins of Modern English society. New York: Routledge, 1991.

Richardson, Robert. The Story of Surgery : an Historical Commentary. Shrewsbury, England: Quiller, 2004.

Acknowledgments

I cannot begin to explain the scope of the gratitude I feel for Brandy Scott. She's worked tirelessly on every one of my books, the short stories, and even this segment. There's no part of this series that she hasn't had a part in reading or editing. I don't know how or why she does what she does, but like manna from heaven, I know better than to question it.

I'd like to thank my fans, who are the reason this book happened. There was a period where I wasn't sure it was going to be published at all, which was a real shame because it is in many people's opinions one of the best books or *the* best book in the series. It's Brandy's favorite, which is why I dedicated it to her. So many people emailed me or spoke to me, pulling for this book, that the publishing went forward despite numerous hurdles.

My parents have been very supportive of this series and my general career with all its financial uncertainties. They ought to have known better, but was I really going to be a doctor or a lawyer? I don't like needles or court rooms. I don't even like the courtroom segments *on Law and Order*. Especially if they involve needles.

My agents have remained by my side despite my dubious earnings: Katie Menick, Howard Morhaim, Kate McKean, Alice Spielgert, and whoever else may be wandering around their office, sorting things - you have my gratitude. Thanks to Talia Goldman for copyediting and Cherri Trotter for cover design.

Speaking of agents, Diana Finch and Jeff Gerecke have been very helpful with their free advice. All you have to do is be their assistant. Liza Dawson was also a huge provider of encouragement.

Jessica Kupillas Hartung is in here because she did me a major favor on the day I was writing these acknowledgments, and also for being an all-around super fan.

To all the people who come up to me in synagogue and ask me if I'm Carol's daughter and if so, they liked my books, I don't know who you are. I should, but it's not as if we've ever worn nametags and it's a big congregation. Cut me some slack. And thank you for reading.

My roommate, Alex Shwarzstein, pays her half of the utilities bill and I love her for it. Also apparently she actually reads and likes my work. That's a bonus.

Reassurance in my career and life choices came from Rebbetzin Chana Henkin and Simi Peters. I wish I didn't have to fly 12 hours to see you guys. I wish I was in Israel all the time, but slowly I'm learning to take life on its terms, not mine. I didn't think I was going to be a Regency romance author, either.

To the Holy One, Blessed be He, I would apologize for having so many of my characters take Your name in vain, but I have a feeling I'm just going to keep doing it, so come to peace with it.

Coming Soon … Book 6 in Our Series

Georgiana and the Wolf
by
Marsha Altman

Look for it online by checking out
www.marshaaltman.com

Prologue

Inspector Robert Audley turned to the mortician and said with annoyance, "You are aware that the body should not have been moved until my approval?"

Monsieur Lambert was an elderly gentleman, and so was excused to sit in the corner of his dusty workshop. "Oui. But Inspector, you were not called when this body was found. You were not called for another day."

Audley frowned. "That is true," he said as he looked at the body again, partially uncovered by his own actions. The corpse of a man named Simon Roux was in a state of ready decomposition, now three days old. Monsieur Roux was found by a shepherd at dawn, and was already stiff by the description of the local guard, so all he had at this point to pinpoint a time of death was that information. It was probably sometime in the early morning, while it was still dark, or the body would have stunk as it did now. Only the mortician's chemicals under his nose prevented Audley from being overwhelmed.

The inspector probed the cold wound on the dead man's neck. He had died quickly after his wounds, as no one survived a slash to the throat, much less three. "These marks – "

"Claws. Definitely."

"I agree," Audley said. "Not a blade, certainly, but have you ever seen three claw marks so evenly spaced?" He took a measurement of one with his forefinger and thumb, and then checked the next, and then the last. "That is very rare on a true animal wound. Also, strange that the animal merely killed him with one swipe and then left the body so intact otherwise."

Old Man Lambert said quietly, "It is odd, yes, Inspector. I have never seen anything like this before. Perhaps this is why you were called."

"Perhaps." He took a last look at the messy, bearded face of Simon Roux. By reputation, he was a known gambler who worked the fields in season and made his living by selling firewood the rest of the year. He was also known to be good with a blade – or at least a hatchet – and one was found on him, unused, at the scene of the crime. Inspector Audley had barely been in town two hours and he already had the impression that the man was not well liked, at least by the female populace. "Were you called to the scene or was the body delivered here by your assistant?"

"I was called, Inspector."

"I will need a list of everyone present, even women and children, when you arrived. Was the marquis there?"

"Non, Inspector. He remained uninvolved until the ... rumors started spreading."

This was when Inspector Audley had been called, by special request of the Marquis, and rode from Paris to his summons immediately. Normally he did not like to be approached about a case from a suspect, but apparently the nobility still held more sway than they were supposed to, because Audley was pulled off a significant strangler case on the docks to attend to this murder in the wilderness with a startling order from above.

Of course, logically, the Marquis was not a suspect. He had no known reason to kill Simon Roux, a man he was not known to associate with. If there were any connections, it was hidden – but Inspector Audley would find it out. That was his profession and his duty, even to a man like Simon Roux.

~~~

The meeting with the marquis was earlier than he expected, until he reminded himself that the country noblemen often ate earlier than city folk. He knew very well that the marquis would want to have him at dinner to parade around the fact that he had brought in (undoubtedly, at his own expense) this superior inspector to investigate the brutal crime. Inspector Audley was not bothered by it, as it would give him a terrific meal and a chance to see the local people in action, from the servants to the marquis himself.

The meeting between them took place precisely at four, when the inspector was often accustomed to taking tea. To his surprise, he was not asked to stand before the noble, who instead offered him a seat and a rather wide selection of flavored teas. "I heard, Inspector, that you are of English descent."

"Yes," Audley said. "My father was an officer. He retired here."

"In Paris?"

"Valognes," he said, making his selection quickly and waving off the servant with sugar cubes. He wanted to preserve his teeth. "He still lives there with my mother and sister."

"But you are the famed inspector of Paris." But the marquis was not an ostentatious noble of old, trying to flatter him openly. He was a quieter man, more intense and serious, almost frightening with his pointed nose and long black hair. He was a widower, but that was all the inspector had at the moment.

"Hardly," Audley said. "My lord, I am afraid I must of course begin with the most basic inquiry – "

"Of course," said the marquis. "I was asleep that night. I went to bed very late, being distracted by a new book. And, I will not deny that I am one to take walks along my lands in the early morning. I enjoy the morning mist, especially this time of year." He sipped his tea. "Do you have a conclusion as to the time of death?"

Audley knew the man was clever, and also guessed that the marquis could likely tell if he was holding back. "Early morning, but likely, very early. Perhaps one, two past midnight."

"Then I was asleep," the marquis said. "I do not know this man – Monsieur Roux?

"Simon Roux, yes."

"I know of him only by reputation. He came to the village a few years ago, after the war, and never fully settled himself. He remained unmarried and was apparently a known womanizer. You know the type, surely?"

"I do." The war brought out the best – and worst – in men. Many were left scarred by it, unable to find their places in this new France, whatever it was to be. "Have you any idea of the foundation of these rumors concerning yourself and Monsieur Roux?"

"None whatsoever. It came as a shock to me, but what good free countryman is not ready and eager to discredit a noble? Even if to stoop so low as to start rumors about ... werewolves, or whatever this nonsense is." He paused. "You know, it was not even a full moon the night of his death."

"So you are aware of such legends?"

"Such are the things told to a child, especially one who lives so close to the woods. Wolves, vampires, witches – that sort of nonsense. I thought we got rid of that nonsense with the revolution, but apparently, not so."

"But somehow, someone started the rumor that you were seen running through the woods that night – or, someone with a wolf's head was seen in the woods wearing your clothing. Am I correct?"

"You are."

Audley made a note in his book. "Have you done an inventory of your wardrobe since the event?"

"No. I had not thought to do so until people seemed to be – taking these ridiculous rumors seriously." He smiled, and Audley could not help but notice his teeth were very pointy. "But – in the dead of night, I imagine one would only have to acquire one splendid coat to give the effect of appearing as me."

"True, but I would appreciate if you would do the inventory as soon as possible, perhaps even before dinner. If a servant can be rooted out, it will make our lives much easier."

"Of course. It will be done." The marquis rose. "If there are no other pressing questions, I must prepare for dinner. You have joined us on a very special evening, Inspector Audley."

"I have?" Audley said, rising with him.

"Yes. My bride – my intended bride – is joining us with her companion. She is studying in a seminary for English women very near here."

"Very convenient." The inspector could not help look at the marquis and be reminded that this man was in his forties and a widower, and a seminary girl could have been hardly more than twenty.

"Our intention. Our families planned this wedding together– hers in England, mine here – but I would not agree to it until I saw her and we felt it was a good match ourselves. So she came to study in the seminary that is but five miles from here, and I have arranged that she may occasionally visit."

"Her name?"

"Lady Heather Littlefield. You shall be introduced tonight, of course." He made motions to leave, and Inspector Audley bowed.

Something struck him. "My Lord – "

The marquis stopped in the doorway and politely turned around. "Yes."

"You said she had a companion?"

"Yes, her friend from school, who accompanies her so she is not alone in a carriage with the guard. I apologize – her name escapes me now. I am quite a bad host." He snapped his fingers. "Ah yes. I remember it."

The inspector readied his pen again. "Yes?"

"I believe it is – Miss Georgiana Bingley."

To be continued…

Put down your book and go to sleep.

SERIOUSLY.

CPSIA information can be obtained at www.ICGtesting.com
Printed in the USA
LVOW131321180912

299289LV00005B/5/P